THE VINYL
Princess

THE VINYL Princess

Yvonne Prinz

HarperTrophyCanada™
An imprint of HarperCollinsPublishersLtd

Published by Harper*Trophy*Canada™, an imprint of HarperCollins Publishers Ltd.

Originally published by Harper*Trophy*Canada™ in a trade paperback edition: January 2010
This digest paperback edition: December 2010

Harper*Trophy*Canada™ is a trademark of HarperCollins Publishers.

HarperCollins books may be purchased for educational, business,
or sales promotional use through our Special Markets Department.

HarperCollins Publishers Ltd
2 Bloor Street East, 20th Floor
Toronto, Ontario, Canada
M4W 1A8

www.harpercollins.ca

Library and Archives Canada Cataloguing in Publication information is available.

ISBN 978-1-55468-517-2

Typography by Alison Klapthor
Printed and bound in the United States

HC 9 8 7 6 5 4 3 2 1

This book is for Karen Pearson. If I am the Vinyl Princess, she is most certainly the Queen.

I sense him in my midst. The air seems to thin when he's near me. I get light-headed. I don't even have to look up but I can't help myself. It's my fourth sighting this week but who's keeping track? He calmly takes in the standoff at the buy counter before carrying on to the bins. Our eyes meet and he nods and offers up a half smile. I follow him with my eyes and reluctantly bring my focus back to the pile of CDs sitting in the middle of the scratched-up blue countertop between Thombo and me like an island no one wants to claim. I remember when Thombo was "Thomas." It wasn't that long ago. He was an okay kid back then but he fell through the cracks and emerged as "Thombo," someone you definitely shouldn't turn your back on.

"This is the same tired pile of crap you brought in

yesterday." I slide the stack of CDs across the counter toward him.

"No, no, man. This stuff is good, it's all good." He twitches and scratches his skinny arm.

"Yeah? So, when did you start listening to Whitesnake and the Grateful Dead?" I ask, looking into his bloodshot eyes.

Thombo's eyes dart around quickly. "You gotta help me out here. It's my sister, man, she's really sick."

I steal a glance at my friend out in the bins. He's flipping through the Bs in the used-CD section. I pull up the sagging waist of my skinny jeans and stand up straighter.

"Yeah? Yesterday you said it was your mom who was sick, and by the way, I saw your sister this morning and she looked fine."

"Let me talk to Bob. Bob's my man."

"Bob isn't here and you know he'd have kicked your ass out of here already."

Thombo thinks for a second or two. "Gimme twenty for the stack. All's I need is a twenty." He slides the pile back toward me like a poker player going all in. His eyes become hopeful again.

"And what do I tell the guy when he comes around looking for the CDs you stole from him and he asks me what you look like and where you live?" I furtively glance out the front window, looking for Laz. Damn it, he should be here by now.

Thombo finally faces the fact that I'm standing firmly between him and his next fix and I'm not budging. He reluctantly puts the stack back into a rumpled paper bag and stalks out the door. He was waiting for me when I arrived this morning, his sweatshirt hood pulled over his head, jumping around while I unlocked the smeared double glass doors. I'm annoyed at Laz. I don't like handling the tweakers alone. I press the worn-out play button on the amplifier. *My Life in the Bush of Ghosts* by David Byrne and Brian Eno starts up, booming African percussion and techno weirdness through eight speakers. It's only the two of us now, alone in the store, but he doesn't look up even though he must feel me watching him. I smooth my spiky hair and then, on second thought, I mess it up again.

The music makes it official: This house of worship is open for business. This is the place where people come to find community; they come here to confess their sins and talk to their gods; they come for validation and understanding; they come here to get their groove on, let their hair down, visit the past, look to the future, find some spirituality, search their souls, get some peace, stir things up, or live a little. This is Bob & Bob Records. This is where I work.

In the infamous words of Billy Joel, "the regular crowd

3

shuffles in": Blind Bill and his ancient Seeing Eye dog, Lucy; Becky, the speed freak, yanking at her red hair and always searching for more Iggy Pop like she doesn't already own it all; Mario, the aging record snoop, hoping we put out more used classical LPs overnight; and a ragtag group of desperadoes: small-time criminals, carrying crumpled bags of stolen CDs and DVDs to sell us, hoping we won't remember that we said no yesterday so they can trade their booty for cash to convert into cheap drugs.

Lazarus arrives in a fog of incense, back from the dead. Jimmy the Rasta dude has set up shop on the sidewalk outside the front doors. He sells incense the way Baskin-Robbins sells ice cream. He offers fifty different scents, each one a different color in a different glass jar, but they all smell exactly the same to me. He never has fewer than ten sticks burning at once. Two years of working here and my clothes reek of it. On the heels of the incense is the perpetual wall of patchouli, Telegraph Avenue's signature scent. If you were to combine the incense, the patchouli and urine, you'd have yourself "Eau de Telegraph Avenue." Someone might actually buy it.

Sometimes, though, on a breezy summer day—like today, for instance—if the wind is blowing just right, you can catch the licorice scent of the wild fennel that grows in the empty lot across the street from the store. That sweet smell means that summer is here. It also means school is

4

out, which means I'm officially full-time at Bob & Bob's for the entire summer. Just me, my beloved stacks of vinyl, a lion's share of the craziest people in the universe and a handful of underpaid, overworked, music-obsessed people who work here with me. In other words: paradise, that is, if you happen to be a reclusive music junkie like me.

The guy starts to leave. He makes eye contact again on the way out. I look away first, embarrassed by my preoccupation with him. He brushes shoulders with Laz on his way out the door. Then he's gone. It's like I imagined the whole thing.

"Laz. Hi. Nice that you could make it in."

Laz doesn't respond. He throws his backpack and his motorcycle helmet under the front counter.

"Coffee?" he asks, heading back out the door.

"No, thanks. Had some."

He shrugs and disappears up the street, leaving me alone again.

A guy in a wool cap stumbles into the store.

"Hey, you got a bathroom I can use?"

"Try the park." I point my pen in the direction of People's Park.

"I'm not that desperate," he says, and stumbles back out again.

I don't blame him. People's Park sits directly behind Bob & Bob Records, and back in the day it was a political hot spot where real live hippies came to protest the Vietnam War. Riots broke out and the National Guard was called in and they stormed the street and shot the protesters with rubber bullets and teargassed them and dragged them off and arrested them. But the protesters didn't give up until the war was ended. You don't really see too much of that kind of passion around here anymore. Most of those hippies are grandparents now and their kids belong to the "me" generation and their kids' kids belong to my generation. Judging by the kids at my school, I wouldn't be expecting a revolution anytime soon. I think that you actually have to talk to start a revolution and they don't talk, they text:

Texter #1 (after watching video on Darfur in social studies class): Dude, we should go demonstrate at the park.
Texter #2: What 4?
Texter #1: Darfur?
Texter #2: Who's Darfur? Is that the new chick?
Texter #1: No. It's a country.
Texter #2: LOL, is that by Narnia?

Anyway, the restroom in People's Park was built about two years ago. It took twenty minutes for it to be transformed into a Wal-Mart for street drugs. I don't even think the people who venture in there to buy their drugs would use those toilets.

I was born here in Berkeley sixteen years ago. My mom named me Allie, short for Alberta. When my mom found out that she was pregnant with me, she did the math and discovered that I'd been conceived on their trip to the Canadian Rockies, a place called Lake Louise in the province of Alberta. She said that the skies were *so* blue, the mountains *so* majestic and the glacier-fed lakes *so* pristinely turquoise there that she had to name me after that place. My mom and dad had long dreamed of taking a "rugged" vacation together (and by rugged I mean a mountain view from the window of the luxury château and optional trail rides through previously mentioned mountains). Later, when I showed up earlier than expected, my mom redid the math and realized that I'd actually been conceived in a rather down-at-the-heels Montreal hotel room on the same trip. But it was too late; I was Allie by then (she named me in utero) and Monty would have been a terrible name for a girl.

I think my mom and dad may have been expecting someone different. I don't really look too much like either of them (and absolutely nothing about me screams pristine glacier-fed lakes, blue skies or majestic mountains) but maybe that's because I put a lot of effort into not looking like them. In my mind, I sort of look like the love child of Sid Vicious and Chrissie Hynde. I doubt I'm really pulling it off but I try damn hard.

Bob, the sole owner of Bob & Bob Records, will wander in when he's good and ready and generally after a couple of morning bong hits. He likes to ease into the day. My job here at Bob & Bob Records is pretty much running the place. I serve as cashier, buy used product, restock the bins, order new product, mark down old product, open the store, close the store, and do the staff schedule. During the school year I work nights and weekends but during the summer I'm here five days a week. Bob hired me back when I was fourteen. I told him I was sixteen. I'm pretty sure he knows I was lying about my age, because I've been the same age for two years now. It's a good thing that Bob keeps things pretty loose around here. Not only was I the youngest person ever to apply at Bob & Bob, I was also the only applicant ever to ace the dreaded "product test," which elevated me to a revered place in Bob & Bob history. The way the test works is: Bob hands you a box of randomly chosen CDs and LPs and you have to sort them by section, like, rock, classical, hip-hop, soul, blues, reggae, pop vocal, gospel, country, folk, jazz, and world. You're allowed three errors. Any more than that and you walk the walk of shame, out of the office, through the bins and out the front door, jobless, not good enough for Bob & Bob.

Bob probably thought I'd be stumped right off the bat, but I breezed through the box like a champ, filing the Johnny Burnette Trio in rockabilly, Horace Andy in reggae, Shonen Knife in rock, Sun Ra in jazz, and Lila Downs in world (Mexico, to be exact). The rest was laughably easy. Country Joe & the Fish? Oh, please (rock). What Bob did not know at the time and has since come to know only too well is that I'm what people in the record store business refer to as a "throwback," an "audiophile," a "record geek." Secretly, though, I'm the Vinyl Princess. My knowledge of music is encyclopedic. Before I got this job, I spent more time in this store than Bob's employees. I owned a decent turntable by the time I was seven and by the time I was twelve my vinyl collection had swelled to nine hundred albums. When I was a toddler, my dad would trot me out at parties and yell out the names of Beatles songs and I would answer with the album they appeared on. I never missed. It's mostly his fault I turned out this way. He started me on music when I was still in the womb, playing records, strumming his guitar, using my mom's belly as a drum kit, dragging her to live shows even in her eighth month when she was as big as a house. In the nine months before I was born, I attended every single concert that came to the Greek Theatre in

Berkeley. As an infant, I never got to hear anything as mundane as "Twinkle, Twinkle, Little Star." My lullabies were taken directly from the Beatles' *White Album*. In nursery school, I taught my classmates all the words to "Rocky Raccoon." The note they sent home was ignored. When I started grade school, I didn't know the national anthem or the Pledge of Allegiance but I could chronologically name every Rolling Stones album ever released.

There's probably only one place on earth where a sixteen-year-old girl with a gift like this could be appreciated, and that's right here at Bob & Bob Records on Telegraph Avenue in Berkeley, California.

My mom thinks I'm crazy, or at least that I will be if I keep working here. When I come home from a long day of filing LPs into the bins she tells me I smell like an octogenarian's attic.

Don't get me wrong. I'm well aware that most girls my age wouldn't be relishing the idea of spending the summer in a musty record store. Certainly this isn't the most happening environment for a girl in the prime of her adolescence and I'm already dreading the endless hookup stories my peers will be broadcasting at school come September. Summer vacation is, after all, backseat mating season for adolescents, and I've fared rather poorly in that area thus far for various reasons. I look in the mirror and I see pretty but not the right kind of pretty. Not the kind that gets asked out; more the kind that gets called *interesting* a lot and left alone. I think I might look like I want that, to be left alone. But I've been looking like this for so long that I don't know how to be someone who says, "Ask me out." To be brutally honest, one might go so far as to say that I've created a life here at Bob's because if it weren't for Bob's I would have no life. Sometimes I even wonder if it's more of a place to hide than anything else. It's not that I'm not open to the experience. I've been groped, kissed badly, and my bra came off once, but I've never been romanced. Is it absurdly old-fashioned to wait for romance? I know that I don't look like the type who craves romance, at least not the storybook kind, but I continue to believe that it's out there somewhere. I've never been delusional enough to think that it could simply walk in the door of Bob & Bob's, but then, a week ago, *he* started showing up and I started wondering for the first time in my two years here if maybe love had come for me. I've got a really corny side that's been thinking lately that maybe this summer will be different. Crazy, right? Anyway, my first love is vinyl. Vinyl lives here and here I am.

Laz returns with a large coffee and a newspaper and settles in at the buy counter to read it. His elbows rest on the counter and long, wavy strands of his black hair dangle down, obscuring his face. Every now and then he calls out a headline and shakes his head. Laz is disgusted with the world in general. He feels that humans have evolved into mass consumers of emptiness and we're all destined to die in a fiery and/or watery death when the planet finally and imminently succumbs to global warming. Laz finds solace in speed metal.

Mornings tend to drag around here and I take advantage of the time to go online and check my brand-new blog, even though Bob has specifically told us we are not to use the computer for our personal business. I will remember to erase my history. Recently (like three days ago), I started a blog called thevinylprincess.com. It started out as an experiment to see if there was anyone out there in the world who cared about music and vinyl the way I do, I mean besides Bob and some of his customers. It occurred to me that if you were a chain-saw juggler and you Googled *chain-saw jugglers* you'd find your people in a matter of seconds, so how hard could it be for me to find *my* people? I'm hoping that if there's enough of us and we all find one another, maybe we can band together and turn the music world around; maybe we can start a movement just like in the sixties in People's Park. We could revolt against corporate rock and downloading and digitizing and Clear Channel. Okay, sure, you won't see vinyl collectors rioting in the streets, but at the very least we could become a vinyl preservation society.

My blog pops onto the screen. It looks a bit understated and a bit basic, as music blogs go (this coming from a girl who didn't really know how a blog worked until six months ago). This morning's blog is an insightful piece about glam rock. I explore the rise and fall of the New York Dolls and continue on with Lou Reed, Roxy Music, David Bowie, Queen and Mott the Hoople. Granted, I wrote this in twenty minutes but in the comments box below the blog is a big fat zero. No comments. I scroll down to the number of hits: twenty-two. Most of them are mine. Maybe there isn't anyone out there. Maybe it's just a barren, postapocalyptic plain of endless asphalt parking lots with empty Starbucks cups blowing around. Or maybe I need to write a better blog, get people thinking, write a mission statement. I flip through music magazines while I'm thinking about this. I favor the British ones like *Mojo* and *Q*; the reviews are better and they stay away from mainstream crap. I'm careful not to bend the pages back too far or spill anything on them because I put them back on the magazine rack when I'm done. I come across a *Mojo* interview with Elvis Costello, whom I adore. The interviewer asks him a question about playing live and Elvis talks about how he'll never stop playing live and then he says something that grabs me by the throat: "I'm not of a mind to record anymore. The MP3 has dismantled the intended shape of an album." That's it!

The MP3 has dismantled the intended shape of an album. I could never have come up with that on my own. I'll quote him in my blog. He'll inspire thousands.

Summer mornings are particularly quiet here on the avenue because in May, when the school year ends, the Cal students head back to whatever cultural vacuums they came from, leaving us blissfully student-free for two and a half months. The population shrinks down to roughly half its size. In the old days, when dinosaurs roamed the earth, students actually shopped at Bob & Bob's for their music, but that was before downloading became de rigueur, effectively killing independent record stores. A lot (a *lot*) of the Cal students are expert downloaders. Bob points this out with increasing frequency. He says the word *downloaders* with extra emphasis, like he's saying *freeloaders*. He's more than a little annoyed that the students seem to have no idea what we're selling here. Groups of earbud-wearing downloaders saunter past the dusty, eclectically decorated windows, oblivious to the treasures inside, searching like lost sheep for the Gap, which closed two years ago. They will never know the joy of flipping through a bin of records, being captivated by the cover art and reading the liner notes. Bob calls them the Lost Generation. He stands at the counter, arms crossed at his chest, watching them out the window, and seethes. He wants someone to blame. Some days he blames technology for tragically altering the way that people get their music with no regard for the music itself; some days he blames the record companies for being oblivious; some days it's corporate America for killing the mom-and-pops, or suburban malls for obvious reasons; and then eventually it all comes back around to Richard Nixon. I'm a little fuzzy on this part of the equation. I'm not entirely sure how a dead president could be responsible for a kid buying an AC/DC CD at Wal-Mart instead of at Bob & Bob's, but Bob's a bit of a conspiracy theorist and he likes nothing more than to explain to unsuspecting customers the exact moment when this country started going to hell. Bob threatens to sell the store daily but the fact is no one would buy it even if he could sell it, which he can't because it's his life, and he also can't because he doesn't own; he leases.

Aidan, the only employee at Bob's who never has to deal with the public, skulks past me. Aidan takes misanthropy to a whole new level. He turns his head slightly my way as acknowledgment (*I see you but I don't want to talk to you*) and nods almost imperceptibly. Aidan prices and processes in a tiny room in the back affectionately known as the Cave. He's tall and whisper thin with a sort of a bloodless look to him. He disappears into his environment like a chameleon. It seems that his only desire in life is not to be noticed. He also owns, I've heard, a pretty badass record collection that took most of his lifetime to accumulate.

"Good morning, Aidan," I greet him enthusiastically. I've spent two years trying to pry him loose. Also, truthfully, I want to underline a contrast between us: I'm extra-effervescent around him because I see some of myself in him and sometimes it scares me.

"Morning," he says quietly, and then he's gone.

"Hey, what's that Frank Zappa album with the song about frosting a cake?" asks my first customer, a kid dressed like a perp. He's got a black baseball cap pulled down over his eyes and he's wearing guyliner. Bits of oily dark hair poke out from underneath his cap, which matches his too-big black satin jacket with red trim. It's zipped all the way up to his pale thin neck. He reeks of cheap cologne, meant to mask days of BO, and it's not working.

"*Sheik Yerbouti*," I tell him, and look back down at my magazine.

"You got a used copy of that?"

"I saw one out there yesterday. Did you check the section?"

"Nah. What's that under?"

"Z." I look at him like he must be kidding.

"Right. Z." He wanders away.

Should I have taken him by the hand and led him over to the Zappa? No. I won't spoon-feed the customers. If you don't know your alphabet, you have no business leaving your house, let alone shopping for premium music.

The store slowly fills up with shoppers and I close my magazine. Blind Bill and his companion, Jeff, are still scouring the blues section. Jeff recites the songlists off the backs of CDs to Bill while Lucy sleeps next to them on the floor. They practically live here. Chet Baker's sweet, sad voice fills the room singing "My Funny Valentine." He sounds so hopeful that it's hard to believe he eventually jumped out a window in Amsterdam. Some people say he was pushed. I know better.

Employees are no longer allowed to choose the music that plays in the store. Bob fills the six-CD carousel before he goes home every night, and if we touch anything other than the play button on the stereo we risk losing all Bob & Bob's privileges, which include borrowing anything in the store for up to two weeks. This rule came about when certain employees started dominating the CD player and certain other employees got bent out of shape about it and one thing led to another and someone got hit in the head with the edge of a CD case and had to go to the emergency room and get eleven stitches. Just for the record, it was a Mötley Crüe CD. So now Bob has to make it in before the entire carousel has played or anarchy will undoubtedly ensue. Fortunately, my musical tastes often intersect with

17

Bob's. I like about half the stuff he loads into the carousel.

Bob appears at noon, disheveled and sleepy. He's wearing a tissue-thin T-shirt advertising a Who concert (that he undoubtedly attended) over another T-shirt that I remember from yesterday. He's not a man who makes complicated wardrobe decisions. His wife, Dao, follows him through the door. Dao and Bob met on one of Bob's many trips to Thailand and they were married on the beach in Phuket six years ago. Dao is all sweetness and smiles until you cross her, and we all know better than that now. Her English isn't very good despite the fact that she always seems to be taking an English class somewhere. I've suggested to Bob that maybe we should all take Thai lessons and make things a whole lot easier around here. Dao memorizes words she hears on television but she often confuses the definitions. She uses the word *runway* for *road* and *top* for *good*, and *guest* for *friend* and *pop* for *put* and *nation* for any sort of place. I like Dao a lot even though we have a tough time communicating. She's informed me many times that I'm a "top guest" to her. Bob adores Dao but they fight like cats and dogs. Dao might be one of the most beautiful women I've ever seen. Her hair is about nine feet long and cascades down her back in a shiny blue-black river. Her features are small and delicate. She has a habit of turning her head to one side when she doesn't quite understand you. This is usually followed by a wide smile, featuring perfectly straight white teeth. You can't help but smile right back at her. She can even get Laz to smile. Dao is Bob's third wife and the only one I've met. The veteran staff members say she's the favorite so far by a long shot. There's a rumor that the first two wives are buried in Bob's backyard. Bob can be difficult.

Dao chirps a smiley "Hello" to everyone as she passes the counter on her way to the office in the back. She was an accountant back in Thailand and she works on the books here at Bob's. Over her shoulder she's carrying a large bright red handbag roughly half her size. It obscures her tiny body and makes her look like a tomato with legs.

Bob stops directly in front of me at the counter.

"Al? Who's that in sound tracks?" He points backward over his shoulder. I follow his finger.

Shorty and Jam, two street people who are regularly ejected from the store, look like they're reenacting a bar fight. Shorty is hanging on to Jam's foot, which is up in the air.

"So I grabbed his foot like this and I stopped the kick. I stopped it dead," says Shorty.

"No way. No goddamn way!" says Jam, his eyes wide in disbelief.

I look at Bob. "We let them back in, remember?"

"No."

"You want me to throw them out?"

"No. I'll talk to them."

He walks over to sound tracks. Shorty and Jam start flipping through vinyl musicals when they see Bob approach. Shorty pulls out a vinyl copy of *The Sound of Music* and pretends to read the back of it.

"Guys. You need to chill or I'll toss you out again, okay?"

"Yeah, okay, Bob, you bet," says Shorty.

Jam stands at attention and salutes Bob. Bob walks back to the office, his shoulders slumped, sighing and shaking his head. Shorty and Jam are a good example of the type of street people who spend most of their time on the avenue. Their behavior ranges from harmless to annoying to extremely cantankerous. These two are unusual even for Telegraph Avenue, because in addition to abusing drugs and alcohol, they also dabble in cross-dressing; they like to wear women's clothing. Not generally a whole outfit; usually just a flourish here and there. Like today, for instance, Jam is wearing a pale pink polyester blouse with a ruffle down the front and Shorty is carrying a beaded handbag.

Jennifer, our resident goth chick and my relief on the cash register, saunters in at twelve fifteen. She's always late and she always has a great excuse. The expression she paints on her otherwise expressionless face daily is slightly smudged at the eyebrows. Jennifer is our least helpful employee unless you happen to be looking for Dead Can Dance or the Cure or Siouxsie and the Banshees.

"Sorry," she says, but she's not. "The damn bus breaks down and we all have to pile off like a bunch of refugees while they find another one for us, like there's just going to be an extra bus sitting around somewhere that they can send right over, like we live in Mayberry or something."

"So, did they find one?"

She shrugs. "I dunno, I took off, got a cab and blew ten bucks on the fare." She yanks off her leather motorcycle jacket and throws it under the register. She checks her slash of red lipstick in a little mirror she keeps in a drawer at the counter and smooths her skirt over her fishnet stockings. She reties the laces on her knee-high Doc Martens and stands up.

"Well, I'm going to lunch." I hate to rain on her rant but I'm late. Jennifer is a victim and lives to complain. She has twenty-seven ex-boyfriends who all did her wrong, parents who abused her, countless friends who abandoned her and an entire system working against her. She'll still be ranting when I get back.

"Go, go. I'm here. Who said you had to wait?" she asks impatiently.

I walk out the front door into the glare and head up the

street, past the head shops and two bookstores, to Swarma, a vegetarian Indian joint. I'm meeting my friend Kit for lunch. She works at a vintage-clothing store just up the avenue from Bob's, and when we're both on the street, we try to eat together. She's seated at a table in the window when I arrive. She's already spooning dal soup into her mouth. Kit wears vintage like no one else. Her outfits look like they were put together by a team of professional costume designers. Today she's wearing an off-white silk blouse with a burgundy velvet fitted vest and a black pleated miniskirt with chunky Mary Jane heels. By contrast, I am wearing a Blondie T-shirt and skinny jeans in need of a wash. I look like the person who should be carrying her luggage.

"Man, are you late. I ordered. Got you the spinach paneer. I hope that's okay."

"Fine." I pull out a chair across from her and sit down. "Jennifer was late again."

"Bitch. What's with that chick?"

I shrug and snap off a piece of papadam. I dip it into a small bowl of mango chutney. A waitress puts a fragrant metal bowl of dark green spinach paneer and a plate of fluffy Frisbee-size discs of naan bread on the table between us.

"Thanks." I smile at her. I take a sip of my water and dig in.

I've known Kit since preschool. We're very tight. We

feel the same way about almost everything but we're nothing alike. Kit gets a *lot* of attention from guys. She coyly pretends not to notice but she knows how to flirt and she does it shamelessly (I am the absolute worst at flirting unless you count blushing violently when a guy looks at me); she's petite (oh, how the boys love that); and she's got enough confidence for both of us. Kit has a sense of feminine adventure that I envy. One of her most admirable qualities is that she can change her mind about anything, unapologetically, at the last second. Somehow, even the nastiest of baristas and waiters don't seem to mind. I have a habit of letting her sit in the driver's seat in these matters. She chickened out of a tattoo a few months ago and I followed suit. We opted for piercings instead (hers is a navel ring and mine was a nose ring until three days later, when I got it caught on a cardigan, which turned out to be a blessing because it's since occurred to me that the whole world, or at least my whole world, is either tattooed or pierced).

Kit also handpicked the boy who delivered each of us our first kiss after rejecting several other candidates at the last second. I should probably also mention that we were eight and we each had to give him a dollar. I can't remember a time when Kit didn't have a boyfriend. I can't remember a time when I did. Kit is handbags and high heels to my backpacks and Converse sneakers. Kit would never set foot on a skateboard, let alone consider it a mode of transportation, and I couldn't live without mine.

In matters pertaining to music, however, Kit lets me lead and she does not judge. I could show up at her house with *The Best of the Partridge Family* under my arm and she'd say, "Cool. Let's put it on." Her knowledge of music runs deep and she has a small collection of rare picture-sleeve 45s, but she's no match for me.

Kit is telling me all about the road trip she and her boyfriend, Niles, are planning for next summer. Niles is a bass player in a garage band called Auntie Depressant. They met when Niles came into the vintage store looking for stage clothes. Kit sold him a white shirt with ruffles on the cuffs and a pair of women's leather capri pants. When I met Niles, I immediately pegged him as one of those guys who works hard to look a lot more dangerous than he is. He went to private school in the Oakland Hills, and his techno-geek parents paid for his private bass guitar lessons. He somehow never has any money and Kit ends up paying for almost everything. Admittedly, he's adorable, and Kit loves him, so I've never shared my real feelings about him with her.

Kit and I have our distinct roles in this relationship. She is the outgoing boy magnet who always arrives with a good story about a boy, and I am the faithful, long-suffering best friend who listens to it and then offers up advice, pretending that I could possibly be qualified to do that.

Kit already has their route mapped out on a dog-eared road map of the U.S. she carries everywhere with her. They're planning on stopping at every kitschy roadside attraction and every indie record store that they can find along the way. Kit's been saving money for this trip for over a year now. I'm going to assume that Niles hasn't saved a dime.

Kit starts to describe to me a record store on her road-trip itinerary, a place called Hot Poop in Walla Walla, Washington, that she found online this morning. It's right next to a vintage-clothing store called Sunset Boulevard. I have a forkful of spinach in midair when he walks past the window. It's him again. Two sightings in a day? Unprecedented. I drop my fork and look up at him. He sees me too. He has the most unusual eyes: pale blue-green but dark rimmed, like an Egyptian cat. Kit sees him too.

"Who is *that*?" she asks, abandoning the road-trip highlights.

I shrug. "I dunno. Probably a customer," I say, embarrassed about my possible crush on a total stranger.

She cranes her neck to watch behind her as he disappears up the avenue. "Cute."

She's right. He is cute. I grin at Kit and dip my fork into the spinach again.

My mom and I live in an ancient low-slung house in the Elmwood District, seven and a half minutes from Bob & Bob's by skateboard. This time of year the wisteria vines dangle the last of their lacy purple flowers through a trellis that hangs over a deep porch out front, where two old, sagging wicker chairs sit empty most of the time. We rarely sit out here, even though it looks pretty inviting. A glass pitcher of frosty lemonade and a basket of mending would look right at home on the little table between the chairs, but we're not the Waltons; we're the Westons, and half of us live somewhere else.

About a year ago, at yet another cocktail party featuring academic blowhards spouting off about something they read in a book or wrote in a book (and likely stole from another book), my mom was discussing her dissertation topic, Pushkin's poetry, with a colleague from her PhD program when my dad turned to her and told her that he didn't want to be married to her anymore. My mom reached for a cheese puff and asked him why not. He said that he didn't think she completed him. My mom was mystified by this. She'd never really completed anything in her life. Half-finished crossword puzzles were scattered about the house, half-read books, half-read articles; piles of clothes that could be worn if they were ironed sat in a basket under the ironing board; half-eaten food filled the fridge; and her half-written dissertation sat in a jumbled pile next to her computer under a half-eaten apple. How on earth could she be expected to complete another human being if she'd never even finished a carton of yogurt?

My dad moved out shortly after that conversation and moved in with Kee Kee, who lives on a massive spread in Santa Cruz. I'm not sure if Kee Kee "completes" my dad, but she's completely rich, so that probably helps. Kee Kee's dad invented some sort of medical software that changed the world (he couldn't have known how much it would change *my* world) and he bought Kee Kee a ranch, so now all she has to do is ride her very expensive Austrian horses all day and kick the help around. While we're on the subject, why are rich girls who ride large animals always named after small dogs? Anyway, my dad hates horses, so he "dabbles" in real estate, a career he sort of fell into when he retired from playing drums in a band. Real estate offices in California are filled with ex–rock stars. They put on suits and pretend they know how to golf, but every now and then a tattoo will emerge from under a sleeve or a skull ring will show up on a finger or a roach clip will peek out of a car ashtray on the way to an open house.

Now my dad and I talk on the phone about things that never mattered when we lived under the same roof, like the weather and school. Sometimes he'll drive to Berkeley and we'll go somewhere stupid to eat. Ever since he moved out, my dad treats me like an appliance that he just pulled from a box and hasn't read the manual for yet. He has no idea how to make it work. Sometimes he'll try to inject Kee Kee into the conversation; like he'll say, "Kee Kee thinks—" and I'll say, "Whoa, stop right there; we both know Kee Kee doesn't think." And then he'll sigh and say, "I wish you would try to get to know her." And I'll say, "Dad, she listens to Dave Matthews. It's not gonna happen."

I leap up the wide, sagging wooden steps to our house, passing Pierre on his way out. He pretends not to know me. Pierre is our cat, although I'm sure he doesn't see it that way. Even as we were rescuing him from certain death at the animal shelter when he was a kitten, he seemed to have complete disdain for us. We decided that he must be French: hence the name.

I yank open the front door and drop my skateboard in the foyer next to a Chinese urn filled with umbrellas that my mom steals from restaurants. I smell exotic spices, which means Ravi is here. My mom and Ravi are sitting at the big French farm table in the dining room with mugs of chai in front of them. My mom bought this table after my dad moved his drum kit out of our dining room and into Kee Kee's house. The dining room had never actually been used for dining before, and we left it empty for a long time, detouring around the big empty space, not sure how to deal with it. The table arrived one afternoon but we didn't actually sit down at it for months. We stood next to it and looked at it a lot, running our hands along the smooth grain of the old wood. Pierre liked to groom himself on it and stretch out in the afternoon sun. Then my mom came home with two old wooden chairs she found at a garage sale and we started eating the occasional meal sitting at it instead of cross-legged on the kitchen counter or standing over the sink or lying in the bathtub. Now the table is a part of us. We like it. It's amazing how much crap you can put on a table and still find room to eat. I often wonder where we put stuff before the table appeared.

Ravi is a professor of literature at UC Berkeley. He's writing a book about Alexander Solzhenitsyn and my mom is his research assistant. Ravi is the classic rumpled-professor stereotype. He wears a threadbare tweed jacket that smells of wet wool and the same corduroy pants year-round. His salt-and-pepper hair falls into little curls at his collar, and his disheveled beard often has crumbs of food in it. He grew up in New Delhi but he's British educated, so even though he looks rumpled, he's always unnecessarily formal. He nods at me when I walk in the door and his dark, expressive eyes wrinkle into a smile.

"Miss Allie. How are you today?"

"I'm good, Ravi, how about you?"

"I'm very good today," he says, pulling strips of fruit leather off a roll. "Your mother has just given me this delicious sweet snack made from apricots."

My mom rolls her eyes at me over her laptop computer. Ravi travels through his life somewhat oblivious to any form of pop culture, but when you introduce him to something new, he's all over it. You have to appreciate that naive enthusiasm.

Ravi spends a lot of time over here because his apartment is teensy, and once my dad left and the massive table arrived, it seemed to make more sense that they work from here. Ravi has written four books and he's won all kinds of literary awards, but it seems to make no difference to the way he lives his life. He doesn't seem to need much to make him happy. He reads books almost every waking moment of his life, and I don't think he has a lot of friends outside his little academic world. My mom likes working for Ravi because she can poach a lot of the research she does for him for her own half-finished dissertation. I also think she likes Ravi. He's a nice person in a bumbling, neurotic sort of way. He's like an East Indian version of Woody Allen.

"Oh, and, Miss Allie?" he remarks. "Thank you for the Tchaikovsky. You're right: It's outstanding, the finest recording of the unfinished symphony that I've ever heard. I don't have any idea how I've lived so long without it in my collection."

"You're welcome, Ravi."

"There's tea on the stove," says my mom.

"Thanks." I wander into the kitchen. The pot of chai sits on the gas. My mom buys the spices in Little India on University Avenue and then she slow-cooks it with the milk and sugar on the stove like they do in India. Ravi taught her how to do this and to my mom it's culinary quantum physics. It's the only thing my mom knows how to cook. I take a mug from the cupboard and pour the fragrant steaming milk into it. I hold it up to my face and inhale. It's glorious, nothing at all like Starbucks.

I balance the mug on a stack of LPs I "borrowed" from Bob & Bob's and make my way upstairs, stopping in front of Suki's door. I press my ear against it and listen for signs of life, a habit I developed soon after she moved in. When my dad moved out, my mom decided to rent out his old office to a student. We cleaned it up and painted the walls a soft green. My mom put an ad in with student housing and Suki arrived on our doorstep the next day. She looked to weigh about ninety pounds soaking wet, and she really was soaking wet. It was pouring rain and she had no rain-coat or umbrella. We showed her the room, she signed the lease, and my mom handed her a stolen umbrella on the way out.

She moved in a week later with her meager belongings and, although she shares a bathroom and the kitchen with us, we never see or hear her. We've never even heard her so much as flush the toilet. Curiosity got the better of us one day and we broke into her room while she was at school. My mom insisted that it isn't technically a break-in if you have a key and you suspect foul play. I'm not sure what she meant by *foul play*. Someone who never makes a peep would seem like the opposite of foul to me. I expected something monastic, and it was rather spare, but Suki had everything she needed in that tiny room: A hot plate and packets of miso soup and green tea were neatly laid out on an empty suitcase on the floor. A tiny desk with her computer and a small collection of books sat up against the only window, and a tidily made futon was rolled out on the floor with a clock next to it. A plain wood-framed mirror hung on the wall with a snapshot of a smiling Japanese family tucked into its frame. Her clothes were lined up in a neat row in the closet. We closed the door and felt incredibly guilty for being such busybodies. We accepted Suki's ghostliness after that, just as she seemed to accept our tendency to shout at each other and play weird music at all hours.

I carry the chai into my room and set it down on the desk next to the chaotic jumble of wires and components that I call my stereo system. I suppose that *system* might not be the right word. None of my pieces came from the same place or even the same era. I have an ancient Technics turntable. I prefer it to the one I grudgingly got recently with a USB plug for making mixes. I have a newish Sony CD player, four Infinity speakers I inherited from my dad, a set of enormous headphones that look like the Professor from *Gilligan's Island* made them out of coconut shells, and a Pioneer amp that looks very mid-eighties to me that I bought at a garage sale for ten bucks. It's a mess to the naked eye but, after years of my tweaking and moving and adjusting, the sound quality is finally magnificent. Two entire walls of my room are lined with wooden cases filled with vinyl LPs, a collection that consumes my thoughts.

I flip through the stack of LPs from Bob's and decide on a European import of David Bowie—*Young Americans*. I slide the vinyl LP out of its jacket, holding it with my fingertips. I love the look of vinyl, the smell of it, the tiny crackles you hear before the song starts. I place it on the turntable, click on my amp and lower the diamond needle on the first song. The honky-tonk piano and sax intro to "Young Americans," possibly—no, definitely—one of the most amazing songs ever recorded, starts up. I arrange myself on my bed with the album cover and my mug. I sip the chai and lie there watching Bowie watching me in all his airbrushed, androgynous perfection. Cigarette smoke curls around his painted fingernails. He dares me not to fall in love. I close my eyes and listen.

As I'm flipping the record over to the B side I hear my mom saying good-bye to Ravi at the front door. She comes up the stairs and leans far enough into my room to lower the volume on my stereo.

"Hey, I've got that thing tonight," she says, running her fingers through her long brown hair and letting it fall onto her shoulders. She looks tired. "I think I'll wear my Nicole Miller."

"Good. I like that dress." I smile at her.

"Would you mind taking your sneakers off the bed? That's gross."

I kick one Converse onto the floor and then the other; they land with a clunk on the rag rug next to the bed.

My mom has recently started roaming the vast and perilous sea of love known as internet dating, searching for her intellectual equal. When it comes to men, my mom's at a bit of a loss. She fell in love with my dad when she was nineteen. He was drumming in a band called Fool's Gold, a retro-Byrdsy, vocally heavy group. They sounded a bit like the Jayhawks. My mom was in the first row, a pretty college girl with a tan and a wide smile. My dad was smitten. Now, at forty-two, my mom says she refuses to give up on men just because Dad turned out to be a huge disappointment. She's taken a sort of "someday my prince will come" attitude to surfing for love, and I hate to discourage her, but I just don't think it works that way. My mom's already been on two dates with toads. The first one was with a guy who listed reading and opera as two of his interests. He made a reservation at Chez Panisse for dinner and my mom ran around like a schoolgirl getting ready for her prom, trying on every piece of clothing she owns. She was home two hours later. Jeff didn't read much beyond the sports page and the backs of cereal boxes, and he'd never actually been to the opera. He was quick to mention that he did write a tax-deductible check to the San Francisco Opera every year on behalf of his business, which had something to do with bilking retirees out of their retirement money. Turns out he was getting his sister-in-law to respond to my mom's emails because he wasn't much of a writer (duh). He snapped his fingers at the waitress at Chez Panisse and that was it for my mom. She pretended to have a migraine and excused herself. She was back from the second date even faster, looking pale, and she wouldn't talk about that one. Now she asks for IQ scores. She's not leaving the house for anything less than one twenty-five. For one forty, she'll even shave her legs. Tonight's date is a civil engineer, a freshly divorced transplant from the Midwest with an IQ of a hundred and twenty-eight, or so he says. Who wouldn't lie about their IQ score? And besides, smart doesn't always mean nice.

Mom reappears in my doorway in the dress, a simple black sleeveless thing that makes her look like the opposite of who she is. She turns around and shows me the back.

"How does my butt look?"

"Good. You might want to consider a thong, though; you have VPL."

"VPL?"

"Visible panty line."

She moves to a mirror on top of my bureau and cranes her head around, straining to catch a glimpse of her butt.

"I can't wear one of those things. They're like medieval torture devices. Why am I supposed to look like I don't wear underpants? Wouldn't a man assume that I have underwear on under this?"

I shrug. "I dunno. It's complicated."

"Do you own a thong?"

"Nope. Kit has one in every color, though." Kit's lingerie collection mystifies me. My collection is not a collection and it could easily belong to an eleven-year-old boy.

My mom spins around and adjusts her breasts in the mirror, fussing with her bra straps. I watch her, thinking, *Shouldn't that be me? Shouldn't I be the one fussing over what to wear on a date while my mom looks on and gives sage advice?*

"Tell me I've at least got this part right. I just spent fifty dollars on a new bra."

"You look great. Almost hot."

"What are you going to do tonight?" she asks me, still working with the bra.

"Nothing much. I'm kind of tired."

"Do you feel okay? You want me to cancel?"

"You wish. No, Mom, you have to go. What if he's great?" I try to look hopeful for her.

"What if he's not?"

"Only one way to find out."

My mom sighs and starts to walk out of my room, her shoulders sagging. Her high heels clack against the hardwood as she walks, leaving divots. At my door she stops and turns. "If this one is horrible, that's it. I'm done."

"Good attitude."

She grimaces and clacks down the hallway like Dead Man Walking.

I watch out my bedroom window as my mom takes the porch stairs gingerly in her heels and heads up the street toward the wine bar where her alleged prince awaits. The irony of this role reversal isn't lost on me: me watching from the window like a worried mother as my mother heads out on a date.

I take off David Bowie and replace him with the Sex Pistols—*Never Mind the Bollocks*. I crank the volume and take the stairs two at a time, arriving in the kitchen in time to see a spider scuttling across the countertop. He's one of the black ones. We have three kinds in the house: the black ones, which are the scariest, the translucent white ones, which can easily be mistaken for small dust bunnies, and then the dangly-legged ones that do push-ups when you try to touch them. I wonder what the different colors do when they run into one another; do spiders have turf wars? Or do they all live a harmonious existence in our house, respectful of one another's space? God knows we've got enough bugs for everyone in this place.

"I'll let you live if you promise not to get any bigger," I tell him. He disappears between the stove and the fridge.

I pull a frozen mushroom pizza out of the freezer, a small ice cave, badly in need of defrosting. I kick the refrigerator door shut with my foot, balancing on the other one to lean over and turn the oven on. I execute a series of complicated pseudo-ballet moves that I made up, over to the cupboard for a glass, keeping perfect time to Johnny Rotten's ragged vocals as he belts out "Holidays in the Sun." My plan is simple: pizza, a little light dinner music while writing a blog update including my plan to take over the world, and a movie—I have my choice of several that I borrowed from Bob & Bob's but I'm leaning toward *On the Waterfront*, an enduring classic, and then, if my mom's not back, a little pacing of the floors, but somehow I get the feeling she'll be home in time for the end of the movie. She loves Marlon Brando like I do.

At five a.m. on Saturday morning, my eyes fly open and I'm wide-awake. Ideas are rushing into my brain at a very high rate of speed. I slide out of bed and walk barefoot across the creaking floor and into the hallway. My mom's bedroom door is shut. She'd better be alone in there. I didn't even hear her come in last night. I go back into my room and turn my computer on. Here's the plan: Not only will my blog contain a powerful mission statement and a daily LP blog, but every week I'll post my top five vinyl picks. Readers will be encouraged to participate in that. Plus I'll publish a Vinyl Princess fanzine anonymously and distribute it to the world through Bob & Bob's and a mailing list that I'll compile through the blog. It's brilliant. I start in on the mission statement:

Welcome to my blog. I am The Vinyl Princess and I am devoted to the preservation and sharing of music in LP form. I have spent countless hours searching for the very best music available on vinyl and I am committed to keeping it safe, sharing it with you and keeping it real. Are you a vinyl junkie too? Share your thoughts with me; share your music with me. You are home. Corporate rock still sucks; downloading is harmful to music and other living organisms.

Music is love.

VP

I put the Elvis Costello quote below that and then I work on the fanzine till I can't see straight. It's only a few pages long but I figure I'll try to put a new issue out each month and, naturally, it will get longer each time. I'll finish it when I get home from work and then take it over to Krishna Copy and print it out. I grab my still-dirty jeans off the floor and pull them on. I search for my bra in all the likely places (under the bed, on the bathroom floor, in with my extension cords) and finally give up and yank a black Stray Cats T-shirt over my head (I am able to go braless, part gift, part curse). While I brush my teeth I wet my free hand and try to arrange my hair into something besides a woodland creature perched on my head. I pull on my sneakers, dash downstairs, pour myself a bowl of cereal and pound it. I'm late.

The weekend scene on the avenue features a whole different kind of shopper. At Bob & Bob's we call them "B and Ts," which stands for "bridge and tunnelers": suburbanites who venture in from the far-flung suburbs over bridges, through tunnels, along endless freeways to participate in the urban experience, get a tattoo, score some drugs and look at the freaks, who purposely act extra-freaky, hoping for handouts.

Some Saturdays, there's a preacher on the corner across the street from the store quoting scripture into a microphone, trying to save some souls. He's got the haunted look of an ex–drug addict or a Vietnam vet. As his voice escalates, his face turns red and the veins in his neck pop out as he waves his thin white arms and works himself into a frenzy. Dark circles of perspiration form in the armpits of his short-sleeved shirt as he alerts all sinners who pass by that the time has come to take Jesus Christ into their hearts. He can't seem to stress enough that we're running out of time before we're all doomed to eternal damnation, but he's been standing on the corner for years and nothing much has changed. No one around here pays too much attention to the Jesus guy. Sometimes I wonder what he does on the Saturdays he's not on the corner. Maybe he mows his lawn or goes to the movies or maybe he has an alternative spot for saving souls.

My only job on weekends at Bob & Bob's is as cashier and phone answerer. There's not much time for anything else; the B and Ts are a needy bunch. There is hand-holding involved. The hours fly by and I answer the same basic questions all day long. "Where's the new Pink, Beyoncé, Avril Lavigne, Gwen Stefani, Nickelback, Lil Wayne?" The answer to that question is, "Right behind you." We keep a rack of CDs right at the front of the store filled with everything that the B and Ts could possibly want or were brainwashed to want by MTV and VH1 or Clear Channel. They have no business in the bowels of the store.

When a fourteen-year-old girl who's trying way too hard to look eighteen leans over the counter snapping her gum and says, "Hey," I ask her how I can help. I can't take my eyes off the raw pink of her freshly pierced nostril. My own personal piercing experience followed by the cardigan fiasco is still pretty fresh in my mind.

"I'm looking for a CD?" She states it in the form of a question.

"Can you be more specific?" I ask, also in the form of a question.

"Yeah. It's by this girl. I heard it on the radio, like, a

thousand times. I can sing it. Should I sing it?" She snaps her gum. Her breath smells like fake watermelon.

"No." We discourage *American Idol* auditions. "Did you happen to see the music video?"

"Um, yeah, sure."

"Okay, turn around and look at that rack behind you. Does anyone pop out at you?"

"*Omigod!* There she is!" She grabs a Lily Allen CD and clutches it to her heart: another satisfied customer.

The phone rings and I grab it. "Bob and Bob's." I cradle it under my chin as I ring up the girl's CD; she vibrates like Paris Hilton's Chihuahua in anticipation.

"Allie, it's me," says my mom. She sounds groggy.

"Did you just get up?" I ask, sounding like her parole officer. I take the girl's crumpled bills and hand her the change. I slip the CD into a psychedelic Bob & Bob's bag and hand it to her.

"Sort of. Sorry I was so late getting in. I hope you didn't worry."

"No," I lie. "I went through all your jewelry and decided what to sell if you were dead."

"Yeah? What did you come up with?"

"Nothing. You have crap jewelry. So, how did it go?"

"He's nice. His name's Jack."

I don't acknowledge the name. "Nice?"

"Well, he's nice and smart and interesting, and kind of funny."

"Funny?" I wasn't prepared for funny. I wasn't even prepared for nice.

"Yes. Funny, like he made me laugh."

"Like out loud or just a chuckle here and there?"

"Out loud."

Bob walks by me and mimes going for coffee or beer; it's the same gesture. I wave at him.

"So, he makes you laugh out loud?" I ask again, doubtfully.

"Yes. Out loud." She starts to lose patience. "Would you prefer he were a serial killer? Could you at least try to be a little more positive?"

I would point out that, this early in the game, it would be foolish to assume he's not a serial killer, but I feel she might not appreciate that. "Sorry. Are you going to see him again?"

"Yes. Thursday. He's coming over for dinner."

"You mean to our house?"

"Yes."

A line is forming at my cash register.

"But we don't do dinner."

"We'll think of something. Let's talk when you get home, okay?"

"Okay." I click the phone off. I start ringing people up, avoiding eye contact so I can analyze my shocking behavior regarding "Jack." Do I not want my mother to be happy? Is that it? What's this nagging discomfort I'm feeling? Am I afraid she'll fall in love and get married and move to the Midwest and have children with "Jack," leaving me alone in that rambling old house with only Suki the ghost and an insolent cat for company? It seems rather unlikely. My mom doesn't even acknowledge the Midwest as a real place and she had her tubes tied ages ago, after I was born. Maybe they'll adopt chubby, happy little Chinese babies, hundreds of them. Love does strange things to people. Look at my dad; he's overlooking an IQ in the negatives to be with a woman he says he loves. I try to put the whole "Jack" thing out of my mind but it hovers in the back of it like a needy first grader with his hand up in the air, trying to get my attention.

To make matters worse, as my "up before dawn" fatigue starts catching up with me, Joey Spinelli, hands-down the coolest guy at my high school, gets in line. He possesses a certain swagger specific to Italians and an old-fashioned brand of handsome that I adore in spite of myself. My only interaction with him was that our lockers were next to each other for a whole school year in tenth grade so I was privy to the comings and goings of his various girlfriends, many of whom were in eleventh grade, all of whom looked like beauty pageant contestants (not only was I not a contestant, I was not even qualified to spray glue on their butts for the swimsuit competition). As Joey moves closer to the front of the line I pretend not to notice him even though he's blinking like neon. Then he's standing right in front of me, Springsteen CD in hand. He looks at me the way he looks at all members of the opposite sex, starting with my slept-on attempt at a retro Joan Jett hairstyle; my unwashed face with traces of yesterday's eyeliner and mascara, the only makeup I ever wear, still lingering somewhere near my eyes, I hope; and down to the Stray Cats, stopping for as long as it takes to appraise my breasts (God, why didn't I keep looking for that bra?); and then down to the counter I'm standing behind, where he's forced to use his imagination regarding my butt. I see a light of recognition go on. Not a bright light, more of a flashlight.

"Heyyyyyyy . . ." He struggles for my name, comes up empty.

"Allie," I offer.

"Right. Allie." He points at me. He looks around. "You work here?"

"Sure hope so, I've been coming here for two years."

He chuckles and leans in a bit. "You look good," he says, giving me the once-over again. He has a way of saying it that makes you understand that he knows his approval means a lot to people.

You look good, I think to myself and, in spite of my inner feminist, I'm thrilled to hear that Joey Spinelli thinks I look good. For an entire school year, I stood six inches away from him several times a day, waiting for him to even notice that I existed, let alone comment on how I looked. "Thanks," I say. I busy myself with ringing up his CD. My cheeks feel hot.

"So, whaddya doing for the summer?"

"You're lookin' at it."

"Yeah, me too. I'm making pizza at my dad's place in Piedmont. You should stop by sometime: Rusty's Pizza on Piedmont Avenue." He digs around in his wallet and comes up with a business card with frayed edges. "Here." He slides it over to me. I pick it up. It's an illustration of a fat little man in a chef's hat tossing a pizza in the air. It says, RUSTY'S—BEST PIZZA THIS SIDE OF ITALY. I flip the card over. It says, _Pamela_, with a phone number.

"You need this?" I show him the back of the card. He thinks for a few seconds.

"Nah, ancient history."

Suddenly, he seems more human to me. Like me, he's working for the summer. He's not at some resort for the insanely handsome. "Okay, maybe I'll see you there." I slide the bag with his CD across the counter.

"Hope so." He takes his bag and saunters out like James Dean. Then he executes the classic film-star turn back. "I mean it," he says over his shoulder. Did he wink at me? I thought I saw him wink.

Well, it took two years and change, but Joey Spinelli finally noticed me. I can't wait to tell Kit.

And while I'm still reeling from my Joey moment, about fifteen minutes before we close the store, *he* walks in the front door. He's wearing dark glasses, though, and he's skulking like he doesn't want to be noticed, but I notice him, all right; I notice the way he walks, the way he holds his mouth, the line of his jaw, the shape of his face. I'm intimate with it all. He walks over to the blues LPs and starts flipping through them, looking at the back of one by Elmore James and then another by Howlin' Wolf. I start my closing duties, keeping one eye on him at all times. I'm disappointed in the sunglasses. I like the idea of our eyes meeting. I like to pretend that we share a secret. Bob is up at the front, running the day's totals, something he likes to do on Saturdays, the only day the store makes any money. I can tell by the look on his face that it wasn't the day he was hoping for.

"I should sell the damn place and move to Florida," he grumbles under his breath like we haven't heard it a thousand times.

I watch my friend in blues meander over to jazz for a while. Then he heads over to world and stops short right in front of Africa. He quickly flips through country after country in a very distracted fashion, sort of the same way I flip through *Sports Illustrated* at the dentist's office because it's all Dr. Gould has in his waiting room. Maybe he's looking for something new to listen to tonight. That happens to me all the time. I get the urge to listen to something that I've never heard before, something that will surprise me, something out of my comfort zone.

Abruptly, he turns on his heel and makes his way to the front door, glancing at me quickly as he passes the counter. He seems to suddenly recognize me and he slides his sunglasses onto the top of his head, exposing his amazing eyes, which look a bit faraway at the moment. He gives me that same half smile again; then he looks as though he's remembered that he left something on the stove at home and stalks out.

I shrug and empty the register of money and Visa slips and trade vouchers to bring to the back for the closeout.

Later, I tell Kit about Joey. She also has a massive crush on him that started in seventh grade, and she can't believe he invited us to his pizza place. Yes, it's "us" now.

Kit pretends to clean her aunt's house while we talk, something she does to earn extra cash for her road trip.

"Well, first of all, it wasn't a formal invitation; it was like a 'maybe I'll see you there' type of thing, and it's not his pizza place; it's his dad's."

"Still. We're going, right?"

"Yuh-huh." I definitely want to see the animal that is Joey Spinelli in his natural environment.

Watching Kit allegedly clean, I can't imagine that Kit's aunt has ever seen Kit's room, because if she had there'd be no way she'd believe that Kit could clean anything, let alone an entire house. I sit in an overstuffed chair with my feet on the coffee table and flip through a *National Geographic* magazine I found next to a stack of coasters with different wine labels on them. A PBS program on gray whales is on TV. I tell Kit about the mystery guy. It's been a big day, boy-wise.

"Do you think he might just be shy?" asks Kit, as she feather-dusts the coffee table around my bare feet and then sits in a chair across from me and kicks off her sandals. She rests her feet on the coffee table sole-to-sole with mine. She feather-dusts her feet.

"I don't know. It was more like moody than shy."

"Uh-huh. I have days like that, fat days. I didn't think guys did, though."

"Unless they're hiding something," I suggest.

"Like what?" Kit's distracted by a whale breaching and

slapping its tail on the water, causing a mini tidal wave.

I honestly don't know the answer to that question. I don't really know anything about this guy. He could be hiding a lot of things, I suppose, or maybe his eyes were tired from partying, or maybe he had a migraine; maybe it's as simple as that. As a rule, though, people who skulk around indoors wearing sunglasses are generally the same kind of people who will carry on an inane cell phone conversation while you're ringing them up; they're generally assholes. But he's not an asshole. He couldn't be. Could he?

"You wanna Popsicle?" asks Kit, leaping out of the big chair and heading for the kitchen.

"What flavor?" I ask.

Kit pulls open the freezer compartment of her aunt's massive refrigerator. "Grape, orange, lemon."

"Grape, please."

She returns with two grape Popsicles and hands me one, plopping back into her chair. We watch the whales frolic carefree in the ocean while we lick our Popsicles. The narrator, who sounds suspiciously like Jean-Luc Picard, captain of the *Enterprise*, soberly tells us how grim the future looks for these animals because global warming is killing off the food that they live on. I'm glad the whales can't hear him. They should enjoy life while they can.

"We should save the whales," I muse.

"Uh-huh. We should." Kit has licked her Popsicle down to a nub. She puts it in her mouth and the stick emerges empty except for a purple stain. She swallows and shows me her purple tongue. I show her mine.

"Joey Spinelli," says Kit. "Man, that guy rocks my world."

"Yeah, mine too."

"He only likes dumb chicks with big boobs."

"Yup."

"Idiot."

"Hey, what do you wanna do tonight?" I ask, changing the subject. It's an unspoken agreement between us that we spend every Saturday night together, because Niles's band is always playing somewhere and the glamour of being the bass player's girlfriend wore off a long time ago. Besides, Kit's sixteen, and most places check ID even if you're with the band. They never seem to check the band's ID, though. Niles is eighteen and he's been playing crappy, hole-in-the-wall clubs since he was sixteen.

"I dunno. There's that party at Brie's but it sounds like a total drag. She said something about board games. What are we, senior citizens?" Kit looks at the clock. "I'd better get the vacuum."

I ease out of my chair. "Call me when you're done."

I walk out the front door and drop my skateboard on

the sidewalk in the direction of home. I've put off going home long enough, I suppose. I really need to work on my fanzine for a while. I know that this "Jack" guy hasn't even set foot in my house, but somehow I'm already considering his presence in my mom's life a full-on home invasion, as though I might wake up tomorrow morning and find him making pancakes in our kitchen and cheerfully asking me if I'd like a cup of "joe." I don't want that pancake-making home invader anywhere near me on a Sunday morning, or ever, for that matter. He probably even leaves the toilet seat up and beard crumbs in the sink and pubic hair in the shower . . . man dirt. I want him out. God, I need a therapist.

My mom is upstairs working when I arrive home. I can tell because Leonard Cohen's *Death of a Ladies' Man* is playing on the stereo and it's turned way up. She hasn't listened to this CD since long before my dad left. Should I read this as some sort of a cryptic red flag? Pierre is lounging on the dining table. I bet he's had a grueling day. He lifts his head slightly as I pass. The cat version of "Oh, it's just you." I walk to the kitchen, open the fridge, not expecting much, close it again and walk up the stairs. My mom's staring at her computer, singing along with Leonard. This would be the perfect opportunity to scare the crap out of her but I decide against it.

"Mom!" I yell above the music.

She turns around and smiles at me. Is she glowing? Is it possible that she's glowing?

"Hi, honey. Can you turn down the music for me?"

I run down the stairs and turn Leonard way down. I run back up again. I need to get a better look at her. I'm still panting from the stairs when she says:

"He called."

"Who?"

"Jack."

"Nicholson?"

"Allie, please."

"What did he say?"

"He said he had a wonderful time last night and he wanted to hear my voice before he boarded his plane."

"Where's he going?"

"Um, I don't know, the Midwest somewhere—one of those M states. Or was it W?" She shrugs and smiles.

And, by the way, she *is* glowing.

I shut the door of my bedroom and start in on today's blog entry:

Janis Joplin—*Cheap Thrills*: This LP should be a seminal part of every vinyl collection. Cover art by Robert Crumb: That's enough reason right there to own this LP, but put it on the turntable and your life will never be the same. Let's start with the best cut: "Summertime." No one pulls it off like Janis (but the *Porgy and Bess* sound track is a close second). She comes from somewhere so deep that you think she might not make it to the end of the song. Mix up a frosty pitcher of lemonade and vodka (in her honor) and let her take you somewhere. "Piece of My Heart," what can I say? She'd have pulled her own heart out of her chest and showed it to you if she could. "Ball and Chain." Nine minutes of two parts bliss and one part agony. Go, Janis.

There were two comments posted yesterday below my blog about glam rock. One was from Jan in Iceland. He tersely told me that I forgot to mention Elton John, who is often overlooked for his important contribution to the glam movement. I comment on his comment: *Thanks, Jan. You're absolutely right. Elton deserves his own issue, though. I'll be sure to devote an entire blog to him in the near future.* The other comment is from Jim in Seattle, who wrote: *Vinyl is dead; downloading is where it's at. Face it, Princess.*

$\mathcal{I}$'m sitting cross-legged on the wooden bench at Krishna Copy, listening to the *zip-whirr-sigh* of the massive copying machine as it prints my *Vinyl Princess* fanzine. To print, collate and staple five hundred copies, it's going to cost me sixty-nine dollars and seventy-two cents, a lot of money for me, but not bad when you consider that I'm looking to start a movement. I wonder what the Black Panthers spent on flyers in the sixties when they got going.

Matt, the clerk who's helping me at Krishna Copy, is throwing in colored paper for free. He seems to recognize what I'm trying to do here and he's solemnly sworn not to spill my identity even if he's tortured or held at gunpoint. It took a long time to settle on a color. I almost went with purple but decided it was too dark. In the end I settled on turquoise, or "pool," as it's called on the paper sample.

Across from me, pinned to the wall, is a huge map of the U.S. I stare at it for a moment, musing about M. (That's right, I'm calling him M now; no more "mystery guy," just M.) One thing I know for sure about M is that he's not from around here. My eyes drift to the South on the map and stop on Greenville, South Carolina. Maybe M is from the South. Maybe he has one of those charming southern accents. It occurs to me that I have yet to hear him speak. Maybe, unlike me, he grew up in a rambling house full of love and good smells and lots of brothers and sisters. The kind of family I always secretly envied, where the dinner table is raucous and big plates of food get passed around and everyone talks over one another and dogs sleep under the table. Once I get to know M he'll fill in all the blanks for me. Then I'll bring him home and show him my record collection and he'll be blown away.

I wonder how M got here. I'm always curious about how people just arrive somewhere; maybe it's because I've been here all my life. I wonder what it feels like to drive into a city and get out of the car and say, "Well, this is it. Guess I'll unpack the car; I'm staying." I wonder if he left a girl behind, or a dog. (Or is he a cat person? No, he definitely looks like a dog person.) Maybe he calls home once a week to check in with his parents and to make sure his dog is okay.

Matt jolts me out of M's life by waving my first fanzine in front of my face. I take it and hold it in my hands. It's fabulous. The cover I designed, a vintage pen-and-ink of an ice princess on skates wearing a tiara, executing an arabesque, using an LP as a skating rink, came out beautifully. I stick my head in the box and breathe in the printer ink smell, destroying about ten thousand brain cells. I pull out my crumpled bills and pay Matt and then I lug the box home. The weight of it feels like a good day's work.

While I've been inventing a fake life for M and attempting to get a real one for myself, my mom has been creating one for *herself*. She's hell-bent on making us look normal by Thursday, although, frankly, I don't think "Jack" is going to buy it. The last few days, she's been coming home with shopping bags filled with cartons of food and scooping it out onto plates as though she cooked it herself and then putting the plates in front of us at the dining table roughly around the time that she thinks normal people eat dinner. Last night we had Dover sole baked in parchment paper with lemon dill sauce, steamed baby carrots and mashed potatoes with truffle oil. It was delicious. The night before that we had grilled jumbo shrimp on a bed of angel hair pasta tossed in pesto sauce. It was also delicious. I'm so onto her, but I'd be an idiot if I said anything. It beats the hell out of chipping a frozen pizza out of the freezer or warming up leftover take-out Chinese noodles and eating them straight from the box. Growing up, I don't recall one meal that we ate at the table as a family. For one thing, there was no table, and we weren't that kind of family anyway. We were like wolves, foraging for ourselves and eating when we were hungry; for my dad that usually meant midnight, but my mom likes to snack all day. She has the eating habits of a gerbil. I like to mix it up. Cereal for dinner is fine but so is lasagna; so are doughnuts. Pizza is great for breakfast; so are bananas; so are doughnuts. I usually eat lunch at work and when I'm off I go up the street to the Japanese place on College Avenue and get a bowl of udon noodles in broth for three bucks. It's the best deal around and the people watching is great. Not as weird as Telegraph—not everyone has abused a controlled substance before ten a.m. It's more of a pharmaceutical crowd, but interesting enough to watch while I slurp my soup.

The food in front of us tonight smacks of "normal," but my mom and I haven't exactly perfected table talk. She reads a big hardcover volume of some dead guy's poetry as she eats, while I read about Robert Plant in *Rolling Stone* magazine. Joe Cocker sings his shaky heart out on the stereo. Occasionally, one or the other of us will announce something newsworthy.

"The liquor store on Telegraph was robbed last night," I offer.

She looks up from her book. "Really? What time?"

"Late. One a.m. No one was hurt." I throw that in for her sake. She hates that I work on Telegraph.

"Did they catch them?" She takes a bite of her maple-glazed salmon.

"Nope, they're still at large," I report darkly.

"Hey, have you seen Pierre lately?"

"No, I haven't. Do you think he did it?" I ask.

"Nah, what would he need money for?"

"Maybe it's not the money; maybe it's the thrill of it." I try to imagine my cat robbing a liquor store. Height would be an issue even if he stood on his back legs. Besides, these guys had a gun. Pierre can't even open a door with his paws, let alone cock a gun. If he could, he really wouldn't need us for anything.

After dinner, we clean up, which entails throwing all the neatly labeled boxes into the refrigerator with the others and washing two plates. I go upstairs to take a phone call from Kit, who seems convinced that Niles is messing around on her. I'm lying on my bed, digesting my third "normal" dinner in a row. My jeans feel snug around my waist.

"When he came to get me last night he didn't even say anything about how I looked."

"Uh-huh, is that all you got?"

"No. I looked at his cell phone while he was in the bathroom and I saw a number on there I didn't recognize. A four-one-five area code."

"That could be anything. You dialed it, didn't you?"

"Of course I did."

"Who was it?"

"I got the voice mail of a girl named Chelsea. She sounded pretty."

"You can tell by someone's voice mail if they're pretty?"

"Yes, I can. I can also tell that she has large breasts."

"Of course you can. You think everyone has bigger breasts than you."

"Well, they do."

"You're petite."

"I'm breastless."

"Well, you can't really ask Niles about this allegedly large-breasted pretty girl named Chelsea, can you?"

"No, but I can catch him in the act. I think he's a lying shithead, don't you?"

"I don't know. I think you might be rushing to judgment. She could be anyone. How are you going to catch him in the act?"

"I'm going to follow him next Saturday night. You have to come with me."

"No, Kit, you know I hate surveillance. What if he sees us?"

"Don't worry; he won't see us."

"Why not?"

"Because it won't be us."

I can't believe I didn't see this coming. Kit is very big on disguises. She gets first pick of whatever comes into the vintage-clothing store that she works in and she prides herself on looking like a completely different person every time she leaves the house. She owns a vast selection of wigs, hats, sunglasses, jewelry and shoes. She'd make a great gumshoe. Not including Halloween (which I won't even get into), I've been dressed as a disgruntled shopper (when Kit needed backup on a complaint about a staff member at a boutique), a Girl Scout (when Kit needed a partner to go door-to-door, collecting empty bottles to support her fake troop), a guy (when Kit needed a pretend boyfriend to make her current boyfriend jealous) and a middle-aged woman (when Kit exceeded the one-per-customer on free samples at the Lancôme cosmetics counter).

"So, will you help me?"

As I'm lying there, Pierre appears in my doorway. He strides purposefully past my bedroom without even a glance in my direction. I jump off the bed and tiptoe to my doorway, poking my head out. Pierre stands in front of

Suki's door and meows. The door opens. Pierre disappears inside. The door shuts.

"Allie? Are you there?" asks Kit.

"Aha!" I say into the phone.

"What?"

"Pierre is cheating on me with a Japanese woman."

"You see what I mean? You can't even trust a male cat."

"Okay, sure, I'll help you. But I'm not wearing a disguise."

"Yes, you are. Call you tomorrow." She hangs up before I can respond.

I pull the Beatles' *Rubber Soul* out of its sleeve and place it on the turntable. The needle drops and "Drive My Car" starts up. I lie there and listen to it, looking up at the ceiling. My eyes close. I imagine M lying next to me, listening, our fingertips touching, feeling the music and the heat of our bodies flowing through his fingers to mine and back again. There's no need for us to talk. That's what it's like with us. We talk without speaking.

The minimart on Telegraph and Alcatraz was robbed last night, and this time someone got hurt. The robbers were surprised when an employee came out of the bathroom holding a *Road & Track* magazine, which they mistook for a gun. One of them shot the guy in the arm. He's going to be okay but I hope he wasn't planning a career as a major league pitcher. Right after that, as if that weren't bad enough, the perps went another couple of blocks down Telegraph and robbed a barbecue place, a pretty bold move. The minimart got them on the security camera but they were wearing ski masks and it was too grainy for a positive ID. How is it that you can get a crystal-clear picture on a cell phone camera but security cameras still deliver the picture quality of your great-aunt's black-and-white TV that she bought in the sixties to watch *I Love Lucy* on?

Bob has put the store on what he's calling "high security alert," which one might take to mean that he's handing out assault rifles and digging foxholes, but all it really means is that we're supposed to report any suspicious-looking characters immediately. That's a bit tricky. Everyone on Telegraph looks at least a little suspicious, even Bob himself. The entire avenue is like one big Fellini film. The only way a person would look even remotely unusual to a Bob & Bob's employee is if that person were actually standing in front of them in a ski mask, waving a gun, and it would be a little late to alert anyone at that point. And who are we supposed to report these suspicious characters to anyway? Homeland Security? Bob? You can't arrest someone just for looking suspicious.

The neighborhood cops even stopped by on their bicycles. (I don't like their chances of catching up to the perps in their getaway car on those bikes, even if they pedaled like the Wicked Witch of the West, and besides, even if they could catch them, what would they do? Ask the robbers to pull over and wait while they get off their bikes and arrest them?) They gave us some helpful tips on what to do in the case of a robbery. They told us not to play the hero. For eight bucks an hour? Don't worry about it. And hand the money over to them cheerfully. We'll hand it over, all right, but cheerfully? We don't even do that for our customers. Record store employees are misanthropes. It goes with the territory. Plus, if you've worked retail for more than six months you will most certainly be suffering from Retail Burnout Syndrome. Even if you were cheerful when you were hired, you won't be for long.

Jennifer and Laz have banded together as self-proclaimed "crime experts." Jennifer knows someone who was shot in the leg (of course she does—spilled blood is only one of her many ghoulish preoccupations), and Laz has started his own perp walk of all the neighborhood unsavories that he's acquainted with. He has a long list of suspects, and I hate to burst his Columbo bubble, but the cops say it's very unlikely that the suspects are from the neighborhood. Still, I think it's nice that the latest crime spree has brought him out of his shell.

I have my own suspects but I'm not saying anything right now. Over the last couple of weeks, I've noticed these two guys hanging around who look a little uptown for this end of Telegraph. Telegraph Avenue runs for miles and becomes Oakland somewhere along the way, but this end, the Berkeley end, is only about six blocks long and ends at the campus. It's like falling down a rabbit hole and arriving in 1967. You notice new people, and these two are definitely a little slick for around here. When I first saw them, right around the same time that the robberies started, I figured that they were dealers moved in from San Francisco or Oakland or some other city, looking for a new customer base. One of my suspects is taller and wears a black wool beanie and a spendy black leather jacket. He wears some expensive-looking pimp bling too. The other one wears a tracksuit and a headband. It's entirely possible that they have a little armed-robbery hobby. Everyone needs a hobby. These two also don't look like the kind of people who would be entirely uncomfortable pointing a gun. I've seen them getting into an illegally parked late-model BMW with slick rims and throbbing woofers. One of them, the one in the tracksuit, was in Bob's last Saturday night buying a hip-hop CD. He was definitely not interested in exchanging pleas-antries with me. Next time I see Shorty and Jam, I'll ask about them. Nothing happens on the street without those two noticing, at least nothing drug-related.

The other thing about neighborhood crime is that it tends not to be too good for business. People like to watch it on the news from the comfort of their La-Z-Boy recliners and shake their heads at the state of the world while they munch on a bag of Cheetos, but they're not keen on getting too close. This has put Bob in a worse-than-usual state of mind and he's filled the CD carousel with Nick Cave and Nina Simone and Jeff Buckley and a few other Gloomy Gus–type singers, consequently depressing everyone in the store until we're all staring out the front window into the fog, which rolled in last night, casting a gray pall over the city. It's the first fog of the summer and I forgot to bring a sweater, so I'm cold and miserable in my Babes in Toyland T-shirt and a denim skirt. Jennifer takes her shift to cover the cash register. She's dressed for all kinds of weather in her knee-high Doc Martens and her leather motorcycle jacket, a year-round uniform. I go out on the floor with a price gun and mark down the soul section. Bob doesn't like product to gather dust, so if the date on the price tag is more than thirty days ago, we mark it down by a dollar. It's a tedious job and you have to keep stopping to change the price on the gun. That gets old fast.

My *Vinyl Princess* fanzines are now in position on the top row of the magazine rack next to all the other zines. After I made room for it, I stood back and tried to be objective. It definitely jumps out at you. Plus, mine's the only free one. I figure I'll give it out to specific customers and then let people take it themselves too. They're obviously not for everyone. This is how it starts: one magazine at a time, and then, before you know what's happening, you're some kind of trendsetter. People want to know your opinion about things and where you shop and who cuts your hair (me) and how you got this movement started. To be honest, no one's picked one up yet, but these things take time. I'll have to be patient. Bob hasn't noticed the zines yet. I'm going to give it a couple of days and then I'll mention it . . . maybe.

Bob spends the afternoon in the cramped office, trying to start a fight with Dao, but she's not having any of it today. Every time I go in there for something, he's picking on her. She keeps her head down and ignores him. I give her a lot of credit for knowing how to handle Bob. Most people bite and before they know it, they're involved in a three-hour rant about the shameful lack of socialized medicine in this country or how we're getting screwed by the North American Free Trade Agreement or something like that. Bob finally gives up on her and comes out onto the floor to work on me for a while.

"Al, can you get to country today too? That section's a mess."

"Sure, Bob, but I did it a week ago; how bad could it be?"

He takes off his reading glasses and rubs his eyes. He puts them back on and regards me over the rims.

"Really? It's only been a week? 'Cause it's a mess. I checked it last night." He tries to look like he honestly cares about the country section, which he absolutely does not except for Gram Parsons, whom we file in rock but a lot of people call him a country artist.

I click the trigger on the price gun and punch him in the arm with it, leaving a red $7.98 price tag stuck to his biceps. He looks at it as though he finds it baffling. He peels it off, folds it into a ball between his fingers and flicks it into the air.

"Did you see that Miles Davis vinyl that came in yesterday?" he asks.

"Yup." I was there. He's referring to a Miles Davis vinyl collectible called *Miles Ahead* with the original cover art from 1957. I'm trying to figure out how I can own it. "It's totally cool."

"Yup."

He tells me again about the time he saw Miles play in New York City, how it blew his mind. I like hearing it again. It's a good story, and Miles is dead now, so I'll never get a chance like that.

"Hey, did you read the piece on Robert Plant in *Rolling Stone?*" he asks.

"Yeah, I did."

Bob nods. This is something we do a lot of: this "blah, blah, blah, fill-in-band." Bob can do it for hours. I'm one of an ever-shortening list of accomplices who can keep up with him. Bob and I talk about Led Zeppelin, Robert Plant, Jimmy Page, the Honey Drippers and on and on, nothing new, really; it's not like we haven't had this conversation before. We get each other going and then we completely lose track of time.

"Did you ever hear him and Jimmy Page do that old Hank Williams Jr. song, 'My Bucket's Got a Hole in It' on that Sun Records tribute album?" asks Bob.

"No. How did I miss that?"

"I've got a copy in the office. Hang on. I'll throw it on for ya." He heads to the office.

I watch Bob for a few seconds and then, out of the corner of my eye, I spy M walking past the front of the store. He glances in at the front counter, at Jennifer. Damn, that should have been me! Maybe he was looking for me. I pretend I have important business in front of the store and bolt out the door and onto the sidewalk, but by the time I get there all I see is the back of M as he walks to the corner, checks for cars and then walks across the street, alongside the empty lot toward campus, his long, lean legs taking him away from me. Damn, damn, damn! I stand there, dangling the gun at my side, watching him disappear, willing him to turn around but he doesn't. Jimmy the Rasta dude grins at me from behind his incense emporium. When I walk back into the store, Laz and Jennifer are standing at the counter, watching me with interest.

"I thought I saw someone suspicious," I say.

They both wait for more.

"But I was wrong."

After work I get myself right home to partake in the fourth meal in four days that my mom will pretend she cooked. This one's no dress rehearsal, though. "Jack" is coming to dinner and she says she's dying for us to meet, something to do with exposing the baggage early in the relationship, I suspect, because I can't imagine any other scenario where that could possibly be true. I muse over M as I roll down the sidewalk on my skateboard. If I'd had half a chance, if I'd even learned his real name and maybe gotten to know him a bit, I could have invited him along tonight. It's the kind of thing where I'd want him along. Maybe he'd even come. Maybe he could use a fake home-cooked meal.

Up ahead I see Florence Kobayashi, our neighbor, hobbling up the sidewalk on her way home from work. I slow down as I come up behind her and jump off my board. Florence is a guard at the Museum of Modern Art in San Francisco. She stands there all day, making sure that people don't touch the priceless paintings or, God forbid, try to make off with them. I'm not really sure what she would do in that particular situation, since she's just over four feet high and weighs about ninety pounds. I guess she would have to radio for backup. I used to think that she probably knew a lot about art or that she might even love it, but when I asked her about it she just shrugged.

"It makes my hips hurt," she told me.

Florence has to stand in one spot for seven hours a day. She's sixty-four years old and she's been working there for ten years. I don't understand why they don't let the guards sit down. She told me that she's learned to sleep standing up like a horse. She wears black sneakers with thick rubber soles, the kind that young boys wear with baggy jeans that hang down around their knees and boxers underneath.

"Hi, Mrs. Kobayashi," I call out.

She turns around, startled, until she recognizes me.

"Oh, hi, Allie," she says.

"How are things at the museum?" I ask.

"Very busy. Matisse, you know?"

"Matisse?"

She nods.

"Very pretty," I say, although I can't visualize one single painting right now.

"Very pretty," she says with zero enthusiasm as she pulls her navy blue sweater tighter around her middle and continues stiffly up the sidewalk, favoring her right side.

When I come up the walk to my house, I'm quite certain I smell bread baking and I know that this simply can't be right. This warm, comforting aroma can't possibly be coming from our house. I pull open the front door and find my mom in the kitchen, her brow furrowed as she reads the back of an empty plastic frozen bread package. She's wearing a soft lavender-colored linen skirt and a white silky blouse. Her hair is piled on her head and escaped tendrils of it cling damply to her pale neck. Her cheeks are flushed. Pierre is not in his usual spot on the dining room table. An abandoned felt catnip mouse lies there in the empty space, cast aside, like us.

"Hi, honey." My mom peers into the oven and sighs.

"What's going on in there?" I ask.

"Well, it says here that you're supposed to let it rise somewhere warm for three hours, but I didn't know that till an hour ago, so I put it in the bathroom while I was showering and I may have splashed some water on it." She sighs again.

"Let me have a look."

My mom stands out of the way and I peer through the glass at the submarine sandwich–size loaf of bread dough sitting in the middle of a baking pan. The drops of water have dried on the surface and resemble a skin disease. It looks anemic and hopeless.

I look at my mom. "What possessed you to bake? We have four bakeries within walking distance."

She shrugs and grabs her purse off the back of a chair. She pulls a five-dollar bill out of her wallet and hands it to me.

"Is that hush money? Because I won't keep quiet for anything less than a twenty."

"Take it. Go to Semifreddi and get a nice loaf of bread. Please."

"Okay, but I think you're giving up too easily. That thing in the oven could have a strong future if you'd just give it a chance."

"Go." She points to the door.

I take my time because I'm compiling a list of LPs for my top five of the week.

So far I've got: Bob Dylan, *Desire*; Pink Floyd, *Ummagumma*; Ornette Coleman, *Something Else!!!!*; Supertramp, *Breakfast in America*; and *The Worst of Jefferson Airplane*. I've decided to incorporate a rating system using little LPs instead of stars, five out of five LPs being the best. I move on to thoughts of M and how I might dazzle him with my music knowledge, maybe even show him my collection someday, throwing something special on my turntable. I spend the rest of the way home, a loaf of Italian batard under my arm, figuring out what that might be. Maybe my British bootleg Bob Dylan *Don't Look Back* outtakes, or a B-side by the Sweet or something by the Nips, Shane MacGowan's original band. I don't have much to go on based on what he's shopped for at Bob's. He'll look at me, amazed, and say something cheesy like, "Where have you been all my life?" or, "You're not like other girls," and, naturally, I'll eat it up.

By the time I open the front door to my house again, "Jack" has arrived and he's situated himself in the middle of our sofa with a glass of white wine in his hand (we have wineglasses?). He regards me the way most adults look at a teenager, sizing me up to decide whether or not I'm going to give him any trouble. I guess he decides I'm not because his mouth turns up into a slow smile and he stands up.

"Allie, I presume." He extends his hand.

"Jack, I presume." I take his hand, which is cold and clammy from the wineglass.

He's wearing khaki chinos, no big sin, but they might be the first pair of khaki chinos ever to come in contact with our sofa. His voice is a little on the high side for a large man. He sits back down on the sofa. His khakis ride up on his ankles, exposing argyle socks. Nice.

"I was just telling your mom that my son is about your age."

I'm not sure what I'm supposed to do with that. Have you noticed that no one ever says that to old people? *You're eighty? Why, I have an uncle that age!*

"Great," I say. "Excuse me." I get myself into the kitchen and hand my mom the bread. Even though everything we're about to eat is coming from a box, she's worked herself into quite a lather. She's carefully composing three salads using

77

components from several boxes and a plastic container of dressing.

"Allie, can you put some music on?"

"Sure, what?"

"I don't know, jazz, classical, something atmospheric?"

"Right."

I return to the living room, noticing the way that the dining table has been set with napkins, silver, crystal candlesticks and what looks to be fine china. It looks like an estate sale. I stick my head back into the kitchen.

"Hey, where'd all this fancy stuff come from?" I whisper.

"It's Grandma's."

"Does she know you took it?"

"I didn't take it. She gave it to me. It's been in a box in the garage."

One might wonder, then, why we've been eating off of mismatched, chipped garage-sale plates all these years when we had access to the queen of England's booty. Sheesh!

I dig through my mom's CD collection, all of which I've given her. I'm acutely aware that I'm being watched. I pull out Joni Mitchell, *Ladies of the Canyon*; Miles Davis, *Sketches of Spain*; Willie Nelson, *Stardust*; and Mark Knopfler, *Ragpicker's Dream*. All of my mom's CDs have her name written across the front of them in black marker. When my dad left there was a lot of "this is mine and that's yours" going on, and my mom wasn't about to let him walk off with anything she cherished, so the day before he moved out she stayed up all night and wrote her name on everything. She probably thought that she was using an erasable marker, or maybe she just didn't care, but it still says her name in big letters on the toaster and the teakettle. I load up the CD carousel and hit play. Jack is flipping through a book on Russian history that he found on the coffee table, or at least he's pretending to. It was probably the best he could find. Most women have a copy of *Vogue* or *People* on their coffee table. My mom has *Smithsonian* magazine and a book on hieroglyphics of the Anasazi Indians in Arizona.

"I think dinner's almost ready," I assure him, perching on the edge of an overstuffed chair across from him.

"Great. It sure smells good."

I nod.

"So, how long have you guys lived here?" he asks, looking around at the cleaned-up version of the disaster that is our home.

I look around too, seeing our house from a first-time visitor's point of view. A chaotic jumble of mismatched, overflowing bookshelves line the walls; African carvings, masks, weird sculpture, and paintings cover every available surface; and all the furniture is draped in brightly colored cotton throws that my mom brought back from her many trips to India in the eighties. I look down at my feet. The Oriental carpet is threadbare and stained. A trail of ants is energetically carrying toast crumbs from the table, onto the carpet and along the wooden floor to a toast-crumb ant banquet in an undisclosed location.

"Forever," I tell him.

Dinner comes off without a hitch, except for one awkward moment when Jack asks how my mom makes her vinaigrette and I have to think fast and pretend to have a coughing fit to distract him. In the end I think he pretty much figured out that my mom was faking it, which is probably a good thing, because she'd never be able to keep this up; sooner or later he'd find the boxes, and we'd be out of money too.

I watch Jack closely and I notice that he seems to really like my mom a lot. He listens to her carefully and laughs easily at her attempts to be funny. My mom behaves like a shy schoolgirl around him, blushing and talking about things that I never even knew she cared about. Why is she trying so hard to impress this guy? I wonder. Has she seen his socks? There are a lot of moments when I wish I could look across the table at M and roll my eyes.

Just as we're digging into our dessert, individual lemon meringue tarts, the phone rings. My mom looks at me and shakes her head slightly. I ignore her, put down my fork and leave the table. I pick the phone up off the coffee table in the living room.

"Hello?" I look at my mom defiantly. Until she gets me a cell phone I'll be answering the phone. She knows that.

"Hello, Miss Allie?"

"Oh, hi, Ravi."

My mom is watching me. Jack is watching me too.

"Hello. How are you this evening, Miss Allie?"

"Great, Ravi. How are you?"

"Very well, thank you. I apologize for calling during the dinner hour but I have something important to tell your mother. May I speak with her, please?"

I look at my mom and point at her and then at the phone. She shakes her head violently. "Sorry, Ravi, she's, uh, unavailable right now."

"Unavailable?"

"Yeah." I move into the kitchen and lower my voice. "She's sort of on a date. Can I get her to call you later?"

"A date?" He sounds mystified. "Are you quite certain?"

"Yeah, I'm pretty sure."

"Yes, well"—his voice catches a bit and he clears his throat—"perhaps you could ask her to call me as soon as possible."

"Will do, Ravi," I tell him. I follow up with a lame "Have a nice night."

He hangs up. That was weird. He sounded so bewildered at the concept of my mom dating.

My mom scrambles to tell Jack all about Ravi. He seems amused at her description of him. It's clear she doesn't want to kick off this relationship with any secrets, and Ravi certainly isn't a secret.

I leave them at the table and head upstairs to listen to Billy Bragg, *Talking with the Taxman About Poetry*. Billy Bragg is featured on today's blog. I was talking to Bob about him today at the store and he told me that Billy used to work in a record store in England in the eighties. He became the socialist voice of the working class in England, and a lot of his music is highly politicized, which is cool, but then he'll come at you with a line like, "She cut her hair and I stopped lovin' her," and a song like "Must I Paint You a Picture?" probably one of the most romantic songs I've ever heard. Then, as if he wasn't cool enough, he took some old Woody Guthrie lyrics that Woody's daughter was hanging on to and turned them into these amazing songs that he recorded with Wilco. The first time I heard "California Stars" from the *Mermaid Avenue* album I thought I would die.

Between songs, I hear my mom and Jack downstairs, talking and laughing. I'm not sure what I was expecting but this Jack guy seems okay. Before I went upstairs, as I was saying good night, I asked him if he likes pancakes.

"Well, sure, doesn't everyone like pancakes?" He smiled like he was humoring a five-year-old. My mom looked at me like I'm an idiot.

All I can say is that he'd better not be here when I get up in the morning. I'm definitely not ready for that.

$\mathcal{K}$it's elaborate scheme to expose her boyfriend, Niles, as a lying shithead involves several steps, the first of which is the two of us assuming new identities. I sit helpless on the toilet lid in Kit's tiny bathroom amid a virtual explosion of idling curling irons and other implements of beauty while Kit applies more makeup to my face than I've ever worn in my entire life. She pins back my own black hair with bobby pins and attaches a wig to my head. I now have waist-length blond hair with bangs. She digs through her eyeglass collection and hands me a pair of tortoise-shell frames. I put them on and check myself out in the bathroom mirror. I look like a prostitute who can do long division. For my final flourish, Kit applies red lipstick to my lips.

"Do this." She smacks her lips together.

I obey. She looks at me critically, studying her work, and then grins. "You are *so* hot!"

"I don't feel hot. I feel stupid."

Kit's own transformation is a little more restricted, because she's using her sister Roxanne's fake ID to get us into the club, so she has to look somewhat like the photo on it. Her wig is red and it's shaped into a pageboy. She's also wearing a hat so that she can obscure some of her face. It's tweed with a narrow brim that she pulls low. I'm wearing knee-high boots with a stacked heel and a short skirt with tights. Kit is wearing a navy pleated skirt with oxfords. Her look is naughty schoolgirl.

I point to the general area of Kit's chest. "What's with the bodacious ta-tas?" I ask.

"Inserts. They're part of the disguise."

"You look a little top-heavy."

"You think so? Should I go smaller?"

"Maybe a little."

Kit disappears into her bedroom and comes back slightly smaller.

"Better," I say.

The plan is to arrive after the band has started playing, try to find a table in the back of the club where it's darker and stay only until after the first break. Kit is convinced that if Niles is cheating on her, the girl will certainly be there tonight. She checked his phone again yesterday and there were two more calls to this Chelsea person. The 415 area code is San Francisco, so she definitely lives in the city.

The club where Niles is playing is in the Mission District of San Francisco, so we walk the four blocks to the BART station to catch the train into the city, Kit comfortable in her oxfords and me tottering awkwardly behind her in my heels.

"Wait up! Why do you get to wear the comfortable shoes, anyway?"

"Sorry. Those boots are the only thing I could find in your size."

Kit has tiny feet. Her shoes look like Christmas tree ornaments. Mine are a size nine. My shoes look like commuter ferries.

On College Avenue we pass a guy pushing a shopping cart with a pit bull puppy in it. He stops to get a load of us.

"Evening, ladies," he says, removing his baseball cap and nodding.

We ignore him and keep walking. By the time we reach the BART station my wig is really starting to itch and I'm overheating. I can feel my makeup melting and I can't stop scratching my face. When we finally get on the train and find a seat, my makeup needs an overhaul. Kit pulls out a Ziploc bag of makeup first aid from her purse and touches me up while the other passengers look on, amused.

We get off at the Mission and Twenty-fourth BART stop. The club is called Boom Box. It's on Mission and Twenty-second. This isn't exactly a safe neighborhood, especially not on a Saturday night, and especially not if you look like a couple of working girls. There's a lot of nasty, gang-related crime that happens here. Laz once saw a drive-by shooting happen right in front of him in broad daylight in this very neighborhood. We walk briskly up Mission Street, away from the station. I try not to twist an ankle walking in the boots. That would definitely slow us down.

Part two of Kit's elaborate plan is that she'll go in the front door of the club with her fake ID and then she'll let me in the back door, because I don't have ID. She knows the club; she's been there before and she's assured me that it will be a breeze. Maneuvers of this nature, in my experience, are never "a breeze." Being the music lover that I am, I have suffered the humiliation of being told *No, Tito, the doorman who's cool with me, is not working tonight*, or *No, my name is not on the list as was promised to me by a Bob's customer*, or *No, that is definitely not me in the photo.*

I leave Kit at the front door and scamper down the alley to the back of the building, carefully avoiding broken glass, puddles of I don't want to know what, piles of garbage, a sleeping homeless person and a vast assortment of used condoms and needles. I stand next to a Dumpster just outside the rotting back door of the club, jumping up and down to the pounding bass of the music in an attempt to avoid having to address the raw fear that's creeping into my bones. My mom thinks I'm at the movies with Kit, and how I wish I were. If I'm raped and left for dead in this alley with no ID, will they know at the morgue to take off my makeup and my wig so that someone can identify me? I picture myself lying on a slab with a Jane Doe tag attached to my big toe. But that's assuming I even make it the morgue. What if my lifeless body is dumped into the Dumpster I'm standing next to, left to rot until some Dumpster diver finds my half-decomposed corpse and tells someone? They'll have to identify me with dental records. Do I even have dental records? After several horrifying minutes, the door swings open and Kit pulls me quickly inside. I stand there a moment, leaning on the filthy wall, gasping for breath, my heart thumping against my chest.

"What took you so damn long?" I yell at her over the music. I feel violent with fear and anger but I also want to cry with relief.

"Sorry, I'm *so* sorry. There was a security guy standing in front of the door. I finally told him someone was getting beaten up in the men's room so he'd move."

We walk along the perimeter of the club to the back and sit down at a table in the shadows. Kit goes to the bar to get us sodas. I slowly start breathing normally again and watch Niles on the stage. He's wearing a plaid kilt and a black T-shirt with the sleeves jaggedly cut off and work boots. His short black hair shoots out in every direction. Right now he's doing a bit of a partnerless polka, hopping from one foot to the other for a two beat. The crowd loves the band, and the jam-packed dance floor moves in unison. Auntie Depressant has a semi-Celtic sound that features a great fiddle player named Jude who's really ripping it up right now. Jude has long golden corkscrew curls that fly around when he plays and enormous blue eyes that guarantee him adoring groupies every night. My focus moves back to Niles and I follow his gaze to the dance floor. He seems to be making eye contact with someone. I crane my head to get a better look. He's grinning at a girl who's dancing with abandon and grinning back. It's clear that they know each other. In fact, I'm pretty sure that they *really* know each other. Her hair is divided into two long mahogany-colored braids that fly out from behind her as she gyrates her hips in time to the music. Her body is entirely different from Kit's. Kit has a sort of a Parker Posey thing going on: cute, a bit pixieish, and thin. In the museum of body types, this girl's body is on an entirely different floor. She has rather large breasts and a long torso with a very curvaceous butt, which is currently encased in a very tight pair of jeans. Her bare, tattooed arms are over her head and she moves like a girl who's very comfortable being looked at. I search for Kit at the neon-lit bar. She's on her way back to the table and she's watching exactly what I'm watching. I cringe.

"Lying, lying shithead," declares Kit as she sits down at the table with two Cokes. She's mesmerized, as though she's watching a movie, hoping for a different ending.

"Have you seen the size of her breasts? They're as big as honeydew melons," she says, without taking her eyes off the girl.

"Uh, no. They're not *that* big," I say, but they are pretty big, and Kit, being obsessed with the smallness of her breasts, is unlikely to let go of this . . . ever. "Hey, maybe they're just flirting with each other. You know how it is with musicians. Maybe it's not what you think."

Kit slowly turns to look at me. "Don't be an idiot, Allie. It's exactly what I think."

"We should go," I suggest. "Don't you think you've seen enough?"

"I'm not leaving till after the first break, like we said."

But we don't have to wait long for that. As soon as the song ends, Chad, the singer and lead guitarist, tells the crowd to stick around 'cause they'll be right back. We watch Niles unplug his bass and lean it against his amp. He's barely gotten one foot off the stage when she descends on him like a vampire. The girl with the braids—Chelsea, I presume—is all over Niles. Not in that "gee, you played really well" way either. More in that "gee, I'd really like to have sex with you right now" way. I look over at Kit. She's watching quietly, blinking tears away. Niles and Chelsea disappear out the back door of the club, arms wrapped around each other. Whatever they're going to do, Kit surely doesn't want to know about it.

"Okay, I think I've seen enough. Let's go." Kit stands up, her chair clattering to the floor behind her. She can't get out of this place fast enough.

I follow her out the front door of the club. She stands on the sidewalk in front of the club, trying to catch her breath.

"Oh, Allie," she says softly, "I feel so stupid."

I wrap my arms around her and she finally breaks down, sobbing. Small groups of people smoking cigarettes watch us with interest.

"C'mon, let's go home."

But we don't. We take BART back to the Embarcadero stop. On the way, we take off our disguises and stuff them into Kit's enormous handbag. I wipe off my makeup with tissues and unpin my hair. After we get off, we walk to a dance club in North Beach where Kit actually does know the doorman. He lets us right in ahead of all the people in line who protest loudly. We drop our stuff on a chair and head straight for the dance floor. Kit closes her eyes and loses herself in the throbbing house music, oblivious to everyone around her, and we dance like that till we have to run up the street to the BART station like Cinderellas at the stroke of midnight and catch the last train across the bridge to Berkeley.

$\mathcal{I}$ completely forgot that I told my dad I would have breakfast with him on Sunday. I'm lying there in a coma, my body desperately clinging to sleep, when my mom flings open my bedroom door. "Your dad," she says, and thrusts the phone at me as though the phone actually were a six-inch-high version of my dad.

"Hello," I say groggily, knowing that I should know what this is about.

"Still on for breakfast? I'm almost at the Bay Bridge," he says. I can hear wind in the phone.

"Yeah, where?" I rub my eyes.

We decide to meet at the Hideaway Café, a ways down from Bob & Bob's on Telegraph; it's a sort of weird, sort of cool greasy spoon. By the time my dad pulls up in his old

Thunderbird convertible (Kee Kee drives a Mercedes), I'm on my second cup of the worst coffee ever, poured by the most annoyed waitress ever, who hates me. I watch out the window while my dad parks the big car, gets out, goes back once for his phone and then again for his wallet. He finally opens the door of the café and spots me. He walks over and kisses me on the cheek (since when?).

"Hey, you look great, Al."

Not possible. My hair, which seems to have rebelled against last night's wig, is pulled back from my face with a bandanna, and three pimples have sprouted on my face overnight, one on my nose and two on my forehead, all of them roughly the size of New Hampshire. It's probably from all that makeup. Today's outfit was pulled partly off my bedroom floor and partly from the laundry basket. I look down at my T-shirt and notice a big oily-looking stain.

I look at my dad. "Wish I could say the same about you," I say moodily. His rugged rock-star looks have faded noticeably since he discovered the good life in Santa Cruz. He looks tired and older somehow. His brown hair is slowly losing the battle to gray. The little gold hoop in his earlobe doesn't quite work for him like it used to. The waitress seems to feel differently. She's magically transformed from annoyed to flirtatious. She hovers with coffee, batting her eyelashes. My dad accepts the coffee she's offering and she's close to walking off with the pot till I clear my throat and point to my cup. She fills mine, embarrassed. I glower at her.

"What's good here?" he asks, looking down at his laminated menu after he gives the waitress his winning smile.

"Nothing. I'm going for eggs and greasy hash browns."

"Me too then . . . and bacon. Kee Kee won't let me eat meat."

"How *are* things on the compound?" I ask after the waitress takes our order, helpfully suggesting fresh-squeezed orange juice. We both decline.

"Good. We just got back from Mendocino."

"What'd you go there for?"

"A yoga retreat."

"You do yoga?"

"Nah, I went kayaking with Moose. Remember Moose, the roadie?"

"Of course I remember Moose." Back when I was a kid, he was a happy, smiley guy with apple cheeks and a ZZ Top beard. He was about the size of a refrigerator and he used to give me licorice and airplane rides. "Does he live up there?"

"Yeah. He has for years now. He got himself a great little place and he's semiretired. He works a bit on a whale-watching boat in Bodega."

Whales make me think of the TV show we watched the other day, which makes me think of Kit. I haven't spoken to her yet this morning. I didn't want to risk waking her, although I doubt she slept much.

"So, was it fun?" I ask.

"Kayaking was great. The yoga heads I could do without."

We make small talk about nothing that either of us is really interested in until the smiling waitress puts our food down in front of us. She's making me miss the annoyed version of herself.

"Anything else? More coffee?" She looks directly at my dad as she says this.

"Can I get some Tabasco sauce?" I ask.

"Of course." She grabs a bottle off the next table and puts it down in front of me without taking her eyes off my dad.

We dig into our breakfast and I tell my dad about the avenue robberies. He feigns interest but he seems distracted. I was planning on telling him all about the blog and the fanzine, something I know he'd be keen on hearing if he were plugged in, but I change my mind. I quickly checked my blog before I left the house. I'm checking it obsessively now. Two comments had appeared on the Janis Joplin blog: one from a girl in Japan who went on in limited English for a while (but I got that she loved Janis) and one comment from that same creep in Seattle who said, *Downloading is king. Long live the king!* What an asshole.

My dad and I watch out the window as a young woman walks by with her arms bent at the elbow and her wrists hovering limply in midair. She holds a sparkly leash in her dangling fingers with a tiny dog at the other end. The other hand holds a cigarette. Her body language is strange, as though she's at a very chic cocktail party or else the Westminster dog show.

"Hey, Al," says my dad, turning his attention back to me. "I've sort of got some news."

"Yeah?"

"Kee Kee's pregnant."

"What?"

"Yeah."

"Jeez, Dad, weren't you using birth control? That's crazy. So what are you going to do? Is it too late for an abortion?"

"No, Al, she wants this . . . we want this."

"Oh." I certainly didn't see *that* coming. Is it my imagination or are both my parents turning into adolescents?

"Be happy for me, Al. It doesn't change what you and I have."

"Well, that's a relief, 'cause I'd sure hate to miss out on

all this." I wave my arm casually around the café.

"Al, c'mon, honey."

The truth is, I don't really care. I'm discovering that once somebody physically moves out of your life, it's impossible for things not to change no matter how hard you try to keep them the same. The place you keep in your heart for that person is always there but it gets smaller and smaller, and I just moved my dad from a spacious loft to a cramped studio. The fact is, he has to make room in his heart for a new baby, and I suspect the place in *his* heart for me will get smaller too. How could it not?

"Can I tell Mom about this?"

"Sure, why not?" He winces slightly.

"She's seeing someone, you know." I throw that in for effect. *Now* he's paying attention.

His eyes change. "She is?"

"Yup." I twist the knife.

"What's his name?"

"Jack."

"What does this 'Jack' character do?"

"I dunno. I do know that he's not a drummer, though." I look at him squarely.

"What's he like?"

"He's great." I refuse to divulge details. What he's probably imagining is much worse.

"You like him?"

"Sure," I lie. I don't even know him.

"Well, good for her. I want her to be happy," he says weakly with a thin smile. He excuses himself to use the restroom.

While my dad's in the bathroom I grab his cell phone off the table and dial Kit's number. She picks up on the first ring. Her voice is thick with crying.

"Hey, it's me."

"Oh, hi." She sniffs.

"Are you okay?" I ask.

"No."

"What are you doing?"

"Calling Chelsea's number and hanging up when she answers."

"You want me to come over?"

"Nah. I think I need to be alone right now. How about later?"

"Sure."

I click the phone off and place it next to my dad's congealed, half-eaten breakfast. He emerges from the bathroom and walks toward me. He still has the swagger of a rock star. His low-slung jeans fit his lean frame perfectly and his belt looks stolen from Mick Jagger's wardrobe. Old habits die hard. The waitress brings the check and she's conveniently included her phone number on it next to a smiley face.

I stand next to my dad's car with him. I always dread the good-bye part of the visit. It's horribly awkward, even after a year, and we both seem to feel obligated to act as though we'll see each other really soon, like tomorrow, or later that day, when we both know that our visits have to be planned and carved out and arranged ahead of time. I can even hear him explaining it to Kee Kee: "Hey, I gotta go see my kid." My dad goes in for a hug and I try to meet him halfway but it comes off weird and uncomfortable. We try to get away from each other as fast as possible so we don't have to do it again. Even when we were allegedly happy, my family was never that touchy-feely. There were hugs in all the obvious places but my dad was far more likely to get close to me by putting on some music and saying, "Al, listen to this; you're gonna flip." And I'd listen, and I'd flip.

I take off on my skateboard up to Shattuck and turn left. I continue down Shattuck for a few blocks to the Sunday flea market in the Ashby BART parking lot. Even though I've never seen M in this neighborhood, I keep an eye peeled for him. It's a habit I've developed. I wonder if M likes kids. I wonder if he's ever thought about having them. I'm never having children. I'd only screw them up.

The flea is huge and you can pretty much get anything

there from a bag of oranges or a kitten to leopardskin car seat covers or a ratchet set. A good crowd of fleagoers meanders from one stall to the next, but I navigate around them and proceed directly to the Dean twins' stall. Don and Dave Dean are identical twins who sell collectible vinyl. They dress exclusively in vintage rockabilly outfits and they sport matching honey-colored pompadours. They always smell slightly of mothballs. I honestly can't tell them apart so I rarely call them by their first names.

"Mr. Dean, Mr. Dean." I greet them as I jump off my skateboard.

"Hey, Allie," they say in unison.

"Anything new?"

"Yeah, check it out, we picked up a box of Japanese imports in Bakersfield you might be interested in," says Don or Dave. He points to a crate on the table.

I flip through them. There's a guy flipping through the crate next to mine. He has vertical hair and very pale skin. He looks older than me but not by much. He's wearing a bowling shirt that says FELLINI PLUMBING across the back and JIMMY on the pocket. He has a small pile of LPs put aside. He goes to the pile and starts pulling out each LP and scrutinizing its condition.

He holds up a Flaming Lips album, *Oh My Gawd!!!...The Flaming Lips* on clear vinyl. "Will you take five for this?" He says this with a heavy New York accent. He must be new around here or else visiting.

Don and Dave look insulted. "Can't do it; that's the original 1987 pressing. It's twenty bucks on eBay. I'll throw in a dollar LP for free if you take it but I can't lower the price," says one of them.

The guy looks torn. He studies his pile again . . . and again. He ends up putting the ten-dollar LP back in the crate. What an idiot. I can't help myself. I swoop in.

"That's a pretty righteous LP you're putting back. You sure you wanna do that? You don't see it around much. It's totally collectible. If you don't take it I will. Even though I already own it."

He regards me from behind his Buddy Holly glasses like I'm an alien. I get that a lot. Guys don't expect a girl to know that stuff, especially out on the street like this.

Don or Dave winks at me.

The guy takes the LP back out of the box and adds it to the pile. The Deans total up his pile and he digs around in his pockets for the money.

"Hey, thanks." He grins at me.

"Don't mention it." I fake a curtsy and he disappears into the crowd.

I settle on a Japanese import of Roxy Music's *Manifesto* that they have marked for ten bucks but they give it to me for eight. The discount is my take for selling the guy on the Flaming Lips.

I suddenly remember my fanzines and I unbuckle my messenger bag and take out a stack.

"Hey, do you think you guys could give these out to your customers for me? I started a blog called 'The Vinyl Princess' and I'm trying to drum up some readers."

Don and Dave each take a copy and flip through it. "This is awesome, Allie," says one of them.

"Cool logo," says the other.

"Hey, I'll tell you what. If you distribute these for me, I'll give you an ad in next month's issue for free."

"Sure, cool," says Don or Dave.

"Deal," says Don or Dave.

I bid the Deans a good day and get back on my board with my new LP under my arm and weave my way through the market and back up Shattuck, headed for home. I turn right on Dwight and I've gone a couple of blocks when I spot the familiar late-model BMW with the fancy rims, parked against the curb next to a plumbing supply store. The black-leather-jacket guy with the bling is leaning up against the car with his arms crossed. No one else is around, the block is deserted, but he keeps looking nervously up and down the street. When he sees me approaching, he gives me an intimidating stare. I zip past him with my eyes to the ground and cross the street on the next corner. That was weird.

Back in my hood, it's like that Monkees song, "Pleasant Valley Sunday." Mrs. Kobayashi is planting flowers under an oak tree in her front yard, wearing a wide-brimmed sun hat. She and I both have Sundays off. I wave to her and walk up the path to my house. I look up at Suki's window and lock eyes with Pierre, who's lying in the open window, gazing down at me lazily. I kick my board up with my heel and carry it into the house.

$\mathcal{M}$y mother and my grandmother are sprawled out in the living room drinking coffee out of big mugs. My grandmother's mug advertises a drug for the prevention of high cholesterol and my mom's says WORLD'S GREATEST GOLFER. The coffee table is laid out with lox and bagels and cream cheese from Saul's Deli. Sections of the *New York Times* are scattered about. This is a Sunday tradition. My grandmother drives over from Walnut Creek, where she lives in an over-fifty community that she's transformed into a kibbutz for blue-hairs. The docile retirees out there didn't know what hit them when tornado Estelle arrived on the scene from New York five years ago with big plans for "improving" things. She worked her way up to president of the condo association in a New York minute and proceeded to Estelle-ize the place. She's had everyone from Ralph Nader to Gloria Steinem out to shake things up in an author series she organized, and canasta tournaments are on the activities schedule permanently, as are ashtanga yoga, kick-boxing and Pilates. She set up a residents' art gallery and a library in the former rec room and she holds weekly salons to talk about books, movies and politics. She's famous for her letter-writing campaigns to government officials: Bill and Hillary Clinton are her pen pals; so is Robert Kennedy Jr., and she's working on Barbra Streisand.

The community van used to take the residents to Safeway for senior discounts on Thursdays; now it takes them to the Museum of Modern Art and the Asian Art Museum for docent-led tours, all arranged by Estelle. She also heads up the now-popular yearly fitness/art/culinary trips to Europe. The children of these people who were counting on healthy inheritances must love watching their money evaporate as Estelle jets their parents off to Tuscany for yet another adventure.

"Allie, gimme a hug, honey." She looks at me over her tiny reading glasses.

"Hi, Estelle." I'm not allowed to call her "Grandma" or, God forbid, "Bubbie." When I complained once she said that my only other option was "Ms. Horowitz."

I hug her and she squeezes me hard and gives me a big

fish-scented kiss on my cheek. I collapse next to her on the sofa and put my feet up on the table. She pats my thigh with her hand. Her fingers are long and thin and tan and she wears a big amethyst ring on her middle finger and a silver band on her thumb. My mom's reading the book review section of the *Times*.

"How was your breakfast?" she asks, lowering the paper to look at me.

I shrug. "Okay. Kee Kee's pregnant, by the way."

My mom and my grandmother lock eyes.

"What a putz," says my grandmother, shaking her head.

My mom seems amused. "Well, that particular honeymoon is over." She looks at me. "Are you okay?"

"Sure. What do I care?"

"That's the spirit," says Estelle, patting my thigh again. "Oy, men. They just can't seem to get past that primal need to spread their seed." She looks at my mom. "When your father proclaimed that he wanted a child—and I have to be honest, I was ambivalent—I said, 'Julian, one child and then I'm right back on birth control.'"

"Gee, Mom, don't get so sentimental; I'm misting up over here."

"Don't act like you were any different. I taught you well."

My mom rolls her eyes.

My grandmother's been married three times, divorced twice and widowed once. She married a doctor, an architect and a retired archaeologist. Even though she's Jewish, she's never had a Jewish husband, which makes my mom half Jewish and me a quarter. My mom's dad was the architect. He died when I was ten. The way the story goes is that my grandfather had a heart attack behind the wheel while they were driving to the Adirondacks to visit their friends Shirley and Maury, who have a summer cabin up there. My grandmother climbed over the seat, took the wheel, and navigated the car safely off the road and then she called 911 on my grandfather's cell phone. While they waited for the ambulance, Estelle tried to keep my grandfather's spirits up by singing show tunes and telling him bad jokes. Just before the ambulance arrived, he turned to my grandmother and he said, "Estelle, you kill me." And then he closed his eyes and died.

Estelle taught my mom to be very independent and, as she was seeing her off to UC Berkeley at eighteen, she announced that she was selling the condo on the Upper West Side of Manhattan and downsizing to a small apartment in the Village, so my mom would have to sleep on the couch in the living room the next time she came home. My mom never went back to New York, and, during her many visits west before and after her divorce from her third husband, Estelle eventually decided that California was a good place to live, even though she had always said New York was the only place on earth she would ever live. She moved out here too. All her friends moved to Florida but she didn't care. She said that New Yorkers go to Florida to die and she felt very much alive.

"How was your week, Estelle?" I ask, pulling the amethyst ring off her finger and putting it on my own. I admire my bejeweled hand.

"Well, let's see. I signed up for a nude drawing class at the art center. That starts in a week. What else? Oh, I went on a date with Stanley Kozinski on Tuesday."

"Who's Stanley Kozinski?" I ask, trying to remove the ring. It won't come off.

"A schmuck who likes to hear himself talk."

"So, no second date?" I stick my middle finger in my mouth, trying to lubricate it.

"God, no. Oh, I bought one of those MP3 thingies for my power walks, a tiny one; it's the size of a matchbook. I love that little thing. My Pilates instructor, Sarah, loaded it up for me with music. Have you seen these things, Allie? They're absolutely amazing."

"This Sarah person, she downloaded all the music on it from the net?"

She shrugs. "I don't know from the net. All I know is that there's more music on this little thing than I'll ever get to. It's fantastic. I've got show tunes, classical, jazz, big band, folk, you name it."

I guess I shouldn't be surprised at this revelation. My grandmother's what I like to call "neonouveau." She embraces anything new like a gadget-hungry adolescent. She's especially vulnerable to TV-advertised exercise doo-dads like the Ab Rocket and the ThighMaster.

The ring finally gives and I slide it off and put it back on her finger.

I leave them to the *Times* and go upstairs to call Kit. She sounds a lot better but I can hear The Smiths' *The Queen Is Dead* playing in the background (music to kill yourself by), so I tell her I'm coming right over. When I get there, I stand on the porch ringing the doorbell for a long time before Kit answers the door in a fuzzy bathrobe. Kit's parents are almost never home. Sometimes, it's like they moved away and forgot to mention it to her. Her dad does something called aerosol research at UC Berkeley. I have no idea what that means. I imagine guys in lab coats, spraying Arrid Extra Dry on one another. Her mom does hospice care, apparently around the clock.

Kit's nose is all pink and raw and there's a trail of used tissues that look like white carnations leading up to her bedroom. We follow them like bread crumbs up the stairs and she shuts the door behind us. I knock about fifty soggy tissues onto the floor and climb onto her bed.

"Have you talked to Niles?" I ask.

"Yeah." Her face hardens. "So, get this: I acted like I wasn't there last night and I said, 'Hey, how was the gig?' And he's all, 'Oh, you know, same old, same old.' So I said, 'What'd you do after?' And he says, 'Me and the boys went out for beers.' And I said, 'Really, the boys? 'Cause I was there, asshole, and that person you left with didn't look like a boy to me.' And then he got really quiet for a minute and then he said, 'Hey, c'mon, baby, you know she doesn't mean anything to me. She's just a groupie. You know how it is. I love *you*, baby. There's no one else for me.' And then I hung up on him."

"Has he called back?"

"Yeah, five times but I'm not picking up." Her eyes well up and she dabs at them with a wad of tissue.

"Good. Wait till you're stronger; then you can kill him."

She nods. I take her free hand and I squeeze it. We lie side by side on her bed, looking up at the ceiling.

I sigh. "Man, what a shithead."

"Yeah, but I'll never meet anyone as cool as that shithead again."

"Yeah, you will."

"No, I won't, and you want to hear something really terrible? All I want to do right now is go over there and be in his arms. How pansy-ass weak is that?"

"I think that's normal. But maybe musicians aren't really the way to go. I don't think they're very good at committed relationships. Too much temptation, you know?" I think my mom might have said this very thing to me once while we waited on the side of the stage for my dad to finish chatting up yet another young female fan so we could go home.

"I know, I know, but the fact is, I still love him and now I have to figure out a way not to and I don't really know how to do that." Her voice catches and she dabs her eyes again.

"I don't either but we'll think of something, okay?" I turn my head and look at her.

She nods. "Hey, do you think it was because my breasts are too small?"

"No, Kit, I don't."

"'Cause you know, I was thinking, I've got all this money saved up for this road trip we were supposed to go on and maybe I should just get the breasts I've always wanted."

"But that's crazy! You're only sixteen; your breasts haven't even finished growing yet."

"What if they have, though? I'll be seventeen in two

months! What if this is all I get?" She looks down at her chest.

"So what? You look great. Kit, you don't want to mess with that stuff."

"Remember Wanda Wilson from middle school?"

"Of course. She took me shoplifting when I was four-teen."

"Well, remember how flat-chested she was?"

"We were fourteen."

"She was fifteen, actually. She got held back in sixth grade."

"Don't expect my jaw to drop. What about her?"

"Well, I saw her the other day on Telegraph and she told me she'd had a boob job and it was the best thing she ever did."

"Well, for someone who had a police record at fourteen, that might be true."

"She even let me feel them."

"Ewwwww!"

"No, that's just it; they felt perfectly natural and they looked fantastic."

"Where did she get the money? No, don't tell me, I don't want to know."

"No. You don't."

"Don't you need permission from your parents?"

"I can get it, and besides, I'll be eighteen soon and then I can do what I want."

"Yeah, like in two years."

"Fourteen months. Anyway, Wanda gave me the name of her doctor. I'm making an appointment."

"Kit, this is crazy. Wait a few days; I'm sure you'll feel different." I try distracting her. "Hey, how about we go over to Joey Spinelli's pizza place on Friday. That would be fun, wouldn't it?"

"Sure, but I wish you'd be more supportive of this. It's what I want."

"I know, but don't you think that the part of you that wants this might be the part that would do anything to get Niles back?"

"No." She rubs her eyes with the palms of her hands and sighs. "I feel awful. I think I'm dehydrated from crying."

"You want me to make you some tea?"

"That would be nice."

While I'm down in the kitchen, waiting for the kettle to boil, I start thinking about Joey Spinelli and how he always goes for a certain "type." I wonder if M's got a type. Could having a type be involuntary? Do we find ourselves drawn to certain physical traits in the opposite sex for no apparent reason? Things like height, skin color, hair color, eye color, breast size, bone structure? Is that all planted in our psyches when we're children or even in the womb, so that we spend our lives searching for someone we've been picturing in the back of our minds forever? What about character traits like sense of humor, intelligence and compassion? Do those all fall by the wayside till we've found our physical match? No wonder relationships rarely work out. Are we filling the gaps with types that we're only too happy to discard when we find something closer to the "picture" we're programmed to find? Or, even worse, do we settle for something close and then go about trying to change our mates into the picture? I guess that would explain a lot of plastic surgery. It seems to me that women, even smart women, are willing to transform their physical selves at their mate's slightest whim. Men, not so much.

I search through the kitchen cupboards and finally find some chamomile tea. I take a mug from the dishwasher and drop the tea bag in. The kettle whistles and I pour the steaming water into the mug and watch the water turn the color of straw. I gaze out the window, thinking about M again. In fact, I'm actually looking forward to work tomorrow because there's a chance in hell that I might see him. It's possible that I'm developing a full-blown obsession with a stranger. I should probably have my head examined.

I hear the shower go on upstairs, a good sign. A shower is always the first step back into the real world. Without even thinking about it, I start to hum a song from the sound track to *South Pacific* called "I'm Gonna Wash That Man Right Outta My Hair." My mom and I have watched that movie together a few times. It's pretty cheesy but I love it.

$\mathscr{M}$onday's daily blog is about Marianne Faithfull's *Broken English*. When I listen to this LP, recorded in 1979, I try to imagine what her life must have been like then. After building a career on sounding fresh and young and folksy, her voice was now raspy and world-weary from years of drug use. She sounds raw and damaged. This album makes me curl into a ball. It was one of the first LPs I ever owned. I bought it at Bob & Bob's.

When I check on yesterday's blog, eight more people have posted comments: seven Europeans and one guy named Gerry, from Louisiana. He posted a comment that says, *Hey, Seattle Guy, you're missing the boat. Vinyl is where it's at. Long live the Vinyl Princess. You rock.* I send Gerry a response, thanking him for the support. I feel my little community slowly growing. Every day my number of hits increases. World domination can't be far off now. I've also noticed that the 'zines are slowly disappearing from the magazine rack. Sure, maybe people are using them for scratch pads but some people have to be reading them too.

M doesn't appear at the store at all on Monday. By Tuesday I'm feeling a little desperate, wringing my hands and watching the door obsessively and occasionally wandering out onto the sidewalk to look up and down the street. This is what it's come to. My moods are now determined by whether or not I see M (and by "see" I mean catch a glimpse of or maybe, if I'm lucky, eye contact). I'm officially pathetic. I'm in love with the idea of a man.

But someone does appear. The guy from the Sunday flea market, the one I shamed into buying the Flaming Lips LP, suddenly materializes in front of me with a stack of used LPs under his arm. Why didn't I see him come in?

"Hi," he says. Then he recognizes me. "Oh, hi."

"Where did you come from?" I ask him suspiciously.

"New York, but that's not important right now." He grins.

"No, I mean when did you come in?"

"Oh, ages ago. I've been digging through the understock." He wipes imaginary dirt off the counter. Then he carefully sets his LPs down and takes a white hankie out of his pocket, wipes his hands on it, folds it carefully and puts it back. His brown hair shoots off his forehead in a wave like the French cartoon character Tintin, and he peers myopically out from behind his horn-rimmed glasses.

"Would you like to purchase those?" I ask.

"Well, maybe, eventually. I'd like to have a look at them first."

He sets to work, carefully sliding each LP out of its jacket and holding it close to his face for inspection. He blows off the specks of lint and looks again, holding it under the light, tipping it one way and then another.

"Do you have any Discwasher?" he asks.

I look at him in disbelief and riffle through the drawer. I pull out the Discwasher liquid and a brush, handing it to him.

"Knock yourself out," I say, pretending to be annoyed, but the truth is I'm fascinated, much the same way a hunter in the jungle might stop to watch another one's technique.

"Thanks." He clearly doesn't care that I might be annoyed.

His LP selection also fascinates me. He has Jimi Hendrix's *BBC sessions*, Sun Ra's *Space Is the Place*, *A Portrait of Patsy Cline*, Nusrat Fateh Ali Khan, Roy Orbison's *Greatest Hits*, and Kate Bush's *The Kick Inside*. That's a pretty eclectic stack of records even for someone who looks like him.

"What's your return policy?" he asks, wiping down the LPs like an expert.

"Seventy-five percent store credit if you return it within seven days with a receipt."

"Store credit? No cash refunds?"

"No cash refunds."

"Hmmm, well, then, do you think you could play this for me?" He slides the Roy Orbison across the counter at me.

"No, sorry. We don't do that."

"Why not?"

"Because, here at Bob and Bob's, we like to provide our customers with a completely positive shopping experience, which includes carefully chosen musical accompaniment. If I put your LP on right in the middle of things, the musical flow would be interrupted and that's just not the way we do things here."

He looks at me like he knows I'm full of crap. He turns around and surveys the empty store. "There're two people in here—oh, wait, I think one of them works here. There's one person in here and he's talking on a cell phone."

I hold my ground. "Look, I just can't do it, okay?"

"Why?"

"Turntable's broken."

"Oh." He scratches his cheek. His fingernails are bitten to the quick. "Do you have a bathroom I can use?"

"No. There's one next door at the Café Med."

"Is it clean?"

"No."

"Are you always this unpleasant?"

That's a good question. Am I? Am I mad at this guy because he's not M? "Are you always this obtuse?" I respond.

"Can you hold on to these while I go next door and possibly contract a life-threatening disease off a toilet seat?"

"No problem." I take his LPs and watch him leave. He almost clips M, who's just walking in the door, in the shoulder. My heart starts to thump. As M walks past me he gives me that same half smile. I'm paralyzed. I try to force my mouth into a smile but I'm so nervous that I think I probably look like I just came from the dentist and the novocaine hasn't worn off yet. He walks over to the used rock CDs and looks around a bit; then he walks back over to me. My heart cartwheels into my throat.

"Hi."

"Hi."

His calm blue-green eyes stay locked on mine as he digs through the front pocket of his jeans. "Sorry, hang on." This is the first time he's spoken to me. I commit it to memory—*Sorry, hang on*. Three little, beautiful words—an apology—sweet. He pulls out a crumpled piece of paper and unfolds it. He reads from the paper. "Yeah, um, I'm look-ing for a Joe Strummer CD. It's called *Streetcore*." His voice is deep but just a touch on the feminine side, with a hint of a somewhere-else accent. He pronounces every letter of every word like someone who didn't go to public school. I gulp him in, his face, his hands, his hair, his eyes, as much of him as I can store in my brain for consumption later.

"Oh, yeah, sure, it's great. The last thing he did before he died."

"Uh-huh. So, do you have it?" His eyes lock onto mine again; my heart leaps back into my throat.

"We should. Let me have a look." I walk out to the used rock CDs with M trailing behind me. I'm acutely aware that he has a full view of my ass. Now he's standing next to me, breathing the same air as me, his shoulder lined up next to mine. It's all I can do not to lean into him. I quickly flip through the section and locate the CD almost immedi-ately. I hope he doesn't notice that my hands are shaking. Will he be dazzled by my Joe Strummer–locating abili-ties? Probably not. I hand him the CD, resisting the urge to "accidentally" touch his hand with mine. He flips it over and reads the back. Is he buying it for someone else? A girl? Or dare I hope that he's stalling so he can keep me here next to him?

"Yeah. That's the one."

"It's great." Is *great* really the only adjective I know?

Then he looks me in the eye and out of nowhere he says, "Hey, you wanna get a coffee later?"

I freeze. "Do I want to get a coffee later?" *Think. Respond. Do something.* "Uh, yeah, sure." I unclench my hand from the CD bin in front of me, where it's turning blue.

"What time you off?"

"Uh . . . five."

"Okay, where would you like to meet?"

I think fast. Not next door—everyone knows me there. Somewhere a little farther away, somewhere quiet. "You know the Bateau Ivre?"

"Not sure that I do."

"It's just up the street, that old house. Next to the grocery store."

"Perfect, five then."

He brings the CD up to the counter with him and I ring him up. He seems to be watching my hands with interest. Are my hands unusual? I've never thought so. Maybe he's a hand guy. Maybe girls' hands drive him insane. Or maybe he's not sure what to say now that he's asked me to meet him. He takes a twenty from his slim wallet and gives it to me, his eyes finally on my face again. He does look a bit nervous. Imagine that: M is nervous over me. I open the register and get his change.

Meanwhile, Annoying New York Guy has reappeared on the scene. He stands there twitching, impatiently waiting for me to finish with M, who seems not to notice him at all. I rack my brain for something clever to say. I come up blank.

I slip one of my fanzines into the bag as I hand it to him. "Have a nice day," I say. *Have a nice day?* Kill me now.

"Thanks, you too. See you later." He smiles at me, a real smile this time, dazzling and unguarded, and walks out. I stand there, watching him leave. The guy I just made a date to see later.

"Hello?" says Annoying New York Guy, tapping the counter impatiently with his skinny fingers.

"Hi." I look at him, uninterested.

He points next door with his thumb. "Everyone in that café is bipolar."

"I know."

"Can I get my LPs?"

"Sure." I grab the stack and hand it to him. I want desperately for him to go away so I can relive the last five minutes and mine it for something salvageable but he's not going anywhere.

"Are you okay? You look a little shaken up."

"No. I'm fine. Are you going to take those?"

"Can I put them on hold and think about it?"

"We hold merchandise for twenty-four hours."

"That's not very long."

"No. It's not. But then, you're not buying a yacht." I grab a bag and slip his LPs into it. "Name?" I ask.

"Zach. Z-A-C-H. Short for Zachary."

I write his name on the bag with a Sharpie and put the bag in the hold bin under the counter.

"Okay, so I'll be back tomorrow. Will you be here?"

"Unfortunately, yes."

"And what's your name?"

"Allie."

"Allie, like Alexandra?"

"Alberta. Long story."

"What, like the song . . . 'Alberta, Alberta, where you been so long'?"

"Nope, longer story." I'm not really interested in discussing the origins of my name right now and my face tells him so. I wonder why M never asked my name.

"Oh. Hi, Allie, I'm Zach."

"I know." I point to the hold bin. "Remember?"

"Right." He stands there for a moment, looking at the magazine rack in front of him. He takes one of my fanzines out of the rack and flips through it, reading.

"Who's the Vinyl Princess?"

"Some girl who used to work here. She quit, though."

"She must have been cool." He folds the zine in half and sticks it in his back pocket. "Well, bye, then." He saunters out of the store like a guy with no particular place to go.

The phone starts to ring and I grab it. I imagine M saying, "Hey, I'm sorry but I have to cancel our date." But it's not M; it's Kit. I exhale.

"Hey. What are you doing?"

"Nothing. Guess who was just in?"

"M?"

"Yup."

"Really? Did he ask you out?"

"Yes! I'm meeting him for coffee later."

"Oh, my *God*! What are you wearing?"

I look down. "Uh, my brown sweater."

"The pilly one?"

"Yeah, and my black jeans."

"Jesus, you want me to bring you something?"

"Won't that make it look like I'm trying too hard?"

"Yeah, probably. Let's not mess with his presumption that you shop at Goodwill."

"Shut up."

"So, I got an appointment with that plastic surgeon."

"Where is he, Silicon Valley?"

"Funny. No, he's in the city, on Market."

"Does he know how old you are?" I watch Aidan walk

past me on his way to the Cave. When I'm on the phone he doesn't feel obligated to even look my way.

"I told his receptionist that I was eighteen. I'll deal with the truth later. But will you come?"

"I don't know. When?"

"Friday, two p.m."

"Well, if you don't mind me expressing my views and opinions on the way."

"Look, it's just a consultation. No big deal."

I sigh. "All right. But let's have some fun afterward, okay? Maybe we'll go to Haight Street or something? It's my day off too, after all."

"Sure, fine."

"Have you heard from Niles?"

"No, but I drop-kicked a box of his shit onto his front porch this morning. I heard the coffee mug he made me for my birthday smashing. I'm sure that sent a message."

"What's the message?"

"'Here's your shit, asshole. And some of it's broken.'"

"Good one. Hey, I gotta go."

"Okay, call me later; I want to hear everything."

"'Kay, bye."

I hang up and start sorting through some LPs that Laz bought over the last few days; I need something to do to keep my mind off my coffee date, and this is my very favorite part of the job because I get to cherry-pick all the good stuff before it hits the bins. But this particular stack is joyless for me. It's all seventies soul and funk with some completely predictable eighties rock thrown in. I price it quickly and drop it into the bin to be filed into the sections. I leave it there as though there's actually a person who might come along and start filing it. As though that person isn't me. Bob comes out of the office looking almost happy. He's in a better mood now that things have quieted down on the avenue. Several days have passed with no reports of any more robberies and it looks like the siege may be over.

"Al, I'm going to the bank," says Bob. He's wearing a cowboy hat that looks like it's been run over a few times and an old Neil Young T-shirt from the *Rust Never Sleeps* tour. He could also use a shave and probably a shower. This is Bob on a good day.

"Sure. Is Dao coming in today?" I ask.

"No. Her mom's visiting from Thailand. She's taking her to Fisherman's Wharf."

I can't imagine why someone from Thailand would want to see Fisherman's Wharf. It's basically a bunch of overpriced tourist traps selling souvenirs of San Francisco that were made in China. You can get a snow globe of a San Francisco cable car but you'd be hard-pressed to find an actual fisherman on Fisherman's Wharf. A morbidly obese couple from Texas with seven fat kids would be a lot easier to spot.

"Okay. See ya later."

Bob walks out into the sunshine with what almost looks like a spring in his step. He stops to talk to Jimmy, the incense salesman. I can see them out there, arms waving, discussing the finer points of being an avenue merchant. When he finishes up with Jimmy, he's still got Precious, who sells jewelry, Celeste, who sells glass water pipes, and Sonia, who does henna tattoos, all of whom Bob will stop to chat with. It'll be at least an hour before he makes it to the bank. It takes Dao five minutes.

Later, on a whim, when Aidan skulks past me (slight nod, almost inaudible hello) on his way out to lunch, I slip back to the Cave and put a *VP* zine on his wooden processing table. Maybe I'm looking for his approval, but maybe I want him to feel a sense of belonging, like, *Hey, you're not the only whacked-out vinyl collector out there; come and join me. I don't bite*.

Then I go back to freaking out about how I'm going to be sitting across from M in a matter of hours, drinking coffee, getting to know him.

$\mathcal{I}$ arrive at the café a couple of minutes after five. He's sitting at a small table waiting for me. He smiles again when he sees me and I sit down across from him. The waiter, a regular Bob & Bob's customer, a classical vinyl collector, takes my order after exchanging a few pleasantries. M already has a cappuccino in front of him.

"Sorry. I'd have introduced you but I don't know your name."

"Joel."

Joel? "I'm Allie."

"Fancy coffee place you picked, Allie." He sips his coffee.

I look around at the high ceilings and the old wooden floors. A pleasant Vivaldi violin concerto plays quietly. "I like this place when I need to get away from the store and hide. Is it too much?"

"No, I like it. It's very peaceful."

Joel has an accent but it's not Southern, more like Eastern but not New York. I can't place it. He doesn't sound like anyone else around here, that's for sure.

"So, where are you from, Joel?"

"Oh, here and there, mostly there. I was born in New Jersey, if that's what you're asking."

"What brings you all the way out to California?"

"I have a buddy out here, a guy from back east, and he said he could set me up with a job and I just thought I'd come out and try it for a while."

"What kind of job?"

A couple, a shapely Latina and her boyfriend, come into the café and take the table across from us. Joel's eyes linger on her until her boyfriend notices and glares at him.

"I do maintenance at the graveyard on Piedmont; you know it?"

"Sure." Everyone from around here knows that graveyard; it's enormous. "You like it?"

"It's okay. Mostly I just ride a lawn mower around and around the gravestones till I'm dizzy." He laughs.

The waiter puts my coffee down in front of me.

"You don't mind all the dead people?"

"Nah." He watches me stir a packet of sugar into my coffee. "Hey, I like that store you work at; it's cool," he says.

"Yeah, I like it too."

"You been there long?"

"Two years."

"Wow, you must run the place. Is this your first job?"

"Yup."

"I heard about the robberies. Are you freaked out about them over there?"

I shrug. "Not really."

"I would be."

"Really?"

"Yeah. I got robbed once."

"You did?"

"Yeah. One of the craziest jobs I ever had was back in Jersey working at a cool old bowling alley for a guy named Giovanni. It was right on the Jersey shore. I was pretty young too, but Giovanni trusted me; he loved me like a son. Man, I never worked so hard in my life. Every morning, before we opened the doors, I was supposed to take the bank deposit from the night before out of the old safe and over to the bank across the street. One morning, I'm walking across the street with the money and I get jumped from behind. I never knew what hit me, never even saw the guy. I went down hard right there on the pavement, in the middle of the road, passed out cold. When I woke up the money was gone and there was a puddle of blood under my head.

Here, I've still got the scar." He pulls his hair back to show me. It's a faint crisscross, about two inches long. I resist the urge to run my finger over it.

"That's brutal. Why would Giovanni let a kid do something so dangerous?"

"He liked having breakfast with his family in the morning before he came in, and I had to get the change for the cash drawers. Anyway, it was a safe neighborhood. I was just unlucky, I guess. The upside was that I got to bowl for free anytime and eat all the pizza I wanted." He stops for a second, considering something. His face darkens. "That place was like home to me, a lot better than my real home."

I'm about to ask about his family but then I catch myself—too early for personal questions. I quickly change directions. "My boss doesn't really trust anyone with money. He'd take it home and stuff it in his mattress every night if he could. He does all the deposits himself. No one even has the combination to the safe. It's a drop safe." God, could I sound any duller? Next thing you know I'll be sharing the California employee tax structure with him.

"I'd trust you with anything. You've got one of those faces."

"One of what faces?"

"The kind you can trust."

"I never thought of myself that way."

"The minute I saw you, I knew you were that kind of person. It's all in the eyes."

He watches me with his cool blue-green eyes. I become self-conscious and look away. I've noticed now that he has a calm way of taking things in. It's unnerving for someone like me, who has to react to everything. In a stolen glance here and there, I absorb him: His shoulders are narrow but he's wearing a black tailored shirt that flatters his build. Something on a silver chain, a medallion of some sort, dangles just inside the first button of his shirt so I can't tell what it is. His jeans are worn but, again, flattering, and they fit just so, and he's wearing a scuffed pair of dark brown work boots. He has an expensive haircut with just a hint of sideburns. I realize that some thought went into this look. None of it is accidental. He wears a slim, tasteful silver watch on his wrist. My own collection of bangles and assorted woven leather bracelets looks cheap and ridiculous in comparison.

I excuse myself to the ladies' room and lock the bathroom door behind me, and I look at my face in the mirror. My cheeks are flushed. I apply lip balm vigorously and try to smooth my ill-fitting sweater. God, it looks like something Shorty and Jam wouldn't even bother with. I rake my fingers through my hair and take a good look at myself. The improvement is minimal.

When I arrive back at the table, Joel is on his cell phone. He flips it shut and lays it on the table. "Sorry, just checking my messages."

I smile and shrug. What I wouldn't give to hear those messages.

"So, you work every night, Allie?"

"No, not every night."

"We should go out sometime. See a movie or something."

"Yeah, we should." Is he asking me out on a real date?

We talk some more, mostly small talk. I start to relax and I even laugh at some of his stories. He seems to have hundreds of them and he tells them in a way that makes you hang on every word. They often feature hilarious situations he's been involved in where he admits that he probably should have known better and then he laughs softly. His life is vastly more interesting than mine but he has a way of looking completely engaged when I speak. Eventually, the waiter drops the check on the table. Joel picks it up and looks around.

"Hey, wanna drink and dash?"

"What?" Is he kidding?

"C'mon. It'd be so easy." He leans in. "Ya think that old-fart waiter would even chase after us?"

I shake my head. "You're kidding, right?"

"Of course." He takes out his wallet and pulls out a five and a one and puts them down on the table.

Later, on my way home, I try to analyze what just happened. Why is it so difficult for me to decipher whether Joel likes me or not? I mean, didn't he suggest a movie date and take down my phone number? And after we left the café, we were standing on the sidewalk and he said, "You're an interesting girl, Allie." And then he touched a strand of my hair that had fallen into my eye and gently pushed it aside. How am I supposed to interpret that? A part of me misses the mystery surrounding M. I'm glad that I know Joel now, but I'd become used to the fabricated story I'd created and I suppose I was a bit in love with it. Joel, the real M, is quite a different person, harder to figure out; even with all the great stories, you get the feeling he's leaving something out, something big. He has this unexplainable thing that I'm incredibly drawn to, this daring, reckless, spontaneous side. You know that he's the first one off the cliff at the swimming hole, the first to knock back a shot or throw a punch or lean in for a kiss. He's the type of guy who's always happy to take you up on a dare, always looking for adventure, never thinks too much about consequences. He has an easy confidence that leaves me breathless and wanting against my better judgment. I've never met anyone else like him.

$\mathcal{W}$ednesday's blog is posted by nine a.m. the next morning. I woke up early, my head spinning with thoughts of Joel. I can't stop thinking about him, and our time together comes back in sound bites and flashes of his hands, his smile, his clothes, his eyes. Since I was awake, I decided to get some work done.

The blog is about Mink DeVille. *Cabretta* (easy to find on vinyl) was their first commercial release. Willy DeVille, band founder and master of the New York ghetto love song (his version of "Spanish Harlem" is soul stirring), was a former all-star drug abuser, about seven feet tall with a reputation for being a real pain in the ass. He was the kind of rock star who could honestly take your breath away when he walked onstage. He's famous for his exploration of Latin rhythms, mariachi, Creole, Cajun, blues, and R & B, and he had, in my opinion, one of the sexiest voices out there (with all due respect to Tom Waits). He lived in New Orleans some of the time, and I was convinced that he was a vampire until he died in August '09. Some might remember him from the *Princess Bride* sound track. His song "Storybook Love" was the best thing about this beautiful Mark Knopfler sound track. I advise readers to get that too.

Inexplicably, my mom is going camping this weekend with Jack. She announced this in the morning before I left for the store. I detected some anxiety in her voice and she wouldn't look me in the eye. My mom has never slept outdoors in her life. She told me that, when she was a kid, Estelle sent her to Jewish summer camp in upstate New York, claiming it would be an excellent "character builder." The campers slept in log cabins on wooden bunk beds but, after three weeks of that, the counselors announced that they were taking the campers on an overnight camping trip in the woods. My mom panicked at the very idea of sleeping outdoors and she faked heatstroke to get out of it. The only person left at camp to watch her was the janitor, an alcoholic with very poor judgment who got my mom drunk on Budweiser. She also told my mom slurred ghost stories and then left her alone in the empty cabin for hours while she drove to the bar in town. My mom was terrified. Who wouldn't be? Her story has all the elements of a classic slasher movie. She always tells that story when someone asks her if she camps, so I'm surprised she didn't tell it to Jack.

Apparently, though, when Jack asked her, my mom somehow thought that by "camping" he obviously meant camping all day and sleeping in a lovely hotel at night with flush toilets and down quilts and four-hundred-thread-count sheets and mints on the pillows. I guess she thought that that's how people over forty camp. Only later, when she'd already accepted, did she realize that when Jack said "camping," he actually meant "camping."

When I arrive home from work, my mom's already in a tailspin over the whole thing. She can't decide whether she should call it off and come clean with him or just go along with it and fake her love for the outdoors like she faked her cooking skills. I think it might be harder to fake your love for the outdoors. When I was a kid I belonged to the Firefly Girls; they're like the Camp Fire Girls except they're not run by right-wing Christians and they don't worship God. Firefly Girls worship nature, so we did a lot of crafty, outdoorsy things with leaves and sticks. We called them "Blair Witch Projects." At the end of the year, we went on an overnight camping trip called a "discovery." The first thing

I discovered was that I never want to sleep outside again. The second thing I discovered was that eating nine s'mores can make you barf.

I lie on the sofa while she reads to me from a book called *Poisonous Insects and Plants of Northern California*.

"Oh, here's a nice one, the brown recluse spider. This one resides in wooded areas. In other words, next to my head while I'm sleeping. 'In a small number of cases, a bite from the brown recluse can produce organ damage with occasional fatalities.'"

"That's the worst-case scenario. How bad can it be? It's called a 'recluse.'"

"It's been my experience that all recluses have a mean streak." She flips through the bug-covered pages, grimacing at the photos.

I muse over the word *reclusive*. Am I reclusive? Am I hiding from the world behind my prized vinyl collection? Am I destined to become an old reclusive vinyl collector with a mean streak, waving my fist at the neighborhood kids with Janis Joplin playing in the background? Would Joel think I was pathetic if he knew how I lived?

I watch my mom, her brow furrowed, concentrating on her bug book. "Mom, why don't you try being yourself with this Jack guy? Why are you suddenly some sort of Martha Stewart in a Girl Scout uniform?"

"Oh, it's not that; it's not that at all. It's just that some-times I wonder if maybe your dad was right. The academic life is starting to lose its appeal for me. Do I really want to spend my life hanging around with people who can quote Shake-spearean sonnets? I don't think it's such a bad idea for me to try some new things. Anyway, at the very least, it's healthy for me to step out of my little world. I've been living in a bubble."

Her words aren't lost on me. Maybe they apply to me too: different bubble, same problem. "Maybe you should bring your bubble camping. Is it bug-proof?"

She laughs. "Hey, what's in your bag, anything for me?"

I dig through my messenger bag and pull out a Ray LaMontagne CD. "You're going to love this guy." I slide the CD into the player and get back on the sofa. The song "Be Here Now" starts and we lie there listening for a while. My mom never talks over new music. We've always been a household of respectful music listeners. When my dad left, it occurred to me that for years our family had communicated mostly by playing music for one another. It was great but we had no idea how to talk to one another. If I came home and heavy metal was playing with the volume turned up, it usu-ally meant my parents had been fighting. If Neil Young or the Byrds or Greg Brown was playing, things were okay. If my mom was trying to torture my dad, she'd put Yoko Ono or Kate Bush on. If nothing was playing, no one was home.

After a couple of songs my mom nods at me.

"I like him. He sounds kind," she says.

Between songs we realize that there's someone knocking on the front door. I turn down the music and my mom goes to answer it.

Ravi is standing on our front porch, holding an enormous plant. He looks a little uncomfortable.

"Hi, Ravi," says my mom, gesturing for him to come in. "I wasn't expecting you today. I have us scheduled for tomorrow morning. Did I get that wrong?"

"No, no. It's just that I was in the neighborhood and I thought I might stop by with a small token of my appreciation." He hands her the plant and my mom stands there holding it for a few seconds and then she puts it on the floor next to her feet.

"Wow, it's heavy. Thank you very much, Ravi."

He smiles nervously.

"Hey, is that a new shirt?" she asks. I lean off the sofa to get a better look. He's wearing an oxford short-sleeved button-down shirt in pale blue. The creases from the package it came in zigzag his chest. I also notice that his unruly beard has been trimmed close to his face and his hair has been cut about an inch. It makes him look much younger.

"Yes. You like it?"

"I do. You look very nice," my mom says sincerely.

Ravi beams. "Thank you very much. Well, I won't keep you any longer."

"That's okay. I'm not busy. Oh, while you're here, I should tell you that I have to move our Monday appointment to the afternoon. Is that okay? I'm going camping for the weekend."

Ravi's face darkens a bit. "Yes, that's fine. Camping?"

"Yeah, crazy, huh?" My mom runs her hands through her hair and lets it fall across her shoulders, a nervous habit she has. "I hope I don't die out there."

"Yes, well, then. I'll see you tomorrow morning."

"Okay. Thanks for the plant. Bye, Ravi." She closes the door and picks up the plant, looking around for a place to set it down. She finally gives up and puts it in the middle of the coffee table. She sits and we both look at the plant thoughtfully. Suddenly, my mom starts to laugh.

"What do you suppose that was all about?"

"You heard the man; he was in the neighborhood." I smirk.

"God, I think he might even have been wearing cologne."

"I think he's sweet."

"He is. Remind me to water that thing, would you?"

We watch the plant some more as though it might hop out of the pot any moment and do a soft-shoe on the coffee table.

"Do you think Ravi's throwing his hat into the ring now that he knows I'm dating?" she asks, finally taking her eyes off the plant and looking at me.

"Not a bad theory, Einstein."

My mom runs her fingers through her hair and looks at the plant again.

Thursday's blog is about the Pogues, more specifically Shane MacGowan, the always inebriated Celtic rebel. The Pogues fired MacGowan, the founder of the band, in 1991, when they couldn't deal with his drunken state anymore. Turned out they signed their own death warrant in the process. Fans weren't interested in the Pogues without Shane. In the blog I advise that you should never buy a Pogues album unless he's on it.

Friday's blog is about the Gram Parsons album *Grievous Angel*. This was the first "country music" album I ever bought. It kicked my ass. Gram called it "cosmic American music." It features a young Emmylou Harris on vocals at the start of her career. Gram died in 1973 in Joshua Tree, California, of a drug overdose. He was twenty-six years old. I told readers that if they don't own this LP, they should find it, buy it and listen to "Hickory Wind" till they weep.

The top five LPs this week are:

The Pogues: *Rum, Sodomy, & the Lash*

(five out of five LPs)

Gram Parsons: *Grievous Angel*

(five out of five LPs)

Neil Young: *After the Gold Rush*

(five out of five LPs)

Marianne Faithfull: *Broken English*

(five out of five LPs)

Emmylou Harris: *Blue Kentucky Girl*

(four out of five LPs)

Within one hour of my posting, eighteen people posted comments on the Gram Parsons blog: people from Europe, some repeats from the other day; most of them live in Amsterdam, one guy from Norway and two people from Denmark. One girl from Vermont and a few people from the South. Most of them wrote about the first moment they heard Gram Parsons and the way it made them feel. One comment that stopped me in my tracks said:

```
Gram's music was a ripple that became
a wave in the years following his
death. One can't help but be moved
by Gram's music. Thanks, VP, for
choosing this LP. It's important.
```

He signed it,

A Fan, Berkeley, CA.

Berkeley? Could it have been posted by Joel? Is it possible that he took my fanzine out of the bag and read it and that he knows it's me? Who else could have sent it? Aidan? Then I remember that Zach took my zine the other day too, but that post just doesn't sound like him.

The blog is taking up more and more of my time. On top of the actual writing, people are also sending me their addresses so I can send them a fanzine. The only way I can keep up is to work on it at Bob & Bob's. I'm finding myself typing away madly whenever I get the chance. The zines at the store are steadily disappearing now. I never see anyone taking them but the stack keeps getting smaller and smaller. Are people actually reading it? I've noticed that whenever I work on the blog, I feel good. I don't feel reclusive or weird. I feel like I'm doing something good for the world, gathering like-minded people together in solidarity. I often imagine all of the vinyl lovers I've amassed, standing together in a circle in the middle of a big field somewhere, and I would stand in the middle like an angelic cult leader, and we would all be smiling and feeling the love. Pretty cheesy, but there it is.

On Friday, as promised, I escort Kit to her appointment

with the plastic surgeon. The barter system is alive and well in our friendship, so in exchange, I've asked her to spend the weekend at my house while my mom's camping. The idea of rambling around the house all weekend with Suki, the ghost, and Pierre, the traitorous cat, for company isn't very appealing. Kit's agreed, saying that the change of scenery will probably do her good. She hasn't stopped longing for Niles to appear on her doorstep, hat in hand, begging for forgiveness. She wouldn't forgive him in a million years but it's nice to be asked.

I left my mom to her precamping anxiety. She'd packed and unpacked and repacked several times. I informed her that she might not need two skirts or even one, for that matter, and a cashmere wrap was definitely out of the question. I told her she should stick to stuff that looked like "gear" but she looked confused. "Things with lots of zippers and Velcro and straps made of polar fleece or some sort of moisture-wicking fabric," I told her. To her I was speaking gibberish. I loaned her a pair of cargo shorts and a hoodie and a down-filled vest and left her to figure out the rest for herself. I didn't want to do the big good-bye because I thought it would just add to her anxiety if I acted as though I might never see her again.

Kit and I arrive at the plastic surgeon's office just before two p.m. It's on the seventeenth floor of a pretty deluxe high-rise office building with a gazillion-dollar view of the entire city and the bay. The furniture in the waiting room is high-end buttery leather in quiet earth tones that sighs when you sink into it and the walls are hung with giant black-and-white photos of women who would have you believe that they've altered themselves to perfection under the capable hands of Dr. Mayer when in fact they're models in their early twenties with bodies like gazelles. There's a glass fountain at one end of the large waiting room trickling water into a trough. No doubt the designer assured the doctor that it would be calming to his patients but all it does is make you have to pee. The unblinking receptionist has been nipped and tucked into an android and it looks like it might hurt for her to smile, so she doesn't. Most of the patients waiting are women. They sit in the leather chairs looking like the victims of mortar attack. One part or another of their faces is wrapped in white gauze and some of them resemble mummies who've come partially unfurled. We're the youngest people in the room but not by much. After Kit checks in with the stone-faced android we take our seats next to a young woman whose nose is taped up. Each of her eyes has a purple half-moon under it. She looks about twenty. No one in the room is making eye contact or talking with anyone else. There is no solidarity here. No one is trading war stories. Everyone is furiously flipping through magazines, so we follow suit. I select *Better Homes and Gardens* and Kit reads the *Economist*. Neither of us is really reading. The magazines are props so we can take in the room. I watch Kit peer over her magazine at a woman sitting across from us who looks like she's in tremendous pain. She winces every time she moves. Kit leans over to me and whispers sagely, "Liposuction." As the minutes pass I can sense Kit's anxiety. She fidgets and sighs impatiently and sits at attention whenever a patient enters the waiting room from the consultation rooms beyond the frosted-glass door.

By the time Kit's name is called, half the mortar attack victims have disappeared and I've resorted to reading shortcake recipes. Kit makes it clear that she wants to go in alone and I don't argue, but I'm actually dying to meet the guy who's paying for this view by playing Dr. Frankenstein. I get to thinking about Joel again and the way he looked at that curvy woman in the café. Would I be willing to change my body for someone like Joel? I rarely get around to even putting on a skirt. Not that putting on a skirt makes a whole lot of difference. I'm far from curvy. From the back, I could even be mistaken for a boy. Maybe I need to start putting more effort into the way I look. I grab a fashion magazine and flip through it quickly. I stare at a photo of a slender model featuring curves that don't look like her own. Maybe I just need some good lingerie: a little lift here, a little redistribution there. If I'm going to compete with all the curvy women in the world for someone like Joel, I'm going to have to make some serious changes.

Kit is gone for over half an hour and I somehow imagine her emerging looking completely different, like Jessica Rabbit or something, but she strolls out looking like she always has.

"Ready?" she asks.

"No, I need to finish this article on organizing your spice rack."

"Hah. Let's go."

I drop the magazine and we pull open the heavy exotic-wood doors that were probably harvested from the disappearing rain forest and escape into the hallway leading to the sleek elevators. I press the down button.

"So?"

Kit looks up at the descending numbers. "So, you were right."

"Right about what?"

"This was a really stupid idea."

"I never said that."

The elevator arrives and we get in. The door closes quietly and we stand next to each other, waiting to feel the high-speed drop in our stomachs.

"Yeah, you pretty much did, but it's okay; you were right."

"What happened in there?"

"Well. He took a picture of me and then he showed me a computer-generated picture of what I would look like 'enhanced.'"

"And?"

"And I looked like someone trying to be someone else. I didn't look like me anymore. And then I thought, 'Well, maybe I do want to be someone else, but not this person in the photo.' The 'me' in the photo looked so desperate. Then Dr. Mayer started telling me about things like the incision, the anesthesia, the recovery time and the side effects, oh, and pain management . . . *pain* management! Then he showed me some implants. They're these little sacs filled with saline solution, and he put one in my hand and it felt so creepy that I pulled my hand back and it dropped on the floor, and when I looked down at it, it looked exactly like one of those purplish jellyfish that wash up onshore at the beach sometimes. They just lie there, waiting to die. Dr. Mayer leaned over and picked it up and there was lint all over it and I thought, 'How can I let someone who doesn't even stay on top of the vacuuming around here cut my breasts open?' So I said I would think about it and I left."

The elevator swishes open and we enter the massive echoing marble lobby.

"I'm really glad you're going to think about this."

Kit's face changes. "You know what? I think I'm done thinking about it. I was already having my doubts in the waiting room. All those people, trying to be someone else. Is it really going to make them happy? I don't think I'm one of those people. They depressed me."

We walk out into the sunshine, happy to be outside. While we were up there the gray blanket of fog pulled back, revealing a rare, gorgeous day in the city. We hop on a Muni bus and watch the neighborhoods roll by the window. We get off on Haight Street and let ourselves be swept along up the street by the hard-core punks and weirdos. Haight Street is a bit like an edgier Telegraph. Street kids and runaways from across the country end up here, looking for money or drugs or friends or all three. They camp out on the sidewalk like orphans, dressed like extras in a *Mad Max* movie, begging for spare change. The street is lined with funky boutiques and cheap food and bars and bike shops.

Kit seems relieved to be away from Dr. Mayer's office. We walk up the street together, ducking into the weird shops and vintage-clothing stores. Kit finds a black newsboy's cap and a pair of vintage sunglasses and I get an Andy Warhol T-shirt and a new set of wheels for my skateboard.

Late in the day, the fog unfurls itself back over the bay for the night. We take BART across the bay, get off at Rockridge, and walk over to Piedmont Avenue, where Joey Spinelli's dad's pizza place is. It turns out to be so tiny that we almost walk right past it. It has six tables and no table service. You just tell them what you want at the counter and they call you when it's ready. I order a mushroom-and-olive with extra sauce from a young girl at the counter. Next to her, a barrel-chested guy with a heavy unibrow and oily black hair is throwing pizza dough into the air. There's no sign of Joey anywhere. I sit down at a tiny table with Kit. We look around at the place. Not much in the way of atmosphere. There's a TV mounted in the corner over a bar, and a soccer game is being played by Europeans with floppy hair and great legs. The sound is off. One of the walls is faux brick and the others are covered with off-white high-gloss paint. The tables are draped in red-and-white-checkered plastic tablecloths.

The guy behind the counter calls out that our pizza's ready. I go up to get it. I watch him expertly roll a pizza cutter back and forth. His knuckles are superhairy.

"Hey, is Joey around?" I ask.

"You want Joey? He's deliverin'." He glances up at a clock. "Should be back soon."

"Are you his dad?" I ask.

"Yeah," he says gruffly. I see the resemblance now, the deep-set eyes, the full lips.

"So, who's Rusty?" I point to the retro logo on the menu that's taped to the counter.

"That was Joey's dog, an Irish setter, dumb as a post. He's dead now." He slides the pizza toward me.

"Oh. Thanks." I take my pizza and walk back to the table.

"Who's that?" asks Kit.

"That's Joey in thirty years," I say, putting the pizza down.

Kit looks at the guy for a few seconds. Then she takes a container of hot peppers and starts shaking it vigorously onto the pizza. Her eyes well up with tears.

"What? What is it?" I ask.

She looks up at me. "It's just so sad."

"What is?"

"It's just so sad what we're willing to do for the Joey Spinellis of the world, you know? The mutilating, the tweezing, the enhancing, the plumping, the pinching, the waxing, the starving, the sweating, the bleaching. And for what? So you can wake up next to *that* in thirty years? What are we thinking?"

A tear rolls down each of Kit's cheeks. She blows her nose into a napkin.

"Was I really stupid enough to think that I could get Niles back if I only had the right-size boobs? Was I really willing to do that to myself?" She dabs at her tears.

"Maybe we should get this to go." Kit nods and blows her nose into a napkin. I take the pizza back to the counter, where the young girl has reappeared, and ask her to box it.

We gather up our things and the pizza and walk out the door.

A half a block down the street, with the pizza box under my arm, I look back over my shoulder. Joey is parking a beat-up motorcycle in front of the pizza place. He's wearing low-slung jeans and a white T-shirt pulled tight across his broad chest. He pulls off a helmet and his black curls tumble out. He looks like an underwear model.

$\mathcal{K}$it and I lie side by side in my mom's big bed. An armless sock monkey, the only thing Kit has left of Niles, lies between us. I can smell my mom's shampoo on the pillow. The house is quiet except for the odd creaks and unexplainable sighs emanating from the old walls. There's a breeze from the open window billowing the filmy white curtains and in the dark it looks like a ghost climbing in through the window and then immediately climbing out again.

We're drowsy and close to sleep. The conversation drifts from what we're making for breakfast in the morning—I try to remember if we have eggs—to Niles (what he used to like to eat for breakfast), to clothes, to Steve Buscemi. Now we're discussing indie movies. We take turns adding to the list of our favorites: *Blood Simple, Ghost World, Mystery Train, Donnie Darko, Pieces of April, This Is*

"Hey, I forgot to tell you. I saw M today." Kit yawns.

"Joel," I correct her. I'm wide-awake now.

"Joel, whatever."

"Why didn't you tell me?"

"I am telling you."

"Where?"

"Barney's Burgers on College. He was eating there with some guy."

"What guy?"

"I dunno, just a guy. He was wearing those seventies aviator sunglasses and he looked kind of big. Not tall, just wide-ish."

"What was Joel wearing?"

"I don't know."

"What were they talking about?"

"I don't know, Al, I didn't think to stop and interview them."

"What were they eating?"

"Burgers? Jesus, Allie, this M guy is making you all weird."

"Joel," I correct her.

"I'm going to sleep now. G'night." She rolls over onto her side, facing the wall, and I hear her breathing deepen. I stare at the ceiling, thinking about Joel, wondering what he's doing right now. The fact that he hasn't called has me counting days and trying to figure out what to reasonably expect from him. Is there any chance that he's doing what I'm doing, or is it just crazy to think that I might figure in his thoughts at all?

I hear a door open and then I see Pierre emerge from the shadows, skulking past the open bedroom door. He stops and looks in at us a moment and then he carries on. I can hear him padding lightly down the stairs and then he's crunching his food in the darkened kitchen.

On Saturday morning, after we clean up from our breakfast of leftover pizza, scrambled eggs and maple-glazed dough-nuts, Kit and I walk to our separate jobs together like an old married couple, parting at the corner of Telegraph and Haste. In the world of retail, Saturdays come at you hard and fast and you'd better be ready. I yank open the metal security gate in front of the doors and knock on the glass till Bob appears to let me in. My keys are at the bottom of my messenger bag and digging them out would take for-ever.

Bob's wearing sunglasses and a navy wool beret. The beret is to cover an emerging bald spot and the glasses are to discourage any sort of chatting. Bob doesn't do morning chat. He won't even be speaking in complete sentences until noon. Saturday is the only day Bob opens the store. I'm grateful that he already has the change in the cash drawers done so I can restock the bins and the waterfall racks, which requires little in the way of brain function. Bob has an Ahmad Jamal album playing—swingy jazz, uncharacteristically optimistic of him. I get to work on the bins till I hear Laz knocking at the glass door. I let him in. Jennifer should also technically be here by now but she's been on time only once since she became an employee at the store and that was the day after she was hired. Aidan's not in till noon. He has totally cushy hours.

Through the side window I can see the street preacher setting up on the next corner. I stand there watching for a minute. An unsuspecting regular-looking guy walks by, pushing a stroller with a toddler in it who's disassembling a sandwich. The street preacher rushes over to the guy with his shtick. He's right up in his face, pointing to the sky a couple of times for emphasis, like it's the head office of his company. He hands the guy a pamphlet to go along with the shtick. The guy backs away, shaking his head slightly, and keeps walking. The baby leans out of the stroller and waves good-bye to the preacher, dropping a piece of luncheon meat at his feet. The guy tosses the pamphlet into the garbage can on the corner.

I get back to work. Laz leaves again for his coffee fix

and his last smoke for a while. I lock the door behind him. A couple of people are milling around outside the front doors, waiting for us to open like we're a free soup kitchen. Bob's is a place that makes it onto a lot of people's list of things to do on the weekends—*Take all those crappy LPs from the basement down to Bob & Bob's and convert them into cash so we can buy that flat-screen TV or Ferrari we've been wanting.* People are frequently insulted that the records they bought in college and played a million times till the grooves all but disappeared could be worth so little in today's marketplace. Somehow they thought they were sitting on a gold mine. They're astonished that we might not need another copy of the Doobie Brothers' *Minute by Minute*, or Fleetwood Mac's *Rumors* or the Eagles' *Hotel California*.

At ten thirty, I slide the security gate aside and swing open the glass doors. Laz follows the small group in, holding a gallon-size cup of coffee. Before I go back inside, I look up Telegraph at the umbrellas that line the avenue on Saturdays and Sundays. They belong to the street merchants. It's hard to imagine trying to sell the same tableful of stuff every weekend. At least I have a storeful of music to groove on; at least I'm not standing outside hawking bumper stickers or tie-dye or scented candles.

Kit calls at eleven to ask if we have microwave popcorn in the house.

"No. We don't even have a microwave. Andrew Weil says they give you cancer."

"Who's Andrew Weil?"

"The doctor with the big gray beard. My mom has all his books."

"He says microwaves give you cancer?"

"Uh-huh."

"They also give you microwave popcorn. Did he tell you that?"

"We don't really talk, Dr. Weil and I. We can make it on the stove in a pot, like in the olden days."

"Okay. Is it dead over there? It's dead over here."

I survey the store. We have a minor crowd, all locals. The B and Ts don't arrive for another half hour or so. I was hoping to work on the blog but it will have to wait.

"It's early," I say.

"Oh, wow, it *is* early. I've already had too much coffee. I just told a girl that the skirt she was trying on made her look fat. If Deb heard I would be *so* fired."

"I gotta go. A pack of B and Ts just arrived."

"Later." She hangs up.

A group of suburban indie-rock poseurs hover around the new-release rack, picking up CDs and putting them back. I hear them exclaim at the price of a White Stripes CD.

"This is hella cheaper at Wal-Mart, dude," says one poseur to the other.

How ironic that they're trying to look indie when they've already sold their souls to Wal-Mart. They shuffle zombielike out of the store. I'm glad Bob didn't hear them. His mood would have been altered dramatically. We barely make any money at all on new merchandise. We just can't compete with the prices at the big-box, Satan-owned, corporate stores.

The store eventually fills up with customers and the day starts to look like a regular Saturday. Jennifer comes in late, excuse at the ready (the hot water ran out in her shower just as she was putting conditioner in her hair). I leave her to work the cash register and head out onto the floor to do some upstocking and file in some used LPs. Dao arrives with her mom in tow, a smiling, smaller version of Dao. They disappear into the office. Bob emerges minutes later, sunglasses off, ready for dialogue.

"Hey, Al, do you mind closing tonight with Jennifer? I forgot that I'm taking Dao and her mom to dinner in the city. I'll pay you overtime if you end up staying late, okay?"

"Sure, Bob." I don't mind, actually. I can close the store twice as fast when Bob's not here. He likes to play "blah, blah, blah, fill in band" till all hours. Jennifer will definitely slow me down but I'll give her the easy stuff.

"Cool. Just leave out enough for the cash drawer and throw everything else in the drop safe. I'll organize it tomorrow."

"No problem."

At roughly one p.m. I walk down to Fabulous Falafels, one block toward Kit's store and around the corner, to pick up two falafel pitas that I ordered by phone. There's a girl with a shaved head sitting on the pavement in front of the herb store, smoking a cigarette; a cardboard box full of pit bull puppies sits next to her. The word *free* is scrawled across the front of the box. Ironic.

Fabulous Falafels is humming. Sanje, the owner, makes small talk with me, which somehow always arrives at how the government is screwing him. Even if we start with the weather, we always end up in the same place. Sanje came here from Iran twenty years ago and worked his butt off, and now he owns a chain of little falafel places around Berkeley. He's been audited three times and he's convinced that the government is monitoring him because of racial profiling. I've heard his conspiracy theory hundreds of times, but he makes the best falafel I've ever tasted. They're perfectly crunchy on the outside and creamy on the inside. Fortunately, he's really busy, so I can dart out between customers with a wave over my shoulder. Just as I'm heading back up the sidewalk with my bag of lunch, I spy Joel disappearing around the corner onto Telegraph. I pick up the pace and turn the corner seconds later. I stand there for a minute, watching. He's walking up the street next to a muscular bulldog of a guy with very close-cropped hair who's wearing aviator sunglasses and smoking a cigarette. The guy must be the buddy Joel was talking about. They're having spirited conversation. They might even be arguing. They don't even slow down when they come to Bob & Bob's. Joel doesn't even look into the store to see if I'm working. They continue across the street against the light and up the avenue. The bulldog tosses his lit cigarette onto the sidewalk as they pass in front of the empty lot; a tiny shower of orange sparks jumps off the pavement.

"Did you bring extra hot sauce?" asks Kit, digging through the bag.

I've delivered her lunch because she has no one to cover for her today. Her coworker called in sick (read: hungover).

"Yeah, it's in there."

She dumps the bag upside down and the plastic containers fall onto the counter. She pulls the tinfoil back on her pita and dumps hot sauce on it.

"So you saw them?" I ask, unwrapping my pita.

"Yeah. M—I mean Joel—and that guy; that's the same one I saw him with yesterday. They walked right past the front window two minutes ago." She sips her iced tea through a straw.

We sit together on stools behind the counter and eat our pitas. The place starts to smell like a Middle Eastern restaurant. Customers come and go. The shop is basically a jumble of vintage used clothes that resembles a drag queen's closet. They ran out of room a long time ago so only the very devoted will take the time to pick through the jam-packed racks and piles of stuff, looking for treasures. Kit rings a guy up for a silk tie and a girl for a pale blue angora scarf and an ivory beaded sweater. She gets to play her own music and right now we're listening to Nick Cave and the Bad Seeds' *The Firstborn Is Dead*.

"Hey, so why didn't you call out to him when you saw him? I mean, you have had sort of a date with the guy." Kit squashes her tinfoil into a ball and lobs it into the overflowing trash can.

"I dunno, he seemed preoccupied." I don't feel like mentioning again that he hasn't called either.

"Who cares? He should be preoccupied with thoughts of you, right?"

"I guess." I wish I had her unshakable confidence.

I finish my lunch and head back to Bob's. The store is busy now and the afternoon flies by. Jennifer and I work the cash together, one ringing and one bagging, and that buzzy feeling you get when you do the same thing over and over sets in. Before I know it, Bob and Dao and Dao's mom are heading out the door.

"You've got my cell number, right?" says Bob, patting his pockets till he locates his cell phone.

"Yup. Have fun." I wave to Dao and her mom and they produce matching toothpaste-commercial smiles.

The store starts to slow down as the avenue clears out. The B and Ts get in their SUVs and head back out to the suburbs. The street merchants pack up their tables and the locals get on with their Saturday nights in a more desirable location. We're back to the bare bones of the neighborhood: the weirdos, the street people and the homeless, all of whom have no specific plans for Saturday night.

For the last hour or so before we close I work my way through the back half of the store and clean up the bins to get them ready for tomorrow because I won't be here. An old buddy of Bob's named Roger opens up on Sundays but he rarely touches a bin. He works two days a week, and that's mostly as a favor to Bob and to keep his record collection fresh and interesting. The rest of the time he plays steel guitar in a country band.

Every Picture Tells a Story, by Rod Stewart, my absolute favorite Rod Stewart album, is playing on the stereo and

I'm loving it and silently thanking Bob as "Maggie May" starts to play . . . what a song.

At five minutes till closing, I check the store for stray customers, a major part of the closing procedure. We once found a drugged-out kid curled up on the floor in the country section, and another time we found an employee (ex-employee now) napping in the storeroom behind some boxes. I check the bathroom and make my way up through the office to lock the front door. I hear voices coming from the front of the store and I crack the office door an inch and peer out. Two men in ski masks are standing in front of the cash register pointing a gun at Jennifer. I lunge backward in shock and then catch the door just as it's about to slam. I hold it open an inch. I can't see Jennifer's face without opening the door some more but I can see that the glass front doors are closed and the lock is engaged. I'm afraid to call for help because the phone is right next to Jennifer and they'll see the red light for the line go on. The robbers don't seem to know that anyone is back here. They must have been staking out the place. They would have seen Bob leave and they might have thought they saw me leave too. A little while ago, I went to take some mail that was delivered to us by accident to Mario's Mexican Restaurant around the corner. I came in the back way because it's faster, but no one would know we have a back door. You have to punch a code to bypass the alarm and then it resets itself. They probably thought I was gone if they didn't see me again. I suddenly think about what happened to the kid at the gas station. My heart is beating so fast that I worry they might hear it. I stand there, holding my breath. I've never been so scared in my life. I pray that Jennifer keeps her mouth shut for once. One of the men is telling Jennifer to fill up a Bob & Bob's bag with all the cash from the register. I know from the report I ran recently that there's only about two thousand dollars in the register; the rest is credit card slips, worth nothing to them. Jennifer miraculously does as she's told and hands over the bag.

"Is that it?" demands the smaller of the two men, the one holding the gun. "You'd better not be holding out on me, you little bitch. I don't like being lied to, ya know?" He waves the gun at her.

Jennifer suddenly looks down. The robbers look down. I look at the desk next to me. The red light is on. Someone's using the phone. I completely forgot about Aidan in the Cave. He's still in there. I forgot to look in there. He must be calling the cops. The shorter guy starts toward the back of the store. I close the door of the office and squeeze my eyes shut. I hear the sound of their two voices arguing. I open the door a crack. The tall guy is gesturing at the front door, backing toward it. A siren starts up off in the distance. The short guy changes direction and follows him. I exhale.

The taller guy turns to Jennifer and calls out, "Have a nice evening," as he pushes open the front door. And that's when I know. The voice is unmistakable. I look at his feet. He's wearing brown scuffed work boots. It's Joel.

Joel is the one who's been robbing stores up and down Telegraph. Joel is possibly the one who shot that guy at the gas station. He doesn't care about Joe Strummer. He didn't post that comment on my blog and he doesn't care about my hands. He doesn't care about me. He told me that story about the bowling alley so I'd tell him about the drop safe and that I didn't have the combination. He used me to help him rob Bob & Bob's. He's just a small-time thief. And those two guys in the BMW? They were probably buying plumbing supplies.

$\mathcal{T}$he yowl of the sirens gets closer and closer. Somehow I'd imagined a bunch of cops on bikes pedaling up the street like mad, rushing to my rescue, but the cops who arrive have serious wheels. A posse of them, circling the wagons with blue and red lights flashing, screech to a halt in front of our door. By that time I've called Bob's cell three times but he's not picking up. I left a message but I'm not sure what I said. My hands are still shaking when I unlock the door and let the cops in. Jennifer is a puddle. She looks even paler than usual and she's sitting in a chair in the office mumbling something about quitting this stupid job. I suppose that would be the upside to this whole horrible situation. Aidan has somehow disappeared.

Officer Davis sits down at Bob's desk and starts writing out a report. He may not always get his man but I don't think he ever misses a meal. His navy uniform strains at the buttons and Bob's chair looks like it's meant for a preschooler under his bulk. Three more cops are doing some serious reconnoitering of the situation. Jennifer and I sit in chairs across from Officer Davis as though we're the ones on trial. Is it possible that he thinks this was an inside job?

I haven't had one moment to collect my thoughts. My head is still spinning with the idea that Joel is a criminal. I'm also hurt and embarrassed at the ridiculous fairy tale I've concocted, thinking that maybe he was interested in me. What a first-class idiot I was.

Officer Davis has watched a lot of cop TV. He has the facial expressions and the body language nailed. He keeps confusing us with each other, though, which makes answering questions complicated.

"Now, Jennifer." He looks at me. "You were in the back the whole time, and what exactly did you see from here?"

Jennifer points to me. "She's Allie. She was in the back. I'm Jennifer."

"Right, you're right." He looks at me. "You were in the back, though, right?"

"Yeah."

"And you are?"

"Allie." I'm thinking name tags might move this along.

He writes on his clipboard. "Okay, Allie, describe what you saw."

"Well, not much. I was peeking through a crack in the door. The guy with the gun was stocky and muscular and the other guy was taller, thinner. They both had ski masks on, and gloves."

"Anything else?" he asks me.

I shake my head. I fully realize that I am now lying to an officer of the law, which is probably a felony. It's entirely possible that both these guys have police records and there are probably mug shots in a big book somewhere down at the station for me to point at and say, *That's him. That's the guy.* But I just can't do it. Not tonight anyway.

"Okay . . ." Officer Davis looks at Jennifer, trying to remember her name from five seconds ago. He clicks his ballpoint pen and leans in; the chair complains loudly. "Name again?"

"Jennifer," she says, annoyed.

"Right, Jennifer. Can you tell me anything unusual, anything you noticed that might help us find these guys?"

Jennifer shakes her head.

"Okay, what about clothes? Can you remember what they were wearing?"

"Oh, yeah, they were wearing long-sleeved black sweat-shirts, jeans, sneakers . . . or was it boots?" She looks at me.

I shrug. "I don't remember."

Jennifer continues, "Well, both of them were wearing ski masks and gloves, and they had guns."

"Both of them?" he says.

I turn to look at Jennifer.

"No, wait. One gun. The stocky one had a gun. But it was big."

I imagine the two of them in a bar somewhere, spending Bob's money, wearing ski masks and gloves with a gun lying on the table between them. Then I imagine them at the same bar, singing karaoke on a stage in ski masks. I must be experiencing some kind of posttraumatic, stress-related hysteria. I start to laugh.

"Something funny?" asks Officer Davis.

I feel scolded. "No, nothing."

"Okay, so we all agree here? One gun?"

"Look," says Jennifer, "I've just had a gun pointed at my head. Can we move this along? I need to go home . . . like, soon?"

At that moment Bob bursts through the door, looking much worse for wear than Jennifer and I.

"Oh, thank God you're okay! Are you okay? Is everyone okay?"

"Yeah, Bob, we're fine," I say. Jennifer doesn't respond. I suspect she hasn't quite decided what sort of an angle she wants to take on all of this. Being the victim of a robbery could work out well for her.

"Jennifer?" asks Bob.

"I had a gun pointed at my head! How do you think I am?"

While Bob gets up to speed, the radio attached to Officer Davis's belt starts to chirp. He touches the tiny microphone pinned to his lapel and speaks into it in cop codes. Squawks and static follow. Officer Davis hoists himself out of Bob's chair in slow motion. He puts his hands on his hips, ready for action.

"Well, looks like the perps have struck again—the deli up the street this time. Gotta run. Ladies, here's my card." He hands us each a white business card like he's a used-car salesman. "My direct line is on there. Contact me immediately if anything else comes to you, anything at all; no detail is too small." He hands Bob a copy of the police report. "That's your case number in the top right-hand corner. You can refer to that if you call in. You'll need it for your insurance company too."

The uniforms disappear as quickly as they arrived. We stand there in the empty store, listening to the sirens blaring and then abruptly stopping. The deli is only three blocks away. The three of us look shell-shocked. Suddenly, it's dead quiet. The music must have been turned off by me or Jennifer or the cops; I don't remember. Bob is still holding the pink police report in his hand as though it's a receipt. Somehow it seems like there should be more. Like, if you survived a robbery there should be a postrobbery cocktail party or something like that.

Jennifer reads my mind. "Well, I'm going to find some alcohol and try to forget that I almost died tonight." She grabs her stuff from behind the register and walks out the front door to tell the world about her brush with death. Bob and I watch her leave.

"Yeah. I guess I'm going to go too. It's been a long day."

Bob looks broken. "Hey, Al, I'm really sorry that I wasn't here tonight. It was really messed up of me to expect you to close with Jennifer."

All I want to do is get out of here now. I have an overwhelming desire to go home and crawl underneath my bed and stay there for a few weeks. "Don't worry about it, Bob. How were you supposed to know we'd get robbed?"

We both practically jump out of our skin as the door to the Cave at the back of the store opens. Aidan walks to the front of the store like nothing's happened. Like this is a regular day and his shift just ended. Part of me wants to thank him for practically getting me killed, but then I figure, What's the point? I wonder if Officer Davis realizes that he forgot to interview the employee who actually called 911. I wonder if Aidan would have provided information that I couldn't.

"See you guys on Monday," says Aidan, the height of animation for him.

"Yeah, good night," says Bob.

I grab my backpack and my skateboard and follow Aidan out the front door. A ragtag group of street people has gathered outside and they watch us emerge from the store with interest. Aidan disappears up the street. Shorty and Jam come at me wearing women's skiwear (it's seventy degrees outside) that they probably salvaged from the free box around the corner in People's Park. Shorty's is a bright floral-patterned two-piece and Jam's wearing a purple one-piece. Old lift tickets dangle from the zipper.

"Hey, man. I know who did the crime," says Shorty.

"No, you don't." I sigh and drop my board.

"Yeah, man, I do." He waves his finger at me. "It was the secret service, man. The same people who killed Kurt Cobain, the same people who killed John Lennon. It's a goddamn conspiracy! They're sending out hit men all over the country! They're trying to kill music in this country, man; you'll see. It's been happening since the sixties! I'm right about this."

"We have proof if you wanna see it," offers Jam earnestly.

I kick off on my board and leave them behind. I can still hear them yelling as I glide up the sidewalk. I can even hear their ski pants swishing as they halfheartedly try to chase me down for a few hundred feet. It's hard to run in skiwear when you're drunk.

"Okay, we'll talk about this later then!" yells Shorty.

I coast home on autopilot. I'm not sure I want to process what just happened. It's too much to try to sort through. By the time I get home I'm still numb but I feel a terrible urge to sit down on the front steps of my house and sob. As I come up the steps I see Kit dashing from one window to the next, yanking them open and frantically waving smoke out with a newspaper. I pull open the front door and watch her through a haze of smoke. When she sees me she tries to act natural.

"Oh, hi. You're home."

"What happened?"

"Oh, well, there was a bit of an incident with the pop-corn—you guys should really get a microwave—but don't worry. It's out now. Yup, all under control. Hey, have you got any incense or a scented candle?"

I walk into the kitchen. The remains of a charred pot sits on a burner and the walls around the stove are blackened. Some sort of grayish foam is oozing through the burners and down the front of the oven. Suki is standing in the doorway holding a fire extinguisher I've never seen before and Pierre is standing next to her, looking up at us accusingly. I look at Kit. Her white T-shirt is smeared with black. So is her face.

"Don't worry. I'll clean it up," she says.

I walk out onto the front steps, sit down, put my head in my hands and start to cry.

For postrobbery and post–house fire music, Kit and I choose Gogol Bordello, Flogging Molly, the Dropkick Murphys, and the Talking Heads' *Stop Making Sense* (just so we can hear "Burning Down the House"). We get to work on the mess, scrubbing the walls, wiping down everything in the kitchen, cleaning the stove, airing the place out. I dug around the house and found some scented candles and incense in a drawer by my mom's bed. Apparently, I've stumbled onto her Kama Sutra stash. Also in the drawer are a vibrator and some massage oil (and I really didn't need to know that). We light enough candles and incense to start our own ashram. Kit thought I was crying about the fire, and I suppose I was in a way. She patted my back and told me to look on the bright side: At least now we know how to get Suki out of her room. When I kept crying she realized that something else must have happened and I unloaded the whole story on her in breathy, hysterical bursts. I even told her the part about Joel being the robber. I hadn't planned on telling her that, but then it all came pouring out of me like water through a broken dam. I just couldn't hold it in anymore. I felt a lot better when I was finished. I wiped my face on my T-shirt and took a deep breath.

Kit sat there, stunned. "And I thought *I* had a weird night."

Then she asked me the obvious question. It was hanging in the air above us like a cartoon bubble; I wasn't really ready to hear it out loud yet, even though it had been spinning around in my head for hours: "What are you going to do?"

"I have no idea," I said.

We talk above the raucous pounding music while we clean. It feels good. We're sweaty and grimy and the music is so loud that I can't crawl into a cocoon of self-pity and anger, which would be my first instinct. Kit talks me through my dilemma with an amazing sense of calm one might not expect from someone who, earlier in the evening, almost burned down her best friend's house.

"Well, what if you don't say anything and someone else gets hurt? Wouldn't you feel horrible?" she says, squeezing out a blackened sponge into a sink full of gray soapy water.

"Yes, I'd feel horrible. But what if Joel was raised by thieves or crack addicts, or alcoholic psychopaths who didn't give him any love, people without morals who possibly beat him and burned him with cigarettes and forced him to do horrible things?" I remember the story about the New Jersey bowling alley and how he hinted at a crappy home life. Was that really all a big lie? "What if this is the only life he knows? If I turn him in he'll go to prison and then what? The very thought of anyone, let alone Joel, sitting in a jail cell because of something I said is too much for me to bear."

Kit considers this, nodding sympathetically. "You think his name is really Joel?"

In all the confusion I hadn't considered this. I still don't even know his real name.

Even if Joel (or whoever) was lying about his childhood, and a big part of me wants to believe he wasn't, I'm not the kind of person who snitches. I've never snitched on anyone in my life. Well, actually, that's not true. Once, when I was four, I rolled over on Bradley Wosniak for spitting in Caroline Markus's long brown curls while she slept during naptime in preschool. I wasn't a napper. I saw everything. It was a curse.

Kit suggests that maybe after some sleep, I'll know what to do, but I'm doubtful.

We finish cleaning at four a.m. The house doesn't smell great but it doesn't smell like we had a bonfire in the living room anymore. The kitchen ends up cleaner than it was before we moved in. Kit and I stand there, exhausted and filthy. We look like chimney sweeps. We get out of our clothes and take turns showering and then we finally pass out on my mom's bed with wet hair. What seems like minutes later, I hear the front door downstairs swing open.

"Yoo-hoo! Anybody home? What's burning?" Estelle is making her way quickly up the stairs. She stands in the doorway of my mother's bedroom.

"Girls! Get up! I think something's burning."

I sit up groggily. "Estelle. Relax. There's no fire."

Kit mumbles, "No fire. Go 'way," and rolls over, shutting us out.

"Where's your mom?" demands Estelle, as though she might be trapped in the part of the house that's still ablaze.

"She went camping. Didn't she tell you?" I pull my mom's silk bathrobe on over my tank top and boxers and close my mom's bedroom door behind me. I follow Estelle down the stairs into the living room. She's already pulling containers and bagels out of a bag and looking around suspiciously.

"Something happened here. I've never seen this place so clean."

"Yeah." I rub my eyes and sit on the sofa cross-legged. "Kit accidentally lit the kitchen on fire making popcorn."

"Well, I guess if that's what it takes to get the place cleaned up," she says matter-of-factly, pulling out of her bag a container of Italian ground espresso that she special-orders from Dean & Deluca in New York. She goes into the kitchen. I can hear her filling the coffeemaker with water.

"This kitchen is blinding me," she yells. I hear the sizzle and pop of the coffeemaker kicking in and the smell of coffee drifts into the living room. She reappears and starts arranging food on the coffee table. "Now, where was it you said your mom went?"

"Camping . . . with Jack."

"Camping." She looks at me dubiously.

"Yes." I rub my eyes. "She must have told you."

"There might have been a message on my cell phone. I don't recall the word *camping,* though. What kind of bagel do you want, honey?"

"Have you got poppy?"

She pulls a poppy bagel out of the bag and slices it open with a large knife she brought from the kitchen.

"Shmear?"

"Sure."

She pulls the top off a container of cream cheese and slathers my bagel with it. She opens a package of glistening coral-colored lox and artfully arranges several slices on my bagel.

"Onions?" she asks.

"No, thanks."

She replaces the top half of my bagel and then hands it to me.

"Coffee's coming up." She jumps up and energetically disappears into the kitchen again. I'm starting to understand that I'll be playing the part of my mom this morning. Tradition is important to Estelle but she's not fussy about the cast. She's had perfectly great Thanksgivings with families she barely knows. I wonder what would have happened if I hadn't been here. Would she have hauled Suki out of her room?

Estelle reappears with two steaming mugs of coffee. Somehow she's managed to create foamed milk in our kitchen. I sip my coffee while Estelle prepares a bagel for herself. She finally sits back on the sofa with a sigh, bagel in hand, coffee to her left, *New York Times* in her lap, bare feet on the coffee table, reading glasses perched on the end of her nose. She flips through the sections, looking for the Arts and Leisure section and then the book reviews. Once everything is in place I cease to exist except for the occasional sharing of a headline or a, "Guess who's coming to Carnegie Hall?" Or, "Guess who's showing at MoMA?" Estelle is a modern-art lover. It's part of the "neonouveau" thing. The old masters hold no interest for her; she's all about new, new, new. When she lived in New York, she skulked through back alleys in the meatpacking district seeking out emerging artists' studios, always wanting to be on the cutting edge.

I take my coffee mug and wander out onto the porch. The local paper is sitting on the doormat. Estelle must have stepped over it. As a citizen of the world, Estelle has no use for our local news. She wants the big picture and that can come only from New York. I lean over and pick it up. The headline is brief and to the point:

Telegraph Robbers Strike Again!

I take the paper in with me and unfold it to reveal an old picture of Bob taken back when he was called "the Mayor of Telegraph," back when there was a pulse on the avenue. The caption underneath it says, *Bob Petrovich, owner of Bob & Bob Records*. The article talks about last night's robberies and includes a quote from Bob that says:

"This kind of crime is tough on the avenue retailers. Telegraph has always been a pretty peaceful neighborhood. If they don't catch these guys soon it's only a matter of time before someone gets hurt again or killed. We're all very nervous and it's really bad for business."

"Rudolf Stingel's showing at the Whitney," says Estelle. "He used to live in my building on the Upper West Side. He always wore fabulous shoes." She slurps her coffee and puts it back on the coffee table.

I read the whole robbery article carefully to see if they've uncovered any more details about the perps. It doesn't look like it. The deli owner describes them exactly the same way Jennifer did. I'm not exactly sure what I'm hoping for here. Do I want them to get caught? I suppose it would take the pressure off me. Joel would undoubtedly end up behind bars but it wouldn't be because of me. My head is throbbing. The stress of the last two days is obviously giving me a brain tumor.

I take small bites of my bagel and chew slowly. I decide not to tell Estelle about the robbery right now. It's not that I think she would react badly. She approaches any situation with her version of calm. I just don't want to think about it for a while. The whole thing has become a hollow pain in the pit of my stomach (probably an ulcer). It's hard to go from thinking that a person is somebody you really want to know to finding out that not only do you not want to know them at all, but they're capable of violence.

Eventually, Kit gets out of bed and joins us in the living room. In our secret sign language she asks me if I've told Estelle about the robbery. I shake my head no. Kit pours herself a coffee and sits next to me on the sofa, picking at a plain bagel. The newspaper is sitting in my lap. She reads the headline over my shoulder and looks at me, wide-eyed.

"Gimme that!" She lunges for it.

"Okay, grabby!" I hand it to her.

Estelle looks over her reading glasses at us and then returns to her paper.

Kit reads the article and then kicks the newspaper under the sofa with her bare foot.

Several minutes pass and then, suddenly, Estelle puts her paper in her lap and pulls off her reading glasses. She looks at me accusingly. "Camping. Do you mean like in a tent?"

"Yes."

"You've heard the summer camp story, haven't you?"

"Yes."

"Your mother despises camping. Anyone in their right mind despises camping. Do you think the cavemen would have camped if they'd had access to luxury condos?"

"No?"

"Who is this Jack guy, anyway?"

I shrug. "Just a guy."

"He must be more than 'just a guy' if he got your mother to sleep in a tent. Where is she going to the bathroom?"

"I don't know."

"Is she so desperate for a man that she's willing to use moss for toilet paper and eat charred animals?"

"I don't think she's doing that." Estelle seems a little fuzzy on the concept of camping.

Estelle shakes her head and stares into space for a moment. Then she puts her reading glasses back on and picks up her newspaper again. Kit kicks me with her foot.

When Estelle has read every word of the *Times* that she's interested in, she packs up her food and her Italian coffee and heads back out to the suburbs in her new lime-green Volkswagen. She's escorting a couple of blue-hairs to an erotic poetry reading in the city this afternoon. God help them. The news of my mother compromising herself to the point of sleeping outdoors has Estelle on a feminist rampage.

Kit has to work at noon and her clothes are all smoky, so she has to stop at home. She gathers up her clothes and her sock monkey and leaves. I'm left alone in the house to contemplate the aftermath of everything. I go upstairs and pick my clothes up off the floor of my mom's bedroom and check the pockets before I put them in the laundry. I pull out Officer Davis's business card. I toss it in the garbage can and immediately dig it out again. I take it into my bedroom and put it next to my bed. I flip it over and then I turn it right side up again. I stand there contemplating the little white rectangle for a minute. The phone rings and I practically jump out of my skin. I guess I'm still a little shaken up.

"Hello?"

"Al, it's me," says my mom.

"Mom? You sound like you're in a bottle."

"I'm in a phone booth. I had to walk a mile in sandals to get to it. I've got three blisters. I don't know how I'm going to make it back to the tent."

"So, how's it going?"

"I don't think I can spend another night out here. The place is surrounded by wild animals. Wait, what am I saying? The campers are wild animals."

"Where's Jack?"

"He went to get more firewood. All he does is chop wood. God, I smell like I've been barbecued."

"Well, then you're really going to like the smell around here."

"What?"

"We had a small kitchen fire. It's all under control but there's a bit of a lingering odor; you'll feel right at home."

"Are you okay?"

"Yeah, but Bob's got robbed last night."

"What?"

"Yup."

"Was anyone hurt?"

"No, but they pulled a gun on Jennifer."

"You mean a *gun* gun?"

"It looked pretty real from where I was standing."

I watch out the window of my bedroom as a large man on a tiny bike pulls a shopping cart full of bulging plastic garbage bags up the street behind him. He moves slowly, like he's a float in a homeless parade. Cars keep honking at him and passing him.

"Well, that's it, I'm coming home," says my mom.

"Okay, but your being here isn't going to change much. I'm happy to be your excuse, but don't come rushing home for me." This is a lie. I want her to come home. I need some adult supervision.

"Are you kidding me? I slept with a rock under my ass last night and I can barely move. I've been peeing in the woods because I just can't face the outhouse. I probably have poison oak. A mosquito bit my eyelid and I look like Quasimodo. We saw a bear yesterday and all the other campers were taking photos, but all I could do was imagine him with my severed arm in his mouth. I'm coming home if I have to hitchhike."

"Okay." My voice trembles a bit but I get it under control. "Don't hitchhike, though. Remember what you told me you would do to me if you ever caught me hitchhiking. Oh, and Estelle was just here; she says you're compromising yourself."

"Great. I have to go." My mom hangs up abruptly. I picture a bear sitting on its haunches, rocking the phone booth back and forth in its giant paws while my mother screams from inside.

Left alone with no distractions, I'm inclined to crawl back into bed and sob for the unforeseeable future. The humiliation and shame and sleep deprivation of the last few days come rushing back to me and I sink into a dark pit of despair. I'm achy and my throat hurts from the smoke. I fight the impulse to hide, and work halfheartedly on my blog for a while. I missed yesterday's entry completely. There are a couple of comments from my regulars asking if I'm okay. One of them is from my Berkeley "Fan." I guess I can eliminate Joel as a possibility. There's also a comment from someone named Elliot in New York. He's a website designer/vinyl junkie and he says he loves what I'm doing and he'd be happy to design my blog site for free if I'm up for it. I write him back immediately:

Dear Elliot,

Really? You would do that for me?

I'm on a pretty tight budget but
I could really use some help. Let
me know what you need from me.
The Vinyl Princess

I write a blog piece on *The Last Waltz,* one of the coolest live records ever recorded and a rad movie directed by Martin Scorsese. It's a farewell concert for the Band recorded in 1976 with an all-star guest list featuring Bob Dylan, Joni Mitchell, Van Morrison, Neil Young, Eric Clapton and Muddy Waters. I pull out the album and put it on while I write about it. The version of "Helpless" with Joni Mitchell and Neil Young makes me feel momentarily euphoric, the way an impossibly sad song can because you feel like you're in good company. I post the blog and scroll down to check how many hits I've had. It says 1,437?! Can that be right? The last time I checked it was forty-one!

In a momentary flash of spontaneity, I throw on some clothes and head out for a walk to clear my head. College Avenue is humming with people brunching and strolling. The morning fog has rolled back right on schedule and revealed a gorgeous midsummer Sunday. I walk up the avenue with my hands in my pockets. The bizarre events of last night keep coming back to me like clips from a cop show on TV. The image of the gun is something I won't be able to forget for a long time. It may as well have been pointed at me. And then hearing Joel say, "Have a nice evening," so pleasant-sounding, just like the day he talked to me for the first time. It chills me.

I walk all the way down to the Rockridge district in Oakland, oblivious to how far I've come until I'm walking underneath the BART station. I pass Olivia's Café, a popular breakfast spot with a patio out front. Something familiar draws my eye, a person sitting alone at a table. It takes me a few seconds to realize that it's Joel. He's reading the same paper I just read. He's reading about the robbery. There's a coffee cup in front of him and the remains of his breakfast. It all looks very civilized, like he's just a guy who lives in the neighborhood, not a ruthless criminal. He senses someone watching him and he looks up and our eyes meet. He darkens and something about the way he looks at me makes me understand that he knows that I know. He's not afraid of me. I'm nothing to him. Anyone who's confident enough to rob two places in ten minutes isn't going to fear someone like me. I'm like a housefly he could smash with his newspaper or some lint he could pick off his sweater and flick away. As he watches me with his calm blue-green eyes, his mouth slowly turns up into a smile and he brings his index finger to his lips. He's only ten feet away from me. He puckers his lips.

"Shhhhhh," he whispers.

A chill runs down my spine. I pick up my pace and duck into a bookstore in the middle of the next block. I head for the magazine racks next to the window and pretend to browse till my heart stops racing. I watch out the window anxiously but I know he wouldn't follow me. He doesn't have to. He was just sending me a message. I heard him loud and clear.

That night I can't sleep at all. When I finally drift off I dream about Joel.

In the dream, he's the M I invented, the nice guy. He and I are walking along a narrow ribbon of a trail cut into the side of a rocky cliff. Above us is a wall of sheer rock, and below us crashing surf. We seem oblivious to the obvious danger and we walk along the trail talking about music, M in front, me following behind. Suddenly, the trail becomes narrower and narrower under our feet and it starts to fall away. Rocks and pebbles clatter hundreds of feet into the surf below us. I grab for M's hand. His face changes into Joel's at the café today. He looks below him at the crashing surf and then he turns to me with a sinister grin and brings his finger to his lips. "Shhhhh," he whispers. I lose my grip on his hand and his fingers slide through my tightly clenched fist, one at a time, till my fist is empty. He falls backward through the air, his arms windmilling, and crashes into the pounding surf below us. I jerk awake. The house is quiet.

In the morning, I leave for work feeling wrung out. My mom is still sleeping. Last night she said something about sleeping for a week. She and Jack arrived home in the late afternoon. My mom was limping and her left eye was almost closed. So much for trying new things. Jack didn't stay long. He looked like an exhausted mother dropping off someone's kid after a really bad playdate.

My mom took a hot bath, praising indoor plumbing. She poured herself a glass of wine and we sat on the sofa while I told her all about the robbery. I left out the part about knowing who did it. I was afraid that she'd react badly and organize a manhunt or something. As it was, she made it pretty clear that she wants me to quit Bob's. She says that no one should have to work in a retail environment where a bulletproof vest is required.

When I arrive at Bob's, I unlock the store and pull the security gate behind me. I feel nervous and jumpy and I look over both shoulders. I slip my hand into the back pocket of my jeans and feel the corners of Officer Davis's card. I stand just inside the door and look around the dusty store. Somehow it looks shell-shocked. Can a store look like a victim of a crime?

For the first time since the new in-store-music rule, Bob has forgotten to load the carousel. I can tell because it's still full of Roger's quirky brand of country music from yesterday. (Roger has a special deal with Bob. He gets to play his own music on Sundays.) I empty the carousel and fill it with my own picks: the first Crosby, Stills & Nash album, Teddy Thompson's *Upfront & Down Low*, Ryan Adams's *Heartbreaker*, Steve Earle's *Jerusalem*, Neil Young's *After the Gold Rush*, Patty Griffin's *1,000 Kisses*. I guess I'm in a rootsy mood.

Laz arrives. He's already been briefed about the robbery by Jennifer (I'm pretty sure that, in her version, she escaped death by using her wits and her catlike reflexes). I'm relieved that I don't have to revisit the whole thing. Laz seems to have lost his enthusiasm for it too. He hunches over his newspaper, sipping coffee.

Minutes after I swing open the doors at ten thirty, Zach from New York walks in carrying a well-used Bob & Bob bag.

"Allie." He smiles. He looks relieved to see me. "I heard there was a little trouble over the weekend." He sets the bag carefully on the counter in front of me, after brushing it off with his hand and then wiping his hand on his pants. His hair is especially animated today, jumping off his forehead abruptly in a tidal wave, as though he slept on his face.

"Yeah. You need some credit?"

"Oh, yeah." He pulls two LPs out of the bag. "These two were a little disappointing."

"Okay." I grab the credit slips pad and start to write out a credit for him.

"So, were you here when it happened?"

"Yes, actually, I was." I keep my head down.

"Man, I thought stuff like that only happened in New York. Do they have any suspects?"

I look up at him and it suddenly occurs to me that he was standing right next to Joel in this very spot, days before it happened.

"No," I reply. I look at him evenly.

"Well, don't worry; they'll catch them. These guys always mess up sooner or later."

I look back down at the credit slip.

"Hey, you know, I've been meaning to tell you. That day at the flea market, when you told me to buy that Flaming Lips LP, you were right on about it. That record is flat-out cool."

I manage a smile.

"Are you okay?"

I shrug and bite my lip. Why am I always a mess around this guy?

Then he does something really strange. He leans over the counter and squeezes my shoulder. I really wasn't expecting that, especially not from him. Somehow it brings my emotions even closer to the surface. I blink back tears.

"Hey, don't worry. It's really okay to be freaked out for a while. My friend in New York? His apartment got robbed and you couldn't even look at him for a whole week without him bursting into tears. It was mostly because they took his comic book collection, but still, it's not easy. You feel violated."

I nod. "Yeah, I guess that's it."

I hand him his credit slip and he takes it, carefully folds it, origami style, and slides it into his thin wallet. He starts to leave.

"Hey, aren't you going to shop?"

"Can't right now. I'll be back later. See ya."

Did I just ask this extremely annoying person to stay? Has it really come to that?

I check my email. Elliot from New York has already gotten back to me. He wants me to send him my logo and he'll take care of the rest. He's going to set it up so that you can access my old blogs by date or alphabetically by band or artist's name. He says that all I have to do is mention that he designed it with a link. Cool.

Bob arrives around noon, wearing his darkest sunglasses,

which indicate his worst possible mood. He wears sunglasses like mood rings. Dao trails behind him and stops to tell me in her broken TV English that the store has insurance but there's a one-thousand-dollar deductible, which hardly makes it worthwhile, since there was only nineteen hundred dollars in cash in the register that night, and if they make a claim the insurance will go up. I suppose that now is a bad time to tell Bob that Jennifer called and she's decided to take a few days off due to a bad case of posttraumatic stress disorder. Laz told me he saw her table-dancing at a bar on San Pablo late Saturday night. I'm sure it's part of the healing process.

The afternoon drags. The atmosphere in the store fluctuates between gloomy and despondent. I work on my five LPs of the week: the Cowboy Junkies' *The Trinity Session* (four out of five LPs); *The Doors* (five out of five LPs); Morrissey's *Viva Hate* (five out of five LPs); Little Feat, *Time Loves a Hero* (four out of five LPs); and Tom Waits, *Frank's Wild Years* (five out of five LPs).

Late in the day, Zach reappears with a CD case in hand. He places it on the counter in front of me. Could it be a mix CD, the mating call of the romantically challenged? *Please. Let it not be that.*

"What's this?" I ask, picking it up. There's a giant moth on the cover. It looks like he cut it out of a *National Geographic* magazine.

"A mix CD. I made it for you." He beams.

"Hey, thanks. I'll listen to it tonight."

"Cool." He stands there a moment. Awkwardness sets in. "Okay, so I'll see ya."

"Yeah. See ya."

He starts to leave. "Oh, by the way, there're two guys in wedding dresses out front." He walks out the door.

Almost immediately, through the window, Shorty and Jam appear in wedding wear. Jam is wearing a flowing white satin dress with a modest train and embroidered roses on the bodice. A veil is bobby-pinned to his greasy, stringy hair. The fact that he's missing a front tooth isn't helping. The hem of the dress is already black with dirt. Shorty is wearing an off-the-shoulder bridesmaid's dress with a full skirt in coral. His bony shoulders jut out like coat hangers, and his dirty jeans and oversize boots emerge from underneath the cocktail hem. The dresses look all too familiar to me. It takes me a moment to realize that they belong to my mom.

I pick up the phone and dial my home number.

My mom picks up on the first ring. "Hello."

"Hey, whatcha doin'?" I ask.

"Cleaning out my closet."

"Getting rid of some stuff?"

"That's right."

"Did you put some things in the free box?"

"Yeah, two whole garbage bags."

"Well, I guess that would explain the two drug addicts out in front of the store, parading around in your wedding dress and that hideous bridesmaid's dress you wore at Aunt Shirley's wedding."

"Huh?"

"Yeah."

"Does the one wearing the bridesmaid's dress at least look better in it than I did?"

"Only slightly. God, Mom, your wedding dress in the free box?"

"Oh, who cares? I just need to move on with my life. Besides, I've always hated that thing."

"Okay, well, I'll see you later. In the meantime, I'll be down here, not moving on. I'll be watching a low-rent, creepy, drag-queen version of your wedding."

"Sorry, honey."

I hang up the phone and watch Shorty and Jam pass a bottle of something back and forth.

My parents didn't get married until I was five. I was the flower girl. I cried during the ceremony because I saw my aunt Shirley crying and I thought we were supposed to. The minister had a long beard and dark glasses. He was a yoga instructor. He scared the crap out of me. It wasn't until the reception that I realized that it was supposed to be a celebration. I threw up wedding cake on my white patent-leather shoes.

I know what it means when closets get cleaned out and old, once meaningful bits of our lives get discarded. The last time it happened was right after my dad moved out. My mom purged herself of anything even remotely reminiscent of my dad. She put everything into garbage bags (I went through them later and rescued some cassettes and a Black Sabbath T-shirt) and then she sat next to the phone, waiting for him to call and tell her he'd made a horrible mistake. He never did.

I'm guessing, in this case, she's waiting for a call from Jack. The answering of the phone on the first ring was a dead giveaway. It's funny that my mom got rid of every connection to my dad after he left but she hung on to the wedding dress for a while. Isn't it a custom that moms sometimes hang on to the dress because they think their daughter might wear it at her wedding? Has my mom already given up on my love life? Is she assuming I'll never marry?

Jam takes a drunken swing at Shorty. I exhale slowly.

When I get home from work, I have to step over several garbage bags of discarded clothes lined up in the front hallway. My mom and Ravi are working at the dining table. Ravi has taken his transformation one step further. All his facial hair has disappeared, revealing a strong, smooth jawline, and he's wearing another new shirt in crisp striped cotton. He looks fresh and youthful. The lack of facial hair makes his eyes look enormous. My mom's eye, on the other hand, is still swollen halfway shut and she looks like she could use a shower. She's wearing sweats and a torn gray T-shirt. Her wedding dress goes in the free box but this outfit she hangs on to? The scene looks like a reverse *Beauty and the Beast*.

"Hi, Ravi."

"Hello, Miss Allie," he says.

"You look good, Ravi. Sort of like your own younger brother."

He blushes. "Thank you."

I look at my mom. "Your wedding dress is filthy. I hope you're happy."

She glares at me out of her one good eye. I stomp up the stairs to my room to call Kit.

"So. Did you call the cops yet?" asks Kit for the fourteenth time today.

"No. I can't. I mean, I will . . . I think . . . Damn!" I try to speak quietly into the phone.

"Even after yesterday? C'mon, Al, the guy's a hardened criminal."

"You don't know that."

"Uh-huh, I do. And I was hoping that I wouldn't have to say this out loud, but he's dangerous and he knows you know. You have thought of that, haven't you?"

"Of course I have." Nonstop, actually. I've also thought about the way he took such an interest in me that day at the café, the way he told me all those stories and listened to me talk about my life, such as it is, pretending to care, the way he moved my hair out of my face. It's unbearable for me to come to grips with the fact that he was just setting me up. He didn't seem at all dangerous that day. He seemed like a lot of fun. I keep hoping that there's a chance that I'm wrong about him and that maybe it wasn't him that night. I keep hoping that maybe none of this actually happened. But, unless I can sell myself on an evil-twin theory, I don't have much.

"Look, let's do this together, okay? We'll go down to the police station tomorrow morning and tell them what we know."

"I don't know, I don't know . . . Okay, yes, let's do it." I squeeze my eyes shut, hiding from the decision I just made.

"Good. Look, you'll feel better when it's done. You know it's the right thing."

"Okay, okay. Let's stop talking about it or I'll talk myself out of it again."

"Sure. By the way, Niles called me today and I actually picked up. He wants to talk to me."

"What did you say?"

"I said he *was* talking to me and he said, 'No. In person.'"

"I said I didn't think it was a good idea and then he begged me. I think he may even have cried. Apparently, and it took him a while to figure this out, probably because he couldn't get past her breasts, but he recently came to the conclusion that Chelsea is an idiot. Imagine my surprise. From where I was sitting she radiated intelligence. Anyway, he says she's moved on already. She told him she was happy to keep seeing him but it wouldn't be exclusive because she's sort of into drummers now."

"Wow." I don't really see how this story redeems Niles in any way but I decide to keep that to myself.

"Yeah, all boobs, no brains."

"So, will you see him?"

"Yes. I told him to meet me at Café Dirt tomorrow night."

Café Dirt is what we call the coffee place on the corner of College and Ashby because you can smell the bathrooms while you stand in the coffee line. Gross.

"You think you'll give him another chance?"

"I dunno. I really don't."

I love how Kit's convinced that Joel belongs on death

206

row, but Niles she's considering pardoning. Is there any doubt that love is truly blind?

"What time tomorrow morning? Should I pick you up at your house?"

"Yeah, um, how about ten?"

"Okay."

"Fighting crime on our day off, how fun. Whatever will we do afterward, buy a Batphone?"

I try to laugh but I can't. "See you tomorrow," I say.

I hang up the phone and flip through my vinyl till I find Pink Floyd's *Dark Side of the Moon*. I put it on the turntable and sit on my bed with my eyes closed, listening. It would be nice if there were a sign that I'm doing the right thing. Kit's giving Niles another chance. Should I be giving M a chance to turn himself in? Who am I kidding? That's not happening. It's time to let go of the fantasy M. I think about the dream again, how I'm letting go of his hand, letting go of him, letting him fall.

I suppose a dream is as good a sign as any.

I sit at my computer and type in my blog address. As I'm waiting for it to load it occurs to me that my blog has become my soft place to fall. I've succeeded, finally, in finding a group of friends (sure, they're in cyberspace but they're real people) who've also been looking for a place to connect. I've started noticing that the same people check in almost every day, plus a bunch of new ones. Forty-three people have responded to the *Last Waltz* blog and it's only been posted for twenty-four hours. They're waiting like eager children, waiting to see what I'll talk about next. I've decided that I'm going to charge a fifteen-dollar subscription fee for a year's worth of *Vinyl Princess* fanzines. The postage is killing me, especially to Europe. Anyway, vinyl collectors are used to getting money orders because they're always buying records through the mail. I have to start thinking about next month's issue. It's going to be bigger and better in a whole bunch of ways. I've also decided that I'm going to produce six issues a year. I can't knock one out a month. I'll lose my mind.

My Berkeley Fan has posted a new comment. I've started going to his comments first (and yes, I sure hope it's a guy).

VP,

I bought The Last Waltz at a tiny
record store in the East Village when
I was fourteen. That was a tough year
for me but I think it helped. I bet
I listened to it five hundred times.
Somehow I knew you would get to it—you

know, any day now I shall be released.

Thank you.

Your Fan in Berkeley

The East Village? That means he's from New York. I think about Zach and then quickly dismiss the thought. No way.

There are only a handful of scenarios where you might find yourself at the Berkeley police station on a Tuesday morning. The obvious one is that you're escorted in wearing handcuffs because you've done something very bad. Another scenario is that you're the victim of someone else's very bad thing and you're here to tell someone about it. Finally, there are the friends, relatives and loved ones of the person who's done a very bad thing who've come to pick them up or bail them out. There's a tragic element to every one of these scenarios.

Looking around, I see very few of our kind sitting in the waiting area: that is to say, two teenage girls holding decaf mochas, casually dropping by to offer evidence in an ongoing robbery investigation. Although the tragic element exists, it's a little harder to spot in our case. It seems to me, though, that the longer you're inside the station, the more tragic things become.

Immediately upon walking through the doors, I felt a sense of guilt wash over me. Maybe that's why people confess to crimes they haven't committed. It's not them; it's this place. Now, standing at the reception desk, I have half a mind to confess to the robberies myself. I've called ahead and Officer Davis assured me that we should "come on down to the station," but no one seems to know where he is, so we're forced to take a seat on a wooden bench and inhale disinfectant and desperation while they locate him. We try to avoid eye contact with our benchmates, who regard us suspiciously. Even a toddler sitting on his mother's lap gives us the stink-eye. A man across the hall is hunched over a pay phone, having a protracted conversation with his wife or his girlfriend.

"Look, baby. . . . Okay . . . I know I said that but . . . No, this is it, I promise. . . . No, you can't do that. . . . I own half of it. . . . How will I get to work? . . . C'mon, baby . . . if you could just come and get me. . . . No, I know . . . but I mean it this time. . . . I love you. . . . No . . . don't hang up. . . . Baby . . . don't hang up! . . . Hello? . . ." He bangs the receiver against the phone and walks away, leaving it dangling.

While we sit there waiting, I start thinking about *Reggatta de Blanc*, by the Police. Great record. I walk up to the front desk and write it across my palm with a pen attached to a chain. I *must* blog about that album; it's *so* cool.

Finally, Officer Davis appears, wiping his hands on a paper towel. I imagine him scarfing down a submarine sandwich in the janitor's closet, ignoring his pages.

"Allie?" he asks, looking from me to Kit and back to me again. He has no recollection of who I am. You have to wonder if he'll ever make detective with his unbelievably bad eye for details.

"That's me." I wave my hand.

"C'mon back." He holds open the low wooden gate that separates us and we walk through it. We follow him up the stairs to a large room filled with desks that looks remarkably like the set of *NYPD Blue*. Officer Davis points to two chairs in front of a desk with his nameplate on it. We take our seats and he eases himself into a leather chair on wheels behind the desk and rifles through a stack of files in his in-box till he locates the right one. There's a photo in a frame sitting on his desk: a woman with a fat kid on either side of her, one boy and one girl. They're all wearing Mickey Mouse ears and Goofy is standing behind them with his arms around the group. I imagine Officer Davis was the photographer.

"So." He looks at me. "You remembered something else about the robbery?"

"Yes, well, sort of. I actually know who did it."

"You do?" He looks dubious, like maybe he thinks I've been watching too much *CSI* on television.

"Well, I have a first name for one of them—Joel, probably an alias," I say, attempting cop talk, "but I have a good description of them. We both do." I look at Kit, who nods vigorously.

"Really?" He crosses his arms and leans back in his leather chair. It complains loudly. He still looks doubtful. As an afterthought he leans forward and grabs a pencil. He writes *Joel* with a question mark after it on the file.

"So, what makes you suspect this Joel fella and his buddy?"

"Well, we both work on Telegraph, as you know, and a few weeks ago we started to notice these two guys hanging around the neighborhood."

"And what made them stand out?"

What am I supposed to say here? *Oh, one of them was gorgeous and I fell madly in love with him and foolishly imagined a future where he and I were together all the time?* I clear my throat. "Well, they were new. We'd never seen them before, and one of them, the one who calls himself Joel, came into the record store while I was working and pretended to be looking for something, and I think he was scoping the place out." Okay, now I really sound like a whacked-out *CSI* watcher.

"You do, do you?" He's digging around in his ear with his pinkie now. He examines his finger and wipes it on his pants. "And you only recently made the connection?"

My heart starts to pound. Good question. Officer Davis is sharper than I thought. "Yeah, um, you know, I just sort of put it together all of a sudden."

"So?"

"So, the night of the robbery, when he spoke, I recognized his voice." I'm definitely not telling him about our coffee date. Kit and I discussed it on the way over. I don't want to be *that* connected to the crime.

"What did he say?"

"He said, 'Have a nice evening.'" Now that I'm saying it out loud it really does sound absurd.

"That's it? 'Have a nice evening'? You recognized his voice in four words after only hearing it once?"

"He has a very distinctive voice. Oh, and I recognized his boots too."

Officer Davis rubs his face with his thick hands. "Do you girls think you could recognize either of these two guys if you saw a photo of them?"

Kit looks at me. We both say yes.

Officer Davis presses a button on his phone and speaks into it. "Rebecca, I gotta couple of gals here who say they can identify the Telegraph robbers. Can we get the mug books out? Let's give them California for now, okay?"

"You got it," says the speaker.

He takes his finger off the button. "So, we're going to get you to look at some photos. It's probably best that you don't discuss this with each other as you're looking. It could push you in the wrong direction. Just let me know if you come across anything that looks familiar. We'll start with California and go from there, okay? If you don't find what you're looking for today, we'll set you up with a sketch artist so we have something to go on here at the station. Okay?"

"Um, this Joel guy, he had sort of an East Coast accent, maybe New Jersey."

Officer Davis narrows his eyes. His hand goes for the button. "Rebecca, bring New Jersey too, okay?"

"Yep," says the box.

The books are enormous. In each photo, the man wears the same expression. A few pages in, I figure out what it is: regret. I start to get depressed almost immediately. Kit sits on a rolling chair at one desk and I sit at another, flipping through photos earnestly at first, looking for our man, but soon we both become despondent. The room is completely airless. What were we expecting this to be like? Looking through a wedding album or an album of someone's trip to Paris?

We don't find them in California or New Jersey, so we branch out to Texas, Florida and Nevada, all the bad-guy states, I guess. Two hours pass and we're still suspectless. Our credibility seems to be slipping away. Officer Davis brings in a sketch artist (is there actually a guy with a sketch pad and charcoal just sitting in another room waiting for moments like this?). We start with the bulldog. Since we only caught a glimpse of him, it's tough to describe him. Kit saw him twice so I let her do most of the talking. For some reason, both of us recall that he was wearing cowboy boots in some kind of exotic leather, like ostrich or crocodile, but the artist doesn't draw the feet, just the head and shoulders. We end up with something that looks remarkably like the guy we saw. He looks very menacing. I wonder if he'd be flattered by this rendering. I tell the artist that he's very good but he seems not to care. I want to ask him if he rents himself out to birthday parties and bar mitzvahs to draw those giant-head, tiny-body caricatures for party guests or if this is his full-time gig. I think better of it. We start on Joel. Kit rolls her eyes at me when I use words like *sea glass green* to describe his eyes, and then I go into minute detail to describe his dark, long eyelashes. I describe him so perfectly to the artist that the final result scares me. I ask for a copy and he looks at me a little strangely but he makes me a copy of it. When he hands it to me he says, "This is police property. Don't tell anyone I did this."

Kit and I are allowed to leave but we're supposed to come back tomorrow and look at more photos. We both have to work tomorrow, but Officer Davis says we can come in after work. He points out with a chuckle that the station is open twenty-four hours for our convenience. I get the feeling that this is something he says a lot.

When I get home from my long day at the police station, my mom looks almost back to normal. Her eye is sagging only slightly now and it makes her look a bit sad. She's showered, washed her hair and applied makeup. She's wearing a fitted purple long-sleeved dress. She looks nice.

"Is that new?" I ask.

"Yeah, you like it? I just bought it today." She smooths the fabric over her hips.

"Yes. You look great. Where are you going?"

"Out for dinner with Jack. I guess he's over the camping fiasco."

"Mom, camping is not a date; it's an endurance test. If you can survive camping with someone, you should marry them on the way home."

She digs around in her bag and comes up with a lipstick. I watch her apply it in the mirror by the front door. Her lips have grown thinner over the years and I think she looks better without lipstick, but I would never tell her that.

"There was no danger of that on this trip. In fact, if we had been married, we probably would have gotten divorced on the way home."

When Jack arrives to pick my mom up, I already know by his face that the relationship is over. I can tell that my mom knows too but she still gets her shawl, waves good-bye to me and walks out to the car with him. I watch out the window as he holds the passenger door open for her and closes it carefully once she's in. I'm overwhelmed by the urge to run outside and throw a rock at his head. I suppose he thinks he's doing the right thing, the gentlemanly thing, taking my mom out to a restaurant so he can tell her it could never work between them, so that he can dump her over dessert, like maybe there's some dignity in that. He has not a clue about what a great person she is. He has no idea how smart and funny and wonderful she can be when she has access to indoor plumbing and a concierge and a warm bed. Who the hell does he think he is in his khakis and his argyle socks, waltzing into our lives from some loser town in the middle of nowhere, expecting dinner, expecting her to put up a tent, expecting her to act normal, when really all my mom's good at, all she's ever been good at, is being brilliant?

I throw a frozen pizza into the oven and flop onto the

sofa. I start watching a DVD of *Summer of '42*, periodically checking for Jack's car out the front window, bracing myself for my mom's return. I know I should be working on my blog but tonight I just can't. The car pulls up when I'm on the second-to-last scene of the movie, where Hermie goes to Dorothy's house and finds it empty and he's reading the note she left him, telling him why she had to leave and that she'll never forget him. Two pieces of cold pizza sit congealing on the coffee table. Jack doesn't walk my mom to the door and I know she told him not to. I hear her key in the lock. She walks in, still fresh in her new dress, and sits down next to me on the sofa. She kicks off her heels and pulls her feet up under her.

"How'd it go?" I ask.

"Oh, you know." She looks at the TV. "Is this *Summer of '42*?"

"Yeah."

Hermie is standing in front of Dorothy's beach house as an adult.

She watches the TV for a moment. A tear rolls down her cheek.

"Mom," I say, sitting up and touching her shoulder. "Forget it. He's an asshole."

"I know. Shit."

I go into the kitchen and pour her a glass of white wine.

I set it in front of her and she looks at me gratefully and takes a sip.

"Thanks, doll face, you're the best."

I push my bare feet against her thigh. "You are," I tell her.

*K*it and I are reluctantly making our way to the police station for the second time in two days to serve hard time. We're not so keen on the whole idea anymore. At first it felt like the right thing to do; it felt like we were helping fight crime and maybe even saving a life, but the place fills us with dread now. It's one big, bad vibe and it's exhausting to think about going through those books again, looking at those faces, dealing with Officer Davis, even sitting on the bench in the waiting room with a whole new set of tragic characters.

When we're a block away from Telegraph, a cop car whizzes past us, lights on, siren whining, then another cop car, then an ambulance, then a fire truck. They all turn left onto Telegraph, going the wrong way on a one-way street.

Kit and I look at each other and turn around and follow them. It doesn't take long for us to catch up with the cops. They're only a block and a half away. They're all parked out in front of Fabulous Falafels with their lights still flashing. The EMTs are unloading two stretchers from the ambulance and rushing them into the restaurant. The cops already have everything blocked off and a couple of them are keeping people out of the area. Kit and I stand on the periphery and strain to see what's going on. Kit sees a friend of hers in the crowd, a guy who used to work with her. He works at Mario's now.

"Darnell!" She waves at him.

"Hey!" He walks over to us like he just spotted us at a social event. He's sipping on a Frappuccino.

"Did you see what happened?"

"Man, you didn't hear the gunshots? The Telegraph Avenue robbers, man, that's who it was. Tried to rob Sanje but he was havin' none of that. He came out of the back with a shotgun and *Blam! Blam! Blam!* He blew those two away. Man, it's a bloodbath in there. One man down, one injured." He sips his drink, his eyes wide.

My heart starts to pound.

Through the window of the restaurant I can sort of make out Sanje. He's sitting in a chair while a cop interviews him. He's making a lot of hand gestures. Another cop emerges from the restaurant carrying a large assault rifle. It looks almost cartoonish, like something Elmer Fudd might carry during rabbit season. Does Sanje have some sort of weapons arsenal back there, hidden amid the tahini and the pita bread? Or did he figure that sooner or later these guys were going to get around to him and he'd better find something to protect himself with? I peruse the small crowd. Behind us, Bob is standing next to Jimmy the Rasta dude. I catch his eye and he waves at me. Shorty and Jam are here too. They're working the crowd, trying to drum up a little dinner (Colt 45) money, but no one pays much attention to them even though Jam is wearing a hot-pink boa around his neck and Shorty's wearing a pillbox hat and carrying a matching handbag.

The first stretcher emerges, wheeled out by an EMT on either side. I know it's Joel immediately. He has a big piece of gauze strapped to his right thigh but the blood is soaking through it quickly. He's pale as a corpse but conscious. His jeans are cut open and there's blood all over them. His hands are streaked with drying blood too. He's grimacing in pain but underneath that he has the same look on his face as all the men in the mug shot book: regret. Kit grabs my clammy hand and we watch as he passes within a few feet of us. The medallion around his neck that I couldn't read before is dangling off to the side. It's a Saint Christopher medallion.

The EMTs collapse the stretcher's wheeled legs and slide it into the ambulance. They jump in after him and slam the doors behind them. The ambulance takes off seconds later, howling up the street. Another ambulance pulls in right behind it. Two more EMTs roll the other stretcher out of the restaurant. The urgency is missing from their steps. The stretcher rolls past us with a blue sheet over it, covering the face. A snakeskin cowboy boot pokes out from under the sheet. They load this stretcher slowly and drive away without turning on the siren. Kit and I exchange a grim look. Another cop car comes sailing around the corner and parks next to the others. Officer Davis eases himself out from behind the wheel and lumbers into the restaurant. He probably resents having to put down his sandwich for this.

The crowd that's gathered starts to disperse but Kit and I stand there for a while, dumbstruck at what we've just seen. Eventually, the cops escort Sanje out of the restaurant and into the back of a police cruiser. He looks directly at the crowd. His face registers no fear at all. In fact, he looks almost smug, like he just provided the neighborhood with a much-needed service. A few people in the crowd start to applaud when they see him but most of us just gape at him, not sure what to think. Even in this neighborhood, we don't see vigilantism of this magnitude very often. A couple of months ago, there was this punk-ass graffiti artist tagging all the businesses up and down the avenue in broad daylight. One afternoon he tags a panel van that belongs to Gus, a Greek guy who owns the produce stand that the van was parked in front of. Gus chases the kid and tackles him. He throws the kid down on the sidewalk and sits on him, grabs his spray paint can and sprays his face with it. Needless to say, the kid stopped tagging the avenue. That's about the height of it around here. You really don't hear about business owners blowing thieves away with assault rifles.

My head is pounding. Lately I've been dealing with too many things that are way outside my comfort level: robberies, dead bodies, police stations and mug shots. I'm ready to hide under my bed again but when I get home my mom takes one look at my face and tells me we're going for sushi. I'm up for it. I could use a break from my life in the form of a California roll. From the look on my pale face, she's probably also getting a sense that I'm running a bit wild and it's time for a parental update. We walk up the street together, passing Florence, who's watering her new flower beds. We say hello and compliment her flowers.

"Did you start a fire in your house?" she asks, looking accusingly at me.

I'd forgotten all about it. "Yeah. Just a small one."

"I smelled it, the smoke . . . very bad. You should be more careful. Silly girl. You'll burn down the neighborhood."

She doesn't know the half of it. "Sure, Florence, I will."

Over miso soup and sashimi, I tell my mom about the whole M/Joel business. She watches me tell the story like I'm unraveling the plot of a James Bond film. When I finish, she stares at me in disbelief. Then she looks like she wants to kill me; then she hugs me like she's glad I'm alive.

"Allie, what in the hell were you thinking? He could have killed you!"

The sushi chef puts an order of yellowtail down in front of us and glances at my mom.

"I know that but I didn't want to be a snitch, and anyway, it didn't matter; we never did find him in the mug-shot books, so it probably wouldn't have made much difference if we'd gone down to the station a couple of days earlier."

"Sure it would have. They send those sketches across the country. If someone had recognized him, the cops might have found out who they are."

"Yeah, but that doesn't mean that they'd find them, just because they might know their names."

She waves my comments aside with her hand. "Okay. Look. You have to tell me this stuff. No more secrets. Why would you keep something like that to yourself?"

"I did tell you about the robbery part but you were camping with Jack when it happened."

She winces at the memory. "God, I'm a horrible mother."

"What are you talking about? You're a mediocre mother. Horrible is much too strong a word."

She pinches my arm. "Promise, promise, promise me you'll talk to me if anything like this ever happens again. You're a sixteen-year-old girl; you're not an FBI operative. You're supposed to be having fun, not chasing criminals around town."

"Who's chasing? I wasn't chasing."

"Promise," she says sternly.

"Okay, I promise."

"Good. And I want you to quit that job."

"Mom, they caught them. One of them is dead. One of them can't walk. I don't think I'm in danger anymore."

"For now you're not but what about the next time? Yesterday I saw a help-wanted sign in the window of that muffin place on Euclid. Why don't you apply there?"

"Muffins? Mom, you want me on antidepressants? You want me to weigh three hundred pounds?"

"Okay, you're right; forget the muffins, but I want you to look for a different job. I mean it this time."

"Sure, Mom. I will," I lie. Personally, I think the danger has passed. My mother might believe that there's danger lurking around every corner waiting to point a gun in my face, but before Joel and his buddy arrived on the scene, nothing much happened on Telegraph that represented real crime.

My mom sips her tea, looking thoughtful. "Hey, can I ask you something? You helped me put my personal ad online. Is there anything in there that would suggest to anyone that I'm outdoorsy?"

"No. We specifically tried to make you sound indoorsy."

A Japanese waitress refills our green tea.

"Okay, so, since Jack contacted *me* and asked *me* out, shouldn't it be *his* problem if I'm not quite ready to dangle off the side of Mount Everest? I mean, why would he contact me at all when I'm clearly not his type?"

"You've been thinking about this all day, haven't you?"

"A little."

"Well, maybe he was attracted to your photo and he thought he could make you drink the Kool-Aid, or I mean the Gatorade, and convert you into one of them, you know?"

"'Them'?"

"Yeah, people who own gear and consider polar fleece the height of fashion and live on PowerBars and have bike racks on their cars."

"Oh. Them." She rolls her eyes. "Allie, I can't go back in there."

"In where?"

"That world: the picking, the waiting to be picked, the daring to be hopeful only to be disappointed. I'd rather be alone and sad and celibate for the rest of my life. At least I'll finish my dissertation."

I chew my sushi thoughtfully. "We should kill Jack. I know a guy." I think about Sanje's big gun.

She laughs. "You wanna hear the crazy part? I wasn't really that into him. I think I talked myself into it because he's the exact opposite of your dad."

"Oh, by the way, he called yesterday. Kee Kee's been told by her ob/gyn that she can't ride horses for the rest of her pregnancy. And that's not even the best part. She's banned his drums from the house; she's afraid they'll upset the fetus. He had to move his kit out to the stables with the horses. Apparently, he gets his own stall but he has to share the hay with the other horses. He's only allowed to drum during the day while the horses are out in the paddock. Kee Kee also brought a trainer over from Germany to work the horses till the baby comes. I think he said her name was Ingrid, or was it Ingaborg? Anyway, when she's not on horseback, swearing at the horses in German, she walks around the property slapping a riding crop against her leather boots."

My mom smirks. "Thanks, Al. I feel a lot better."

"Don't mention it." I sip my tea and pat her hand. "You

see, in the end we're all miserable. It's the human condition."

I'm so exhausted that night that I can barely climb the stairs to bed. I feel like I could sleep for a year. I fall into bed and pass out. In the middle of the night I wake with a start. I lie there in the dark and think about Joel. He's probably in a hospital bed right now with a cop sitting in a chair outside the door. I wonder if he's on painkillers or if he's awake and alone and afraid of what's going to happen to him. Is he thinking about his dead friend? Were they even friends? I wonder if he has a good lawyer or if he'll have to use a public defender. I wonder where his real parents live and if they've been notified. Will they be surprised to hear he's in trouble? Will they even care? Does he have any brothers or sisters? Is anyone sitting on a plane or a bus right now, traveling through the dead of night to be at his side? Are they looking out the window into the dark, trying to figure out what went wrong?

I click on the lamp and get out of bed to look for my backpack. I slide the rolled-up drawing of Joel out and unroll it. After what's happened, I look at him differently, almost with pity. I flatten it out and slide it between two records in the blues section of my shelf.

I wake up early on Thursday morning determined to work on my deeply neglected blog. Today's blog (and yesterday's and tomorrow's) is about sound tracks on LP. Yesterday I explored *The Mission* sound track by Ennio Morricone. I think this is my favorite instrumental sound track. Turns out it's a lot of people's. Comments were through the roof. I had to mention *Ragtime* by Randy Newman too, because it's impossible to leave out if you're discussing sound tracks. Today I'm discussing *Reservoir Dogs*: best sound track featuring previously recorded songs, and a kick-ass movie too. What the hell happened to Quentin Tarantino, anyway? *Kill Bill?* Puleeeeese. I tell readers to stay tuned 'cause we're doing sound tracks all week.

Elliot has sent me a mockup of the blog, not live yet. I

love it. I love Elliot. He's some sort of blog-designing genius. I have to think of a cool way to repay him. The logo looks fantastic and everything is all organized into its own little box. There're little LP bullets to click on different sections, and the daily blogs have album cover art to go with them. He also included simple directions for me to do my daily updates myself. I feel like I'm elevated in the blogosphere hierarchy now, if there is one. Elliot asked me if I wanted to post a picture of myself and I said no. I want my readers to imagine me. I also suspect that they would totally freak out if they found out that I'm sixteen.

My mom's still in bed when I head downstairs. I open the front door to see Joel's face staring at me from the front page of the newspaper on my doormat. His real name is William "Billy" Hennessy. He's wanted in three states—New York, Massachusetts and Pennsylvania—for armed robbery. His partner in crime, also known as "the dead guy," is next to him on the page. His name was Richard Sacci. He's wanted in the same three states plus Maine for assault, armed robbery, identity theft and auto theft—charming. Both of them are from Baltimore originally, but something tells me that they haven't been home in a while. It's anybody's guess as to how they ended up all the way out here on the West Coast.

My mom joins me at the table and I read the news story

out loud to her as she drinks tea curled up in a chair in her silk robe:

"'It appears that a crime spree involving the armed robbery of several Telegraph Avenue businesses has finally come to an end, leaving one suspect dead and another seriously wounded. Early yesterday evening, William Hennessy, twenty, and Richard Sacci, twenty-five, attempted to rob Fabulous Falafels on Dwight and Telegraph in Berkeley, when the proprietor, Arash Azari, formerly of Iran, gave fire, mortally wounding Sacci and seriously wounding Hennessy.'

"Wait a second. Sanje's name is Arash Azari?"

My mom shrugs. "He probably changed it. Sanje is an Indian name. Maybe he didn't want people to know he was Iranian. That's funny, though; Arash is a hero in Persian folklore."

I continue:

"'Azari has been charged with possession of an illegal firearm but he was released late last evening after extensive questioning. Hennessy is listed in stable condition and will be taken into custody following his release from the hospital. Many of the merchants on Telegraph expressed relief at the grisly end to this spree. Most of the merchants were grateful to Azari, whom they know as Sanje, and describe as an honest, law-abiding business owner. Bob Petrovich, owner of Bob and Bob Records, said that although he doesn't condone gun ownership of any kind, he was happy that the whole thing was finally over and that residents and business owners could start to feel safe on Telegraph again.'"

"That's a bit of a stretch, isn't it? Safe on Telegraph Avenue?" She takes the paper from me and looks at the photos.

"No. It *was* safe before all this."

My mom looks at me, starts to say something, and then looks back at the newspaper.

"This William Hennessy guy has an interesting face; I see what you mean about him, very unusual eyes."

"Yeah, maybe I'll write to him in prison."

My mom shoots me a look.

"Kidding."

"I'm sending you to a convent. I should have done it ages ago." She sips her tea.

I purposely go a block out of my way to get to Bob's so I can pass by the falafel place. There's yellow crime-scene tape over the glass door and the place is locked up tight. I press my face against it and peer inside. Tables and chairs are scattered about and overturned. It looks as though someone has halfheartedly tried to mop up the blood but there're still smears of it on the walls and on the floor. One of the glass windows is shattered into a snowflake and a wooden board has been hammered in place in front of it. On the board, someone has spray-painted *Al-Qaeda* in big black letters. Someone else has crossed it out and written *Hero* underneath it in red spray paint.

Things at Bob's are almost back to normal. Jennifer is late but she's announced her plans to return to work today, an auspicious occasion for all of us. Bob arrives wearing sunglasses with pale blue lenses. It really doesn't get much better than that.

"So, did you like it?"

I look up from my *Mojo* magazine. Somehow I know I'm in trouble.

"Like what?"

"The CD I made you?" says Zach. He's wearing a navy-blue gas station employee's jacket with FRANK embroidered in red on the right side of his chest.

My face registers guilt. I frantically try to remember where I put that thing.

"Awwww, come on!" He throws his hands up in the air and looks up at the ceiling. "You didn't even listen to it?"

"I've been a bit busy. I'm sorry."

"Yeah, sure, whatever." He waves away my excuse. He looks wounded.

"I said I was sorry."

He shifts gears. "Hey, I guess you heard about the

robbery last night, huh?" He scratches his cheek.

"Yeah, I was there."

"What? Like, you saw it happen?" He scratches the top of his head now. It occurs to me that he has the body language of a chimp.

"No, just the aftermath."

"Gruesome, huh?"

"Quite."

"That falafel guy's pretty ominous and I'm sure I don't have to tell you that his falafel is outstanding. Where do you suppose he learned to shoot like that?"

"He was in the army. He told me that once. I think it was the Iranian army." I imagine the Iranian army to be fierce and war-ready, although I really have no idea about these things.

He nods. "The Artesh."

"How'd you know that?"

He shrugs. "They asked me to join once but I told them I was busy."

I smile. "Are you a student here?"

"I am now. I'm starting in the fall. I'm a freshman. How about you?"

"Nah, I've got another year of high school and then I don't know."

"So that would make you . . ."

"Ambitionless?"

"No, I meant your age."

"I'll be seventeen in a couple of months." Why couldn't I just say sixteen? What's wrong with sixteen? I'm not applying to be his girlfriend.

"I'm eighteen."

I nod. Not that I care. "Why are you here already? Most of the students don't get here till a week before school starts."

A bright orange Mohawk zips past the front door and we're both distracted for a second. Zach runs a hand through his hair several times until it stands at attention.

"Uh, why am I here already? Because my parents threw me out."

"Really?"

"Sort of. My mom's a doctor and she's going to Africa to work for two years. She sublet our apartment in Manhattan and I think she'd have a hard time explaining the shadowy guy who lives in the back bedroom to the new tenants."

"What about your dad?"

"Well, naturally my parents are divorced. My dad's a writer and he lives in Amagansett."

"Where's that?"

"Exactly. It's in the Hamptons. It used to be what people called quaint but now it's summer camp for rich people

237

from Manhattan. My dad writes all day and goes to the bar at night, gets drunk and hits on all the young local women, sort of like Ernest Hemingway but about half as charming and half as talented. He's impossible to live with and his house is tiny and he hates to be disturbed when he's writing, so I would have to stay outside most of the time and, well, you get the picture."

"So you came here alone for the whole summer?"

"Yes. Trust me: It was the right thing to do. Even though I live in what appears to be a former janitor's closet."

"Aren't you lonely?"

"Nah, I make friends fast."

"You have friends already?"

He looks a little hurt and I realize that he may have been referring to me as a friend. He rebounds quickly. "Not really, although I am pretty friendly with the guy who roots through my trash can every morning; I'm actually working up to asking him to lunch. And the UPS guy and I are on a first-name basis."

"What's his name?"

"Ned."

Zach must live close to Bob's, because Ned is our UPS guy too.

Jennifer finally arrives in a gust of perfume and attitude. She looks disappointed at the lack of fanfare marking her return, although Laz shaved for the first time in several days. Once she's on the register, I'm free to roam. I walk out from behind the counter. It's awkward without the counter between us. Zach seems surprised at my legs. Perhaps he was more comfortable thinking of me as a Muppet.

"So, are you looking for anything special today?"

"You say that like you're oblivious to the rituals and habits of the average obsessive, half-crazy record collector, like it's even possible that I could be looking for one specific thing."

"Just doing my job. Don't worry; I know your kind." I *am* his kind, but I'm not copping to it.

Zach pulls a small leather-bound notebook from the front pocket of his plaid golf pants.

"I'm looking for these." He hands me the book. I flip through it. Every line of every page is filled with his small, precise handwriting in bold black ink. Some of the lines are carefully crossed out in the same black ink using a ruler. There must be hundreds of items listed in here, maybe thousands. He hovers close. I can tell he's nervous about me holding the notebook. It's all he can do not to snatch it away from me. It's his lifeline. I look up at him. He looks embarrassed, like I've just seen him naked.

I hand the notebook back to him. "Well, we've been expecting you."

He stuffs the book back into his pocket. "Actually, not that I want to get too specific or anything, but I was wondering if you had *Christmas and the Beads of Sweat* by Laura Nyro on vinyl."

"Actually, I think we do. I saw one come in the other day. Check the section." I point him in the right direction but there's no need; he's memorized the layout of the store.

Jennifer hails me from the counter; she needs a bathroom break. She's been working for fifteen minutes.

Half an hour later I'm still covering the register when Zach checks out. He's got three LPs. I know that I'll probably see at least one of them back here in the next few days.

"Oh, good, you found the Laura Nyro."

"Yeah. It's in decent shape too."

He also has Nick Drake's *Bryter Layter* and Bob Dylan's *Planet Waves*. I happen to own both those LPs. Who's the crazy record collector now? I put his LPs in a bag and hand them over. Zach looks as though he's going to implode. He's twitching and scratching and I know he wants to ask me something. I wait for it.

"Hey, uh, I was just wondering. Maybe you want to hang out sometime? You know, away from here."

"Oh, um . . . hmmm, it's been kind of a weird week, you know, and . . ."

"That's okay, never mind. Stupid question. Sorry."

"No, no, it's not that, it's just—"

"Hey, forget it, okay?"

"Okay."

He takes his bag and he's out the front door. Through the side window, I watch him walk quickly away from the store, muttering to himself and shaking his head. Joke Man, a street person who sells jokes for a dollar, gets in his face but Zach pushes past him like a bulldozer and disappears up the street.

I don't have time to think about what just happened. It seems that all the excitement in the neighborhood has triggered a minirevival. Some customers I haven't seen in forever have been coming in over the last few days. This morning I rang up a deejay called DJ QT. I haven't seen him in months. He spent four hundred dollars on club music.

Right after Zach leaves, the girls from Leather Tongue Video come in and buy a bunch of used movies for their ultracool movie-rental store in the Mission. I haven't seen them in ages. It feels like the old days at Bob & Bob's.

I rush over to meet Kit for lunch at Swarma and I unload on her about Zach.

"I feel bad. I do. I made him feel like crap."

"You can't date someone just because you don't want to hurt their feelings. That's absurd. I'm having the chickpeas; what are you getting?"

"Spinach paneer."

Kit rolls her eyes. "You always get the paneer."

"That's because I like it."

The waitress takes our order and returns with two mango lassis in tall glasses. We sip the sweet, creamy drink through straws. Ever since Kit and I were six years old, every drink that gets put in front of us signals an unofficial race to be the first one to finish it.

"So, tell me what you were going to tell me when you couldn't talk before."

"Yeah. Niles." She noisily drains her lassi. I'm right behind her but she's the clear winner. "As you know, I met him for coffee at Café Dirt and, well, let me just preface this by saying that I looked fabulous. Remember that hot little Pucci dress?"

I nod.

"Well, I wore that with my skinny boots and I got this new bra that lifts and adds an entire cup size." She demonstrates with a hand hovering over each of her breasts as though I couldn't possibly imagine a cup size. "So, he's already there when I get there and he tells me I look great, which I do, and he's completely remorseful and all, 'Baby, I can't live without you,' and, 'You're the best thing that ever happened to me,' and we're getting cozy and he's kissing me and I'm kissing him back and it all feels pretty good and we're talking about doing that road trip together after all, and then his cell phone rings and, because he's a freaking idiot, he pulls it out of his jeans and looks at it and I say, 'Who is it?' And he says it's a guy who wants to buy his old amp. But he doesn't know that I've got Chelsea's number memorized and I catch a glimpse of the number and it's hers. So then he puts his phone on vibrate and the thing is vibrating all over the damn place. It's like it's doing a tap dance across the table. I finally grab the phone and look at the missed calls and it's her, her, her."

"*Liar!*" I exclaim.

"That's right. He's trying to get me back while she's still in the picture."

"So what did you do?"

"I walked out. Then I remembered that my purse was still hanging on the back of the chair, so I walk back in and he's sitting there, talking on his cell phone, and guess who he's talking to?"

"No!"

"Yes."

"How do you know?"

"'Cause I yanked it out of his hand and said, 'Who's this?'" And she said, 'Who's this?' and I said, 'Niles's ex-girlfriend,' and I flipped it shut and handed it back to him. Then I walked out for real."

"Awesome."

The waitress sets our food in front of us.

"Yeah, and you know what's weird? I don't feel so bad anymore. It's like I just needed to have a moment like that so I could convince myself that I'm doing the right thing." She takes a bite of her chickpeas and smiles at me confidently.

"That's fantastic."

"I know. So, anyway, I still have the money, and here's what I'm thinking. I'm thinking about buying a used car and you and I can do the road trip. How does that sound?"

"Great, but you don't even have a driver's license."

"So I'll get one. No big deal. In fact, we can both get one so we can take turns driving."

I hesitate. "Okay . . . but . . ." I think about my blog. Would I be able to write it from the road? Maybe. Maybe I could blog about those indie record stores that Kit's been talking about. I could talk about the LPs I pick up along the way. That might be a really cool feature.

"Look, it's not like I'm leaving in the morning. We've got almost a year to plan it. Think about it. It'll be great. We'll *Thelma and Louise* our way across the country."

It does sound fun, but there's a lot that has to take place before we're driving down the highway together, fancy-free, looking for adventure. So what's the harm in saying yes? The cool thing about being best friends is that you can make big plans even if there's only a slim chance in hell that they'll ever happen.

"Okay, I'm in." I smile.

Kit grins. "Cool."

$\mathcal{Z}$ach's mix brings me to my knees.

A couple of days after I completely insulted him, I'm at my computer, writing a blog about the sound track for *Paris, Texas*, by Ry Cooder, when it suddenly occurs to me where I put Zach's CD: I slid it between the jazz and blues sections of my LPs because I knew that I'd lose it otherwise. I jump up from my chair and there it is. Right where I left it. I put it into my player and look at the case. There's no song list; maybe that's a test. He starts out with an R. L. Burnside tune, "Come on In," all rich and bluesy and dripping with the South. Cut two is Louis Armstrong and Ella Fitzgerald singing "Under a Blanket of Blue." Then he revs it up a bit with "Beer, Gas, Ride Forever" by John Doe and then it's just one surprise after another: Elvis Costello, "Hidden Charms"; Crowded House, "Mean to Me"; John

Lennon, "Be-Bop-A-Lula"; the Triffids, "Estuary Bed"; Joe Strummer, "Johnny Appleseed"; Ruthie Foster, "Runaway Soul"; the June Brides, "Every Conversation"; the Kinks, "All of My Friends Are Here"; Jesse Malin, "Brooklyn"; Joe Ely, "All Just to Get to You"; Ry Cooder, "Across the Borderline"; Tom Waits, "Green Grass"; the Frames, "Lay Me Down"; King Creosote, "Home in a Sentence"; Iggy Pop, "The Passenger"; Nick Cave, "God's Hotel"; Johnny Cash "Sunday Morning Coming Down"; Junior Wells with Buddy Guy, "Mystery Train"; Small Faces, "Runaway"; Del Amitri, "Driving with the Brakes On"; Son Volt, "Tear Stained Eye"; the Music Lovers, "The Former Miss Ontario"; the Felice Brothers, "Frankie's Gun"; and then, just when you think you can't take it anymore, he finishes the whole thing off with "She" by Gram Parsons.

Just for the record, I'm a girl who considers herself the all-time reigning queen of the mix. My mixes are legendary but, I have to admit, not one of them even comes close to the CD Zach made for me. If I'd never met Zach before and I was handed the mix and told to listen to it, I would probably propose marriage, sight unseen, or I'd at least offer to be his girlfriend. I abandon the blog and listen to the CD over again with my eyes closed.

There's that thing that can happen to you when you meet somebody and you don't consider them extraordinary at all and then they do something like play the cello or write amazing poetry or sing and suddenly you look at them completely differently. That's how I'm feeling about Zach right now. Then I feel a pang of guilt. I'm pretty sure that the reason he hasn't been around the store is because I turned him down the other day. I guess he's a lot more sensitive than I thought. He has to emerge sometime, though; I mean, where else is the guy gonna shop for that list of his, eBay? I have to figure out a way to smoke him out of his hole. I'm pretty sure now that he's my Berkeley Fan. Maybe I can get to him through my blog. I quickly finish up the piece on *Paris, Texas* and then I write a blog extra: "The Art of the Mix":

> Sorry to interrupt sound track week but someone just gave me a mix that rocked my Gypsy soul and I couldn't wait till next week to talk about it. I just had to share it with you.

I list the cuts from the mix, and then I continue with:

> An unexpected mix like this can take you somewhere; it can make you feel nostalgic and renewed or it can completely undo you. But anyone who collects vinyl already knows that. Share the song list from your

favorite mixes with the Vinyl Princess and tell me and my readers where they came from. Those are stories I'd love to read. Oh, and thank you, Berkeley Fan; who knew you were so good?

On Sunday afternoon, the temperature rises and hovers in the mid-eighties. My mom and Kit and I decide to do what three women who find themselves in the humiliating position of being discarded by the respective men in their lives (sure, in my case it was never really "on," but I still feel rejected somehow, not that I expect anyone to understand that) do: We decide to get ourselves to the beach and soak up some sun. The summer is slipping away from us and we haven't so much as dipped our toes in the water.

We pack up my mom's old Volvo with an umbrella, towels, food, drinks, books, sunscreen and an air mattress and drive off to Lake Anza, a tiny puddle of a lake with a sandy beach in the Berkeley Hills (now, this is my mom's idea of camping: a hot shower in your own home at the end of the day to wash the sand from your various crevices). My mom steers the Volvo around the parking lot a couple of times before we spy a parking spot. A dilapidated VW van with a Deadhead sticker on its bumper is pulling out just as we round the corner. The park is packed with stroller-pushing, picnic-carrying, baby-juggling families, and the air smells of briny sunscreen and corn dogs. Boom boxes blaring hip-hop compete for airtime. We fight for position on the sand and unroll our towels and set up our umbrella. My mom digs into her book bag and settles in on her towel to read. Kit and I strip down to our bathing suits and carry the air mattress down to the shore. We inch our way into the chilly water and paddle the mattress out to the deep water, where it's less likely to be contaminated by baby urine. Kit crawls onto the mattress and lies on her back. I dangle off the end of it like an outboard motor, kicking us in a wide circle. The noise from the beach echoes over the water to us: parents yelling at their kids, kids having water fights, the lifeguard yelling at the people who dare to swim outside the designated swim area. It all sounds so pleasant from out here, those sounds that are so specific to summer and water and beaches that you can't help but enjoy them. A mother duck and her ducklings paddle past us, making sweet little quacking noises at one another.

"I'm so happy right now." Kit sighs, looking up at the sky. "We never do this. How come we never do this?"

"I don't know. Let's come here as much as we can before the summer ends."

"God, this has been one of the weirdest summers ever. Hasn't it?"

"Yeah." I look back at the beach, scanning it for our umbrella. My mom hasn't moved.

"I wonder what Niles is doing today," muses Kit.

"Probably sleeping off a hangover in that putrid cave of his."

"Yeah, probably. That room was pretty rank, wasn't it?"

"Very nasty."

"I remember one time there was this lingering odor of rotting meat in there and we couldn't figure out what it was. His mom went crazy and started threatening to throw him out, but about a week later he finally found a half-eaten submarine sandwich under his bed. It was all green. He thought it was a sneaker. Then he pretended he was going to eat it."

"Ewww. That is *so* Homer Simpson."

"Hey, there's an upside I never thought of before. Maybe my next boyfriend won't be a slob."

"Maybe. Or maybe he won't be an asshole. Okay, get off. It's my turn to ride."

"Five more minutes."

I pull up next to her and flip the mattress. Kit tumbles into the lake and comes up sputtering and splashing.

"What the hell was that?"

"You looked hot."

"That's *so* mean."

I scramble onto the mattress and she starts kicking from the end.

"This is hard. I can't get any momentum."

"Kick harder."

"My foot just touched something slimy." She peers into the green water. "Are there sharks in here?"

"Keep kicking. Sharks hate that." I lie there and watch a bunch of cotton-ball clouds float across the sky, chasing one another in slow motion. Kit stops kicking and hangs off the back of the air mattress.

"I just peed," she announces.

"You did not."

"I did so."

"That's revolting."

Back on the beach, Kit and I stretch out, exposing our extra-white skin to the sun for the first time all summer. It feels warm and delicious and we don't care if we burn. My mom has fallen asleep with her book in front of her. That's what you get when you read *Jewels of the Tsars: The Romanovs and Imperial Russia.* This is her idea of beach reading?

I dig into the food bag and pull out the grapes and watermelon slices and potato chips. We eat and watch people. My mom wakes up hungry and I pass her the snacks.

Now all three of us are watching people. I guess that's what you do at a beach: You watch people; people watch you. Interesting.

A while later, a man in a black Speedo seems to appear from out of nowhere. He approaches the shore and strides confidently into the water up to his muscular calves and pulls a pair of dark swim goggles down over his eyes. From behind, he looks like a fitter version of Ravi. I look over at my mom. She's watching him too. We're all watching him. Just before the man expertly enters the water and swims away, he does a little half turn to each side to stretch his shoulders. My mom and I catch a glimpse of his profile. It *is* Ravi!

"Hey, isn't that that Ravi guy your mom works for?" asks Kit, pointing.

"Yeah," I reply, mystified. My mom and I look at each other.

"Wow, 'Sporty Ravi,'" says Kit.

My mom shields her eyes from the sun and watches Ravi cut cleanly through the water, barely disturbing it, like he's been swimming all his life.

"Are we sure it's him?" she asks.

"Yeah. It's him. Who knew that *that* was hiding under all the corduroy and tweed?"

"Gee, how long do you suppose he's been doing this?"

"I dunno, maybe he's always done it." I watch Ravi turn around at the end of the swim lane and start back the other way.

"I had no idea." She can't seem to take her eyes off him. "We should have brought binoculars."

"Mom, your mouth is open."

"Do you think he's seeing anyone?" asks Kit.

I glare at her. She looks at me and mouths, *What?*

"We should go," says my mom suddenly.

"Right now? Don't you want to say hi?"

"Oh, no. He could be in there for hours."

"No, he won't, Mom; he's not swimming the English Channel."

"Well, I don't know. I don't want to make him uncomfortable."

I don't think Ravi is the one who would be uncomfortable, but we pack up the towels and books and lower the umbrella and drag everything back across the sand to the parking lot.

"Hey, you know what we should do?" asks my mom as we walk back to the car.

"What?" I ask.

"We should have a barbecue!" she says, sounding like someone who's had tons of them.

"Yeah! We should!" says Kit, a little too eager to start lighting fires at my house again.

On our way home in the car, the barbecue gets downsized to take-out pizza because we realize that we're missing a few of the necessary components required for a barbecue, namely a barbecue. At first we entertain the idea of buying one, but we're all sticky and wet, and shopping for a barbecue in wet bathing suits doesn't sound very appealing.

After we unload all the wet beach stuff, I quickly run upstairs and check my blog. There're a couple of comments, one about sound tracks; a couple of people have sent me their mix lists. Nothing from my Berkeley Fan.

Kit and I walk down to Arinell's to get the pizza and my mom makes a salad and we put Nancy Sinatra and Brian Setzer on the stereo and talk with our mouths full and tell the worst jokes ever. After dinner, Kit goes home and I go upstairs and call my dad. He left a message on the machine while we were out that I should call. I try his cell first but he doesn't pick up, so I dial his home number. Kee Kee picks up on the second ring. Her voice is thick, like she's been sleeping with the phone next to her head. I ask her politely if my dad is there. Her voice gets all syrupy:

"No, honey. He's not here. He went to band practice."

"Oh, um . . . okay." I decide not to confront her on what in the hell she means by that. "Could you tell him that I called?"

"Sure I will. Bye-bye."

I click off the phone and sit there staring at it for a minute.

My dad's in a band?

* * *

The last entry for sound track week is Peter Gabriel's sound track for *The Last Temptation of Christ*, officially called *Passion: Music for The Last Temptation of Christ*. This LP, when I heard it for the first time, turned me inside out. I actually wasn't even a Peter Gabriel fan till I heard this. I post the blog but then I remember that I can't close off the week without mentioning *Local Hero* by Marc Knopfler, beautiful, haunting Celtic music, some of Knopfler's best work. I put that in as an afterthought and then I remember *The Good, the Bad and the Ugly* sound track, by Ennio Morricone (sound track week wouldn't be complete without it).

Still no comment from Berkeley Fan.

It's part of my routine now to skateboard by the falafel place on my way to work. I can't really say why. Maybe it's my way of whistling past the graveyard, or maybe I'm likening it to my own life, with its boarded-up front and yellow crime-scene tape and blood on the floor.

On Monday, though, it's all different. I stand across the street next to my board and watch two men carefully hoist a new window into place, replacing the broken one. The front door is propped open and the tables and chairs from inside are piled onto the sidewalk patio. A man in white overalls with a do-rag tied over his hair rolls fresh paint onto the walls inside. There's a paint-spattered tarp covering the floor but I'm willing to bet that there's not a drop of blood left on that floor underneath it. I don't see Sanje anywhere, but there's no doubt in my mind that he's behind all this. He's moving on, starting over. I think about that Tom Waits song "New Coat of Paint," where he sings, "All your scribbled lovedreams are lost or thrown away," and then I kick off on my board and glide around the corner to Bob's.

My dad got back to me last night at about eleven just as I was brushing my teeth. I told him to hang on a second while I rinsed. My dad's joining a band is need-to-know information.

The band is called Hong Kong High. They needed a new drummer because theirs just went into rehab. He's twenty-one. They auditioned a lot of kids but none of them was as good as my dad, so they hired him. The average age of the band members is twenty-three, but with my dad on board it's up to twenty-eight. I asked him if he thought he might be a little old for this stuff and he said, "Al, you're acting like I'm *old* old. Do you have any idea how old Jimmy Page and Robert Plant are?" I guess he's got a point there. I asked him which bands influence Hong Kong High and he said they told him but he wasn't familiar with any of them. He mentioned Fall Out Boy, My Chemical Romance and AFI, bands my dad would never listen to, but it's only a matter of time before he gets hold of that particular steering wheel and takes over the driving. He can be very charismatic when he wants something.

This morning, my blog was packed with posted comments about sound tracks on LP. I'm no longer the sole blogger on my blog. I've become a moderator. I give the participants a topic and shout, "Go!" and they're off. Remy from Antwerp usually checks in first, and then Thor from Norway, and then Tex from New York, and Susan from Austin, and Norman from New Hampshire, and Sula from Iceland and on and on. Don't these people ever sleep? Oh, and they don't always talk to just me anymore; they talk to one another. Plus, I found out yesterday that my blog got linked to a lot of other blogs without my even doing anything, so I got a whole bunch of readers from other music blogs. It's totally crazy. Still nothing from my "Fan" in Berkeley.

I was in a sentimental mood when I chose today's LP to blog about; maybe it was because my dad joined a band, but I got to thinking about when we all lived in the house together, so I blogged about Simon and Garfunkel's *Bookends*. This is my favorite Simon and Garfunkel album. It was a staple in our house when I was a kid (I especially loved "At the Zoo"). I usually like to listen to this LP in the fall because all the songs seem to be about the seasons changing or winter approaching or the end of something. Summer's almost over and a lot of things have been changing around here lately, so it seemed appropriate.

Shortly after I open the store and Laz and I take up our respective positions at the front counter, a scrawny kid I've never seen before sets off the security alarm next to the checkout, which means he's either been shoplifting or he has a steel plate in his head. Judging by the size of him (he's about twice as big as when he arrived thirty minutes ago), he's got a lot of product stashed under his oversize clothes. Considering how slowly Laz moves the rest of the time—sort of reminiscent of a record store gargoyle—it's hard not to be impressed by his agility during shoplifting incidents. He utilizes a two-part maneuver: The first part involves him swinging his leg out in front of the retreating shoplifter and catching him just at the front of his shins. The shoplifter goes down hard, dislodging the stolen product, which comes clattering to the floor around him. In part two of the maneuver, Laz straddles the kid, pulling his right arm behind him, immobilizing him. I pick up the product from around him and stack it into a neat pile next to the cash register.

"Hey, you're breaking my arm!"

Laz ignores that. "Okay, kid, you're not in Wal-Mart anymore. Here's how it works at Bob's. You unload anything else you might have in your clothes and we tally up everything you've ripped off and then you pay for it. The only catch is that you don't get the merchandise; we do.

After that, my assistant here takes your photo and we add it to 'Bob's Book of Banned Butt-heads.' The *butt-head* part refers to anyone stupid enough to try to rip off Bob's. Once you appear in this book, you are never to set foot in this store again. Do you understand?"

"What if I don't have any money?"

"Good question," says Laz. "Allie, what if he doesn't have any money?"

I stand next to him, my foot next to his hand. "In that case, you're allowed a choice. We call the cops or we call your parents. Up to you."

The kid groans.

"Okay, I'm going to help you to your feet and then you're going to give me everything else you have. I should warn you that if you try to run at this point, I will give chase and I will catch you, and when I do I'll kick your ass into next Tuesday. Got it?"

The kid nods. He pulls three more CDs out of his clothes and I ring everything up. The total comes to ninety-three dollars and twenty-seven cents. The kid opens his wallet and pulls out a hundred-dollar bill. I give him his change and he starts to leave, cursing and shaking his head.

"Not so fast." Laz grabs him and yanks him back in front of me. I pull out the Polaroid camera from the drawer where we keep it for these occasions and snap a photo.

"And now you can go. Thank you for shopping at Bob and Bob Records," says Laz.

The kid can't leave fast enough. I watch his picture come into focus. He looks like a junior version of the men in the mug shots at the police station.

After the shoplifting incident, Laz and I go back to our separate ends of the counter like it never happened.

A geek in a cheap suit walks into the store late in the afternoon, asking for Bob. I fetch him from the office and he comes out and shakes the guy's hand a bit like you might shake the hand of the undertaker who's about to embalm your grandmother. The two of them disappear back into the office with the door locked for the better part of an hour. After that they emerge from the office and walk around the store, stopping to look at product here and there. Laz and I wildly speculate on who the guy could be but we purposely don't come close to naming our biggest fear. After the guy leaves without so much as a glance in our direction, I casually ask Bob about him.

"Oh, he's nobody, just a guy with an idea, you know . . ." he answers evasively.

I spin around and lock eyes with Laz, who shrugs.

When I get home, my mom and Ravi are sitting at the table working. Is it my imagination or is my mom sitting a lot closer to Ravi than she usually does?

"Hi, Ravi. How are you?" I ask.

"Very good, Miss Allie, how are you?"

"I'm pretty good. Hey, how long have you been swimming at Anza?" I ask him. My mom is giving me her warning look and shaking her head.

"Every day now for years. Why, have you seen me there?"

"We were there yesterday. You're a really great swimmer."

"Thank you. When you say you were there, do you mean both of you?" He looks at my mom and then at me. I let her answer that one.

"Yes . . . we, um, didn't want to bother you. You looked so . . . focused." She laughs nervously and runs her fingers through her freshly washed, ultrashiny hair. Ravi sees something in her eyes that he's probably never seen before. He holds her gaze, saying nothing for as long as he dares.

I creep upstairs and leave them to their moment. My work is done.

I check my blog again. I've become obsessive. There's a comment from my Fan in Berkeley. My pulse quickens. I quickly read it:

Bookends? Are you perchance baiting me? "America" has been there for me since I was a kid. It inspired me to run away three times. (I got as far as Grand

```
Central Station but the train schedule
was confusing. Life is so unfair when
you're eleven.) BTW, I own the red
vinyl promo single of "I Am a Rock."
Maybe I'll show it to you sometime.
Your Fan in Berkeley
```

I comment back:

```
Hey, Berkeley Fan. Still have the mix
in my player. Dare I return the favor?
BTW, I own that red vinyl promo too.
Not so rare after all. Come by and pick
up your mix sometime. You're missed.
VP
```

I stand in front of my wall of LPs and start composing the mix CD I'm about to make Zach that will blow his mind—that is, if I ever see him again. I pull out Aerosmith, *Toys in the Attic*; Jethro Tull, *Aqualung*; *Buffalo Springfield*; the Byrds, *Sweetheart of the Rodeo*; then I put them all back and start over with a Dusty Springfield album. I add Julie London. This could be my biggest musical challenge yet. When I've got a good-size stack going, my mom appears in my doorway.

"Hey, thanks for that. I could punch you."

"What? You didn't want Ravi to know that you were at the beach? What are you, like, twelve or something?"

"No. I just didn't want him to think I was watching him."

"Why not? 'Cause he was wearing a Speedo?"

"Of course not, but now that you mention it, it really isn't much different from seeing someone in their underwear, is it?"

"Nope, and thanks for the visual."

My mom does a pirouette in her flip-flops with her hands above her head and, for a second, she does look like a twelve-year-old. She's wearing a flowered low-cut sundress and mascara—who is she trying to kid with that?

"We're going out next week."

"Who? You and Ravi?"

"Yes." She sighs. "Me and Ravi."

"Really? Where?"

"The Pharaoh Sanders concert at the Zellerbach, but we're having dinner afterward."

"Ravi . . . that dog."

My mom laughs. "A date with Ravi. Wow, I sure didn't see that coming. Am I horribly shallow because I wasn't interested in the old Ravi?"

"Nah. How were you supposed to be attracted to the Ravi who always had crumbs in his beard and smelled like wet dog?"

"Ugh, that tweed jacket, remember that thing?"

"Who could forget?"

My mom flops onto my bed and watches me search through my LPs.

"What are you doing?"

"Brain surgery," I answer, pulling out another LP, sighing, and putting it back.

"Have you talked to your dad?"

"Yeah. Last night. He joined a band."

She sits up on her elbows. "What, like a real band?"

"What's a real band?"

"One that gets paid."

"Yeah. I think so. They're called Hong Kong High. I looked them up online. They're punk-ass kids. The stuff they do isn't Dad's stuff at all; it's pretty 'out there,' but I think he needed something to do."

My mom snorts. "He'll never outgrow his adolescence. He's living with a spoiled brat, starting a family with her, for God's sake! And now he's joined a band? He's probably old enough to be their father!"

I shrug. Sometimes I wonder if she even remembers that he's still *my* father. She talks about him like he's an ex-employee that we had to let go because we caught him stealing office supplies and now we're allowed to talk trash about him for eternity. I mean, technically, she did fire him but I can't do that. We're bonded for life. He'll always be my dad, whether I like it or not.

My mom sits up and dangles her legs over the side of my bed. She looks down at her bare feet. "There isn't any food in the house."

"I know."

"Are you hungry?"

"Starved."

"Do you want to walk over to the island and get a burrito?"

"Sure." The island isn't actually the name of the place. It's a tiny burrito joint with about four tables surrounded by three different streets, so we've always called it the island. We have no idea what the real name of the place is. They have picnic tables outside and you can sit there and watch the cars drive by on three sides while mariachi music plays on the outdoor speakers. There's a certain charm to that.

My mom slides her feet back into her flip-flops and stands up. I leave my stack of LPs for later. As we stroll over to the island together, talking about boys along the way, I realize that I've spent more time with my mom this summer than I ever remember.

$\mathcal{S}$uki is moving out. She told my mom that she's moving into the house where her boyfriend lives because one of his housemates moved out. First of all: boyfriend? I know Suki's a ghost but how is it possible that my mom and I have never even laid eyes on this guy? Maybe he's a ghost too, or maybe she's lying. Maybe the real reason she's leaving is the hair in the sink, the half-eaten cheese sandwiches on the side of the bathtub, the loud music at all hours and the kitchen fires. Let's face it, my mom and I are not ideal roommates. In our defense, though, we're new at the roommate game. If she had complained even once, we might have changed our behavior . . . maybe.

My mom puts up an ad at student housing again and the very next day, like *Groundhog Day*, another Suki arrives on our doorstep. Her name is Akiko and she's Bizarro Suki.

Akiko looks like a character from a Japanese comic book. Her hair is royal blue. She's wearing striped socks that go up to her midthighs and a miniskirt. Her makeup is glam rock circa 1979 and she's wearing platform shoes. She has an explosive laugh and she tells us she's from Tokyo (duh, really?). We show her the room. Pierre is lying across Suki's futon. He lifts his head and regards us as intruders. Akiko takes the room. She'll move in in two weeks, right after Suki moves out. On the way back down the stairs, Akiko asks us to please keep the cat out of her room because she's allergic. Or at least I think that's what she said. She mimed it out for us, pretending to sneeze. It appears that King Pierre is about to be toppled from his throne. How on earth will he go back to living among us mere peasants?

There's another photo of M/Joel/William on the front page of the newspaper today. There it is, the regretful mug shot. I prefer the drawing, now a collector's item, which I've stashed among my LPs. He's been released from the hospital and he's currently in police custody. He's entered a plea of not guilty to the charges against him. Imagine that? I'm not really sure what happens next but as Tom Waits famously wrote: "You'll need an attorney for this journey." And even the very best attorney couldn't get him off, so I guess he's going to jail, probably San Quentin. It's not far from here, at the end of the Richmond–San Rafael bridge. At least he'll have nice views and an ocean breeze. My mom has a friend who teaches creative writing to the inmates there. Maybe he could write his biography. He could call it *The Big Book of Regret*.

The day of the date arrives and I talk my mom through her usual predate weirdness, and when Ravi arrives to pick her up ten minutes early, holding a bouquet of sunflowers and looking handsomer than ever, she descends the staircase looking like he's never seen her look before. It's not the clothes—she finally settled on jeans and a silk jacket— it's the look on her face. She's looking at him like he's her date, not her disheveled boss, and that's got to make him feel nice.

I say good-bye to those crazy kids and I stroll over to the noodle house on College with the new *Rolling Stone* magazine and my notebook tucked under my arm. I get in line behind a few people and when it's my turn I order a big bowl of udon noodles with tofu and vegetables and an iced green tea and then I pull up a chair at one of the tiny wooden tables scattered around the restaurant. I flip through my notebook; I've almost got the new issue of the *Vinyl Princess* fanzine put together. It's twelve pages long this time. Turns out there's a lot more to say about vinyl than I thought. One of the reasons it's longer now is that I've got little features on some of the LPs from my blog with some of the best posted comments, which are really great, better than anything I could have come up with.

Something moving in my peripheral vision compels me to look up. A few tables away from me, Zach is wiping down an identical table to the one I'm sitting at. I watch, amused, as he scours the tabletop and then lays out his chopsticks, his order number on a metal stand, and a napkin, carefully, at ninety-degree angles. Once he's done that, he pulls out a book and opens it to a bookmarked page. Then he looks up and he sees me. His face changes into that fight-or-flight look you get when you know you're screwed. I smile and wave. He slowly waves with two fingers like bunny ears. Coincidentally, he's wearing a T-shirt with a crudely drawn rabbit on the front. He gets up tentatively and walks over to me.

"Hi."

"Hi."

"So, you're okay. You look okay, that is." The truth is, he looks pale. "I thought that maybe you were sick or something, you know, because you haven't been by the store."

"I'm okay. I've been under a self-imposed house arrest."

"Why? What did you do?"

"Oh, nothing, I just needed a time-out."

"From?"

"Myself."

"So, what got you out again?"

"Hunger. I ran out of crackers and peanut butter."

"Oh. Crunchy or smooth?"

He scratches his forehead. "Smooth."

I should have guessed.

The waitress puts my bowl of steaming udon down in front of me. He sees an opportunity for escape.

"Well. I guess I'll leave you to your noodles." He turns to go.

"No. Sit with me . . . please. Could you?"

He glances around the restaurant with a look of consternation on his face.

"I guess I could. I'll go get my stuff."

He returns and goes through the whole routine again with his half of the table.

"Do you think the virus is contained or should we put on hazmat suits?" I ask him.

"What? Oh . . . this is just something I do. Try to ignore me."

"Will do."

The waitress arrives seconds later with his noodles and he apologizes for switching tables, as though she might care. She walks away while he's in midsentence. He looks closely at his bowl, leans over and smells it, and then he gets to work eating all of one thing and then moving on to the next. Not an easy task when everything is floating in broth. You can tell he was the kind of kid who never let different foods on his plate touch one another, and that was probably just the tip of the iceberg.

"Hey, Zach." I look down at my noodles. "You know that time you asked me out?"

I look up at him. He looks mortified. "I think I remember that," he croaks. "But I wasn't asking you out. I asked you to 'hang out.' There's a difference."

"Oh, yeah? What is it?"

He starts to say something and then he stops. "You know, I'm not sure. Near as I can tell, the only difference is probably that the guy doesn't pay for everything."

"Don't worry about that. I'm a modern woman. Anyway, that was kind of a tough week for me and I wasn't myself that day. I really didn't mean to hurt your feelings."

"You didn't. I don't have feelings." He flattens his hair with his fingers. It immediately springs up again.

"Well, the truth is, I'd really like to 'hang out' with you sometime. That is, if you still want to."

"Oh, okay, sure. Maybe I could call you or something."

"What are you doing after this?"

"What, like tonight?"

"Uh-huh."

"No solid plans. That is, except for the self-imposed house arrest, and that's sort of tentative."

"You could come over to my place if you like. I live about fifty steps in that direction." I point over my shoulder with my chopsticks.

"Okay." I can see him mentally regrouping.

On the way to my house I tell Zach again and in great detail how much I love his mix and why. He takes the opportunity to explain his "process" to me. It's not that different from mine. We both seem to grasp the idea that it's so much more than throwing a bunch of songs on a CD.

We pass by the usual suspects on my end of College Avenue: a guy I refer to as Davy Crockett because he wears a buckskin outfit with fringe hanging off the arms and the legs and a stick through his earlobe about the length of a drinking straw with feathers and bones and beads hanging off it; and Juanita, a large woman with pink cheeks who dresses like a wood nymph and sits outside the Nepalese restaurant day and night, quietly asking for handouts.

I swing open the front door of my house and turn to Zach. "Welcome to Shangri-la."

I look around quickly to assess the damage. It's not too bad if you don't look too closely but then I remember that looking closely is what Zach's all about.

I smile at him. He's slowly taking it all in. He looks nervous.

"You're not going to need to wipe the place down, are you?"

"Was there a fire in here recently?" he asks, sniffing the air and twitching his nose.

"Yeah. Wow, you can smell that?"

"It's overpowering."

"You should get a job searching for bodies in avalanches. I bet you'd be really good at it."

"I have a very sensitive nose, that's all." He looks wounded.

"C'mon upstairs. I'll show you my shrine."

He trails behind me up the stairs to my bedroom. He hesitates in the doorway and takes a deep breath.

"C'mon in. It's safe in here."

"No, it's not that. I just want to inhale that smell, you know, that old vinyl smell. It makes me feel good."

"Good. You can do that from in here."

A lava lamp on my desk bubbles goop around in slow motion. I flick on the light and he stands next to my wall of LPs, looking up, impressed. I take the opportunity to kick a dirty pair of underwear under the bed.

"Whoa. I knew you were a collector but I really wasn't expecting this." He looks at me. "You're a freak."

"That's pretty big talk, coming from you."

"Well, I meant that like . . . from one freak to another . . . respectfully."

"You wanna hear something? Help yourself." I sit back on the bed, propped up on my elbows, watching him.

"I wouldn't know where to start."

He pulls out an LP from my blues section and looks at the back of it. He puts it back in its place and moves on to indie rock, and then punk rock. He holds the albums with the tips of his fingers like they're the Dead Sea scrolls or something. There's nowhere to sit except on my bed. I brush off some crumbs and Zach sits, keeping a polite distance away from me.

An hour later, Jeff Beck is on the turntable and Zach is still treating my bedroom like the Smithsonian. We talk about my records the way normal people talk about basketball trophies or academic awards. He asks me about an LP and I know exactly when I got it, where I got it and even whose collection it originally came from. I know the artist's musical background and I know if they played in any other bands, even if it was only as a sideman, even if it was only for fifteen minutes. Music, to me, is one giant puzzle, and collecting music is about finding all the pieces and trying to fit them together. Like, for instance, the LP Zach is holding right now: Johnny Marr and the Healers. Well, Johnny Marr played with the Smiths; then he joined the The, then Electronic, and then the Healers, plus he was a guest musician on albums by Bryan Ferry, Billy Bragg, Oasis, Crowded House, Beth Orton, Beck, Pet Shop Boys, Lisa Germano, and the Talking Heads. It's like a musical six degrees of separation.

I watch Zach being blown away by my collection and I notice that he seems very calm. He hasn't twitched or scratched his face for over an hour. I realize that this must be his happy place, in a bubble, surrounded by music, and because I'm the owner of the bubble, I don't make him nervous. I can totally relate to that.

"So, when do I get to see yours?" I ask him.

"Most of it's still in New York. I shipped a couple of boxes I couldn't live without. The rest is in storage."

"You think you'll ever move your collection out here?"

He looks at me. "Maybe."

I go downstairs to get us drinks and notice that the red light is blinking on the answering machine. I hit play:

"Hey, it's Kit. Um . . . where are you? I've been calling all night. You really need to get a cell phone . . . and a microwave. I need to talk to you, like right now. Call me . . . now."

A second message plays:

"Oh, and did I mention that it's important? Okay, so . . . call me."

I fill two glasses with lemonade and take them back up to my bedroom.

*I*n most places, the signs that summer is winding down are pretty much the same: The leaves start to turn, the nights get chilly and the days get shorter and shorter. In Berkeley, the most obvious and by far the most disturbing sign that summer is over is the sudden arrival of U-Hauls and storage containers. They materialize on the streets in front of student housing and apartment buildings like miniature villages. The locals are forced to swerve around the boxes like they're part of an obstacle course. It's only a matter of time before every seat in every café is filled with a laptop-gazing, mouse-clicking student and idle conversation becomes a thing of the past. I'm always a bit sad when this happens, mostly because the weirdos and eccentrics get homogenized by all the "normal"-looking students and Berkeley starts looking like anyplace else.

There's no one in the store this morning so I have lots of time to work on my blog. I write a love letter to the Clash and post it.

Shorty and Jam drop by to change their panhandling coins into paper dollars. In celebration of the students' return, Shorty is wearing a simple A-line skirt in taupe and Jam has a purple flower in his hair. They do their part in this transaction by separating the silver into separate piles of nickels, dimes and quarters for me to count, but they manage to get something sticky on every single coin, so I scrub down like a surgeon after they leave. A few seconds later, the phone rings. I grab it, happy for the distraction.

"Bob and Bob's."

"Why didn't you call me back last night!" demands Kit.

"Oh, God, I'm sorry, I totally forgot!" I watch out the window as a minitwister of leaves skitters across the road.

"Okay, so are you ready for this? Auntie Depressant got a record deal."

"Really? With who?"

"Ravage."

"You're kidding. Ravage is good. How did you find out?"

"Niles left a message on my cell last night. He said that he just thought I should know."

"Why?"

"I don't know, probably because he wants me to seethe."

"Are you seething?"

"I won't lie to you. I'm seething a little. I guess I should be bigger about it. He also mentioned that they might be touring with the Dropkick Murphys next summer. Crap! I guess I should call him back."

"What for? He'll just gloat. Don't call him."

"You know what? You're right. I'm not going to call him. See? This is why I needed to talk to you."

"You didn't already call him, did you?"

"No. I swear I didn't. I was six digits in a few times but I aborted the mission every time."

"Good."

"The dreaded students are back; have you noticed?"

"Yeah. I haven't seen them in here, though. . . . Downloading bastards."

"So this morning, I'm at Royal Coffee, running late as usual, and I'm in line behind this girl who's dressed in J.Crew, head to toe, and she's explaining to François, the owner, that he should carry low-carb bagels like they do in the coffee places in L.A. and he says, 'This ain't L.A.,' and she goes on to order a mocha with whipped cream on top. She walks past all of us waiting in line in her plaid kitten heels like she owns the place. I was late for work because of her bullshit."

"Nothing says 'summer's over' like plaid kitten heels straight from the catalog. By the way, where are we eating lunch?" My stomach is already grumbling.

"Sanje's back. We have to go over there."

"He's back? Is he okay?"

"I think he's fine. I'm dying for a falafel."

"I'll meet you there."

"Okay, so, don't call Niles . . . right?"

"I wouldn't."

"Later, dude." She hangs up.

Bob is out on the avenue doing something and I go back to the office to grab a new pad of credit slips. While I'm in there, I see this business card on his desk. It's for one of those companies that sells stuff on eBay for you. I immediately think of the cheap-suit guy. I stand there for a moment, staring at the card, trying to put a scenario together in my head. What circumstances would lead Bob to a place where he'd need the services of someone like this? Is he selling some of the inventory? Why? I refuse to let my mind travel any farther down that road. I'm sure that if something's up Bob will tell us soon enough. I mean, we deserve to know, don't we?

I quickly glance around Bob's desk and then I see

something else. It's Bob's lease for the store. Why would he have it out on the desk like this? I open the office door a crack and check to see if Bob's around. He's not. I shut the door and grab the document. I read carefully through the front page, looking for a date that might tell me something. Then I see it; Bob's lease is up at the end of October, approximately eight weeks from today. I feel like I just got punched in the stomach. The last thing I see on Bob's desk, as I stagger out of the office, is my zine sitting on his desk, open.

I decide not to tell anyone about my discoveries. I could be wrong about everything. I sure hope I'm wrong about everything.

Fabulous Falafels is packed. Sanje is enjoying a level of fame that can be brought about only by blowing away a couple of bad guys Wild West style. The place is sparkling clean and there's a lingering new-paint smell in the air. Kit and I get in line behind a bunch of new students who have no idea. They think that this line is all about the falafels and they're only half-right. Sanje is working the counter and he plays down his role in ending the crime spree when his regular customers ask him about it. He shrugs and waves away their questions with his hand. I'm sure that if he didn't think that the American government was monitoring his every move, he'd be riding an elephant up Telegraph Avenue right now, waving to the crowd.

I'm completely distracted by what I saw on Bob's desk this morning. I can't stop thinking about all the times he's threatened to sell the store. We never took him seriously but maybe the robbery was the last straw. Kit and I get to the front of the line and I shove it to the back of my mind.

Sanje greets us with gusto. "Ladies, welcome to my grand reopening. Free falafel today for my loyal supporters."

"Thanks, Sanje! What for?" I ask. Kit kicks me in the calf. She clearly doesn't think we should question free food.

"I'm feeling especially grateful for what I have today." He waves his arm around, indicating the restaurant, or maybe America.

We order and find two chairs outside on the tiny patio.

"Well, Sanje's drunk with power," says Kit, pulling open her handbag and putting her wallet away.

I sip my iced tea and shrug. "It's not every day that you conquer the enemy."

"So, guess what? I think I might have a date."

"What does that mean?"

"It means that there's this guy; he works at the campus bookstore. . . . I know . . . big yawn, but he shops at the store. His taste in clothes is exquisite, and I've chatted with him a bit, you know, about this and that, mostly clothes and music, and he was in this morning, buying some tailored dress shirts, and somehow talk gets around to how I'm currently single...."

"Somehow?"

"What? I'm not a nun. Anyway, he said we should get together sometime and I gave him my cell phone number."

Kit's phone starts to ring. Her ring tone is Patsy Cline's "I Fall to Pieces." She retrieves it from her bag and looks at the number and then she answers it, holding up her index finger in front of me.

"Hello?"

"Oh, hi, Nelson." She mouths, *It's him*, to me. She turns on her cute, sexy, boys-only voice.

Nelson? I mouth back. She gives me the finger.

"Let me just grab my Day-Timer and see if I'm free." She sits there, doing nothing, and lets a few seconds pass. "Good news, it looks like I can make it.... Okay. What time?... Right, I'll meet you there.... Ciao." She stretches this word into two long syllables.

She flips her phone shut. "Did I say I *might* have a date? I meant I *do* have a date." She puts her phone away.

Sanje delivers our falafels himself. "Eat, eat!" he tells us, acting very much like Marlon Brando in *The Godfather*. We thank him again. He visits with some other tables on his way back inside.

"So, do you really like this Nelson guy or is this spite-dating?"

"No. I like him. He's no Niles, I'll give you that, but I'm pretty sure he doesn't have a bunch of Chelseas buzzing around him either." She opens up her falafel and dumps a container of hot sauce on it.

I lower my eyes.

"Oh, don't look at me like that. Do you think I was stupid enough to believe that Chelsea was Niles's first? I'm not an idiot. I know there were lots of Chelseas. This one just happened to be the one that put me over the edge, that's all."

"It's not like I knew anything," I tell her, because I really didn't. "I just suspected . . . you know . . . rock stars."

"I know." She frowns.

I tell her about my evening with Zach. How he stayed until midnight, sorting through my music collection and obsessing with me over who played in what band with whom before he/she was in this other band, pretty much the same thing I do with Bob except with Zach it felt like maybe there was an extra little something going on, a lingering look here, an arm brushing against an arm there. Kit wants all the details and she's annoyed when there aren't many. Anything short of ripping each other's clothes off is disappointing to her. It's hard to explain to her that obsessing over music with a guy is the height of excitement for me. She also wants to know if this Zach guy is a friend or a "friend." She uses her fingers to mark quotations around the second *friend*. I scoff at her implication and tell her he's just a friend, because I just can't imagine him being anything else to me . . . that is, for now.

Kit leans back in her chair, luxuriating in the warm sun. The fog always disappears at the end of summer and we finally get real summer weather. "Can you believe that summer's almost over? It felt like twenty minutes, didn't it?"

"Ten."

"Ugh. How shitty is it that we have to go back to school?"

"Supershitty."

"How many days left?"

"Eleven and a half."

"Let's make every one of them special, okay?"

"Sure."

After work today I'm going to Krishna to print the second official issue of my zine. It's almost done and it now includes a bunch of new reviews and pieces I've written about my own vinyl finds *plus* a little cartoon about vinyl collectors drawn by Shep, from Virginia, who comments on my blog almost daily. I know that it's going to cost almost twice as much to print the zines but I now have actual subscribers who sent me fifteen dollars each for a year's worth of issues. I opened a bank account especially for my blog money. *Plus*, this little indie record company that distributes vinyl has been reading my blog and they asked me if they could put an ad in the zine and on my blog. I said sure. They're sending me seventy-five bucks. Their ad will go right next to the Dean twins' ad. I can't wait to get the twins a stack of the new issue. This month's color will be hot pink.

*S*everal uneventful days pass with no sign of Zach—not on the phone, not in the store—and then my worst fear is realized: Bob & Bob is closing. After twenty-three years on Telegraph, Bob is finally closing his doors forever. He gathers Laz, Jennifer, me, Aidan and even Roger together in his office just before closing time to announce it to us. His eyes fill with tears and he has to stop several times and compose himself. He and Dao are planning to move into a condominium complex in Sarasota, Florida, where his aging mother lives. All Bob wants to do is fish. I never even knew he liked fishing. He's never mentioned it once. You would think that in two years of talking to me about concerts, musicians, bands, rock stars, guitar licks and bass lines, he might have said just once that he liked fishing. Is it possible that he was doing all that for me? That he would have preferred to talk about fishing but he thought *I* wouldn't ?

The cheap-suit guy is going to take all the high-end collectibles and sell them on eBay and the rest of the stock will be cleared out in a closeout sale, which starts tomorrow. The doors close in eight weeks, or whenever we run out of product, whichever comes first.

We're all speechless, even Jennifer. Bob's been talking about Florida and selling the place for so long that none of us believed that he would ever do it. Technically, he's not selling it, though. He's just going to disassemble it like an old Chevy, sell off the parts and let the rest of it rust away into nothing.

After I hear the news, I stand up, feeling dizzy and sick to my stomach. I walk out of the office before I fall apart. Sure, it's sad that the world has no use for a record store anymore, and it's sad that people think it's okay to download their music off a computer without touching it or smelling it or holding it in their hands, but the saddest thing for me right now is that I feel like I'm losing the place where I live.

I walk slowly to the front of the store and then I gain momentum when I figure out that I need to get out of there. I grab my stuff and rush out the front door. Bob comes out after me but I don't slow down. I don't want him to feel bad; I don't want him to see me fall to pieces and I make it only a block away from the store before that's just what I do. I sit on the bench in front of the Holy Trinity Church and weep. I don't care that the students walking past me stare at me curiously. This is partly their fault. They're devoid of passion. They don't even know that an era is ending while they bustle from class to class, listening to tinny-sounding crap on their iPods. Finally, I wipe my face on my sleeve and stand up.

The house is empty when I arrive home. I walk up the stairs heavily and fall onto my bed, my head at the foot end, looking up at my wall of LPs. Should I box them up and sell them to the Dean twins at the flea? Should I be moving on too? Is this a sign? Or will I carry them around with me the rest of my life from place to place, like family heirlooms that I can't let go of?

I get up off the bed and go in search of the phone. I find it on the top stair and start to dial Kit's number and then I think better of it. I go back into my room and locate the piece of paper that Zach left next to my turntable that night. His name and phone number are written in his neat hand. I dial the number. He picks up on the second ring. "Hello?" He sounds a bit out of breath.

"Hi, it's Allie."

"Hey, hi, are you okay? You sound like you have a cold."

"No."

"What's up?"

"Bob's is closing." I squeeze my eyes shut.

"What? No way, really?"

"Really." I inhale in quakes.

"Are you okay?"

"No."

He pauses. "Uh, you want me to come over?"

"Could you?" I ask.

"Yeah, I just got out of the shower. I'll dry off and come over."

"Thanks." I hang up the phone and watch a small black spider crawl up my wall. He's rushing along as though something extremely important on the ceiling requires his immediate attention. I get up and walk into the bathroom and look at myself in the mirror. I'm badly in need of a haircut, my eyeliner is smeared and my nose is bright red. I wipe my face with a tissue and click off the light.

Zach arrives, out of breath, fifteen minutes later. His hair is still wet from the shower and it lacks vertical clearance. The damp clumps of hair sticking to his head make his face look softer somehow. He follows me up the stairs to my bedroom. I sit on the edge of the bed and he sits down next to me. He puts his arm around my shoulders and I remember the day after the robbery when he squeezed my shoulder and it made me feel better. It's not working today. My eyes well up with tears again. Zach hands me his white handkerchief. I hesitate.

"Take it," he says. "It's clean."

I blow my nose as ladylike as possible. His hankie smells like soap.

"How do you feel?" he asks me.

"I feel like my favorite uncle just died. No, I feel like my favorite person just died."

He pats my shoulder like a big brother.

Somehow, we end up lying side by side on my narrow bed, not talking, listening to Billie Holiday sing mournfully on the stereo, our hands turned out toward each other, fingertips barely touching. I'm exhausted.

The sun drops out of the sky and darkness slowly makes its way across my bedroom and I drift off to sleep.

When I wake up, it takes me a second to remember why I've been sleeping in my clothes on my bed. The day's events come back to me and my heart does a nosedive. The house is quiet except for the continuous sound of the needle hitting the end of the record. A dog barks somewhere in the neighborhood. My eyes adjust to the darkness and I look over at Zach. He's snoring softly. He's taken his glasses off and they're sitting on the little table next to my bed. Without his glasses, his dark eyebrows become the focus of his face. I prop myself up on my elbow and trace one of them with my finger. He jerks awake.

"Sorry. I didn't mean to wake you."

"Did I fall asleep? Was I snoring?"

"No, it's okay."

He feels for his glasses and puts them on slightly askew. He focuses on my face.

"Are you okay?"

"Better."

"Wow, you look so beautiful when you're sad."

"Do not."

"I suppose it would be completely inappropriate if I kissed you right now."

"Yes, completely."

He leans in and presses his lips against mine. It's a soft kiss, not one of those long, lingering, romantic kisses and certainly not one of those adolescent kisses where you suddenly have someone's tongue in your mouth followed by hands everywhere, groping awkwardly. I think that this kiss is a kiss with a future.

My mom arrives home and is curious to know what I'm doing in my darkened bedroom with a guy. She seems relieved when we emerge fully dressed and she gets a look at Zach, who doesn't exactly look like a rapist, skulking out next to me in his rumpled clothes, trying to tame his hair, which has dried into a full-on fright wig.

I say good-bye to Zach at my front door and he says he'll call later. I tell him he better, or else. I fill my mom in on the demise of Bob's and start to cry all over again. I haven't forgotten that tomorrow is registration for high school and I'll be arriving with pink, swollen eyes, looking like I spent the summer sobbing in my bedroom. It's bad enough that I have to go at all. School seems pointless to me now.

My mom tries to console me about Bob's but the truth is, she never really understood why I wanted to spend my days in a dusty little store that smells like mildew, and I'm sure that she's secretly pleased about the whole thing. Plus, she appears to be completely in love with Ravi. It's taking up all her brain space. They've spent almost every moment together since their first date. They do everything but work on Ravi's book. They're like irresponsible teenagers. At the rate they're going, that book will never get published and my mother might well be responsible for Ravi missing out on a Nobel Prize. Fortunately, Ravi's back teaching school in a couple of days and my mom might blow the dust off her dissertation and actually get some work done. I'm really happy that my mom ended up figuring out that the person for her was sitting two feet away from her. I'm even happier that she doesn't have to go back to the internet, but the other night I got up to go to the bathroom and bumped into

Ravi in the hallway in his underwear. He was horrified and I'm still traumatized. My mom acted like it was nothing when I told her the next morning. She actually laughed.

Zach calls me later that night just like he promised. My heart jumps a little at the sound of his voice, surprising me.

"Are you okay?" he asks.

"Yes. Stop asking me that. It is what it is. Bob's is done. It's all over and I just have to deal."

"Right, okay, so we're in recovery mode now?"

"Whatever."

"Hey, can I ask you a question?"

"Sure."

"Why is it called Bob and Bob Records when there's only one Bob?"

"Back when Bob decided to open the store, he was going through a phase. He thought that the only music worth listening to was Bob Dylan and Bob Marley and while he was in some sort of drug-induced state he decided that he was going to open a record store that only sold Dylan and Marley and he'd call it Bob and Bob's. Well, naturally when he came to his senses, he realized what a stupid idea that was but he still liked the name a lot, so he went with it."

"So Bob is actually neither of the Bobs?"

"That's right."

"Interesting. Hey, but what about the blog?" he asks.

"Are you kidding me? The Vinyl Princess lives on."

"Good. The Vinyl Princess rocks."

"Yeah."

"Cool . . . and the zine too, right?"

"Yeah. Sure."

"Well, if you ever need a writer . . ."

"Seriously? You'd write for me?"

"Hell, yes, in a heartbeat. I love that stuff."

"I may take you up on that; it's kind of getting away from me." I remember that the latest hot-pink issue of my fanzine is still sitting in a box next to my bed.

"Hey, when do you go back to school?" he asks.

"I'm not going. I've decided to run wild, start my own pirate ship or something."

"Really?"

"I wish. I register tomorrow. School starts in a week. Oh, God, then I have to think about a new job." I sigh heavily.

"I start school tomorrow," he offers, and I realize I should have asked.

"Are you nervous?"

"Nah. I've got my new *Star Wars* lunch box jammed with peanut-butter sandwiches. What could possibly go wrong?"

"Everything is different now, just when I wanted everything to stay the same."

"No, you didn't. You just think you did because it felt safe."

I guess he might be right about that. Bob & Bob's was my safe place to hide from the world. All my best friends lived there but I guess I always knew better than to think that I could do this forever. You can't hide from the world in a record store. And the blog, and everyone out there who reads it? They're my new family. I have "people" now. I have a responsibility to them. The blog must go on.

Zach and I stay on the phone for an hour and before we hang up we make plans to see each other the next day. I have no idea how I came to be excited about the prospect of spending time with someone like Zach. These are the things in life that you have no control over. One minute you're annoyed as hell at someone; the next minute you're thinking romantic thoughts about them. Life can be funny that way.

*A*fter registration, the precursor to another year of hell, I arrive at Bob's in time to watch Laz and Bob tape giant yellow-and-red banners to the inside of the store windows announcing, EVERYTHING MUST GO. When they've finished, the outside of the store looks like a furniture clearance center; all the cool stuff in the windows is covered up by the banners. Bob & Bob's personality is about to be liquidated.

Bob has cherry-picked the bins and taken out most of the collectibles for the cheap-suit guy to auction off on eBay. The boxes sit at the front of the store, ready and waiting. What's left has to be marked down. Bob and I, armed with price guns loaded with red sale stickers, go through the bins, one by one, reducing everything to rock-bottom prices. I apologize to my friends as I go, whispering to them that they're worth more, that this isn't their fault. Some of them I rescue, spending my last paycheck on them. Bob ran a big ad in three different papers and twenty-three years' worth of customers start to trickle back in to scoop up a piece of Bob's before it disappears forever. Some of them I don't recognize; some I do. I want to ask every one of them the same question: "Where in the hell have you been?"

The mood changes from hour to hour. What starts out dismal quickly turns into a happy reunion as musicians, collectors and assorted music lovers from all over the Bay Area arrive to pay homage, show some solidarity, offer condolences, glance at the casket and take home some great deals. Bob holds court through it all. He almost seems to have been reinstated as the Mayor of Telegraph Avenue, shaking hands, hugging old customers, wiping away a tear, kissing babies, petting dogs and talking about the good old days. A few newspaper reporters arrive to interview Bob. He's only too happy to relate the story of the end of the record store as we know it. Later that afternoon, a van from the local TV station pulls up and Bob stands in front of the store in a Marley T-shirt and sunglasses and tells the perky blonde holding the microphone who's probably never even laid eyes on an LP that music has gone the way of food. People want it fast and cheap and they don't care what it tastes like or where it comes from.

I arrive home exhausted. I'm grimy and I need a shower. I can't imagine eight more weeks of this, but starting next week, I'll be back to part-time till the end of Bob's. On the dining room table there's a note from my mom, held down with a used coffee mug. There's a trace of lipstick on the rim. Hers, a new shade of pink. It's the least she can do for someone who reinvented himself.

Allie,
I'm at Lake Anza with Ravi. Estelle's coming for dinner.
Be home soon.

Estelle, as a rule, does not come for dinner. My mom must be debuting Ravi in his new starring role as her boyfriend. Estelle will be thrilled. She adores Ravi. Even with the crumbs in his beard she was crazy about him. I go upstairs and put Zach's mix on loud while I undress. I walk past Suki's room. The door is wide-open. I stand in the doorway looking in. The room is completely empty except for a bright red fire extinguisher sitting in the middle of the floor. Next to that, Pierre is sleeping curled up on a little oval cat bed that I've never seen before. He opens one eye and regards me for a second and then he shuts it again. Is it possible that all we needed to do to win him over was buy him a cat bed?

After I get out of the shower, I turn down the music and I dial Zach's number, which I've now memorized. He picks up on the ninth ring when I've almost given up.

"Hey, what are you doing? It rang forever." I hear music playing in the background . . . it's Whiskeytown.

"Sorry. I put my phone in the kitchen cupboard by accident while I was cleaning and then I couldn't find it."

"Oh. How was school?"

"Not bad . . . well, actually, I sort of hated it. Plus, I got lost twice and I was late arriving to a seminar. My classes are miles apart. I think I may have crossed a state line. It's an endurance test just to get there. Oh, and the students are a bunch of Philistines, and one of my professors has horrible body odor. He smells like fried onions but more acrid."

"Ewww."

"Don't worry about it, though; things wouldn't be any different at NYU. How was Bob's?"

"Unbelievable. Sort of like a Woodstock reunion but sadder."

"Really?"

"Yeah, Wavy Gravy's coming at the end of the week and Bob's on the six-o'clock news." I look at the clock next to my bed. "In fifteen minutes."

"I don't have a TV."

"That's okay. It would only depress you. Hey, do you want to come over for dinner?"

"Um, okay. I could get into a home-cooked meal."

"Let's not get ahead of ourselves. There will definitely be food but it definitely won't be home-cooked."

"This isn't the official 'meet the parents' dinner invitation, is it?"

"No. It's the official 'meet my mother, her new boyfriend and my weird grandmother' dinner. But they don't know I'm inviting you, so just try to blend in. Come over in half an hour, okay?"

"Okay."

"Oh, and don't use the word *grandmother* around my grandmother. She hates that."

"Got it."

I hear the front door open and my mom's voice, then Ravi's. I get dressed and go downstairs. My mom and Ravi are in the kitchen, looking like they just got back from Saint-Tropez. My mom is wearing a cotton sundress and sandals and her cheeks and shoulders are a bit pink. Ravi's wearing cargo shorts and a tank top. He looks like a J.Crew model.

"Hi, honey. Did you get my note?"

"Yeah. Hi, Ravi."

"Hello, Miss Allie." He still can't quite look me in the eye after the underwear incident the other night.

302

"Ravi, it's been a while. You practically live here. I think we can drop the 'Miss.' What do you think?"

"Yes, of course, you're right."

My mom looks away. I know it's killing her not to somehow tie this into an underwear joke.

"Mom, Zach's coming to dinner too, okay?"

"The guy from the other night?" She grins. "Sure."

I wish she would stop acting like Zach is such a nerd that he couldn't possibly be anything to worry about. I realize that going from M to Zach is rather a large leap in the complete opposite direction, but I'm sure that Zach has a dangerous, unpredictable side that I have yet to discover. Maybe one day I'll walk in on him listening to Throbbing Gristle or something crazy like that.

My mom and Ravi get to work emptying a grocery bag onto the counter. Ravi wants to know all about the demise of Bob's and I fill him in while my mom rinses lettuce in the sink for a salad.

"Is that all we're having?" I ask her.

As if in answer to my question, Estelle pushes open the front door with her foot. Her arms are loaded down with bags. Estelle's not much of a cook either but her takeout skills are masterful.

"I've got chicken; I need help!" she calls out.

Ravi rushes to help her, taking the bags. She gets a good

look at him. "My God, Ravi, you look fabulous. Did you get an extreme makeover?"

"Estelle, cut it out," scolds my mom.

"What'd I do?" She shrugs. "C'mere, Allie." She bear-hugs me and kisses my cheek loudly. "Can you fix me up with a glass of wine, sweetie? It's in one of the bags."

I root around and find the wine opener and glasses while Estelle pulls Ravi over to the sofa and engages him in conversation, making it abundantly clear that she approves of this union. I open the wine and pour two glasses, set-ting them down in front of her and Ravi. She's already deep into it with him: something about agrarian cultures versus nomadic cultures, specifically Mongolian nomads with regard to environmental sustainability.

I shove the crap to one side of the dining table and set five places. My mom puts the food out in the containers it came in. There's no pretending here; we all know who she is. Zach arrives and I introduce him to Estelle, who smells New Yorker on him. She abandons Ravi and commences interrogating Zach about his "people." New Yorkers have this thing where they can move across the country and stay there for twenty years but they still consider their New York address home. Turns out that Estelle and Zach lived a short fourteen blocks away from each other in Manhat-tan and further questioning reveals that Zach's mom and

Estelle belonged to the same Y, and if that's not enough, they both swam in the pool at the Y on Wednesday mornings during free swim. It's entirely possible that they passed each other in the water. They're practically sisters. I'm not involved in this conversation so I put on some music, a nice mix of world, specifically Césaria Évora, Ry Cooder's *A Meeting by the River* and some easy jazz.

When we sit down to eat, everyone is too engrossed in conversation to notice Zach lining up his silverware at right angles and finishing one type of food entirely before moving on to the next. He also wipes his hands on his napkin incessantly, as though he's trying to remove an imaginary stain.

Ravi asks me if I'll be looking for a new job now that Bob's is closing.

"Bob's is closing?" asks Estelle, the way you would ask if rain is expected that day.

"Yes," I say. "Forever." I try to sound dramatic.

Estelle, never without an opinion, gives us her take on the whole thing.

"You know," she says, picking a piece of chicken out of her teeth, "I used to save everything: ticket stubs, greeting cards, birth announcements, invitations, corsages, playbills, and then, one day, after three marriages, I'm moving into a new condo clear across the country and I say to myself, 'Estelle, what is all this stuff? It's an old pile of paper and dried flowers. It means nothing. The memories are all up here.'" She points to her forehead. "These record stores, they've gone the way of the dodo bird. No one wants to carry those big LPs around anymore. The world has moved on. Out with the old, in with the new. You should get rid of all those records and get yourself a nice iPod, honey. You can put all your music on it. They're fantastic." She sits back and wipes her hands on a napkin, her point made. Zach looks across the table at me and rolls his eyes.

Halfway through dinner, Pierre appears at the top of the stairs, watching us a moment. Then he slowly descends like royalty deigning to move among the commoners. He pads over to the sofa and leaps up to the spot that Estelle recently vacated. He curls up and closes his eyes. My mom and I look on, amused. I guess we're better than nothing.

When it's time for Zach to leave, Estelle hugs him and kisses him hard on the cheek like he's her long-lost grandson. She's already invited him to attend a lecture series she's organized out at the compound and he's graciously accepted, schedule permitting.

Ravi follows shortly after. His classes start in the morning and he has to work on his syllabus. Estelle leaves too, reminding us that she brought the food so she shouldn't have to help clean up.

My mom and I sit on the sofa next to Pierre, who seems mildly annoyed at first but stays where he is. I find the remote and turn on our tiny TV in time to catch the ten-o'clock news. They rerun the Bob & Bob story. We watch Bob, standing in front of those stupid banners, speaking into a microphone held by the reporter with her dyed blond hair and her overwhitened teeth. Bob's shoulders are stooped and he looks defeated as he explains about record stores dying out across the country and how it's become impossible to make a living selling music. Shorty and Jam appear behind him, hyperaware of the camera, wearing black cocktail dresses and black armbands in solidarity. They stand solemnly side by side, like funeral attendees, nodding in agreement with Bob and waving drunkenly to the camera. The reporter finishes with Bob and the camera zooms in tight on her face.

"Well, Janet, I guess that means we'll all have to download our music now. You heard it right here in Berkeley. Record stores are a thing of the past." She says it with a smile, like she's describing something new and minty fresh.

The camera cuts back to Janet, the anchorwoman.

"I guess so, Diane. I'll have to get my son to teach me. He's a computer whiz and he's only eight!" She chuckles and they move on to the next story.

I turn off the TV and my mom and I get up and start to clean up the remains of dinner.

$\mathcal{I}$'ve been avoiding Bob's for weeks, taking a different route to school, pretending that the events of the summer haven't altered me, but I finally got up the nerve to walk past it today on my way home from school. Clouds are bunching up in the sky and rain can't be too far off. Approaching Bob's, it feels like I'm visiting someone for the first time in a graveyard after I've buried them. I'm not so keen to see it in its new "condition." There's a big FOR LEASE sign in the window with the Realtor's name and number on it. I peer into the darkened windows at the empty space. With all the bins taken out it looks pretty big in there. Years of concert posters are still plastered all over the walls. I know each one by heart. The emptiness of the place overwhelms me with sadness. I stand there with my forehead pressed against the grimy glass for a while.

A lot of homeless people have taken up residence in front of the store. There's no one to tell them to move along and the wooden overhang keeps the sun off them. Among them, sitting on the pavement with their backs against the empty store, I see Shorty and Jam. They're in rough shape. Their eyes are glassy and unfocused and they don't even recognize me. They're wearing stained jeans and T-shirts, nothing pretty from the free box. Cool nights and rain lie ahead, and being homeless on famous Telegraph Avenue will probably start to lose its appeal.

I saw Bob one more time just before he left for Florida. He was at the post office putting in his change of address. Dao had already gone down there to start getting them set up. He looked happy to see me. We stood there for a few minutes and talked about the new life he was heading to and I wished him well and told him that I hope he catches a lot of fish. For a second there it looked like we might start up a good "blah, blah, blah, fill in band," but it never happened. I watched him walk toward his old van and I felt like I might sit down and cry but then it passed. I was okay.

After Bob's closed, the only half-decent job I could find was at a coffee bar across from campus run by a crazy Italian guy named Agostino. He taught me how to pull a good strong espresso and foam the milk perfectly. The place is really busy and I barely get a moment to catch my breath during a shift. The tips are lousy too. Zach has deemed it filthy but he still comes to visit me whenever I'm working. There are two almost cool things about the job. One is that I get to pick the music we play. The other is that Agostino lets me distribute my zines there, not as ideal as a record store but they're getting out into the world. Some of my old Bob & Bob's customers come in from time to time but we hardly ever talk about music.

Kit still works at the vintage-clothing store. She sees Nelson but she's quick to tell you that she's not in love, and she doesn't call him her boyfriend even though he calls her his girlfriend. She says she's not ready for anything heavy right now so he just has to deal. She spends a lot of time planning our road trip in the not-too-distant future and she's all signed up for driving lessons.

My mom and Ravi are madly in love.

My dad quit Hong Kong High after only three gigs. He said the final straw was when the bass player barfed into his kick drum after a gig just because it was round and looked vaguely like a toilet. He picked up a gig playing in a backup band for a jazz singer who works in casino cocktail lounges and fancy nightclubs around northern California and Nevada. Her name is Leona Miles. She's fifty-seven.

Kee Kee is due in the spring. My dad will be a father for the second time in his life . . . that we know of.

I rarely think about M/Joel/William anymore, but when I do, I try to think of him not in a jail cell but living the life I imagined for him in South Carolina with his big happy family and his dog. I hope he's sitting on a wooden porch swing writing in a journal or maybe reading his way through the classics. The other day I came across the drawing of him that the sketch artist copied for me that day at the police station. I decided that it was time to throw it away. I really hope M gets another chance at his life.

Pierre has started sleeping on my bed at night. We jockey for position and I usually end up clinging to the edge while he sprawls out luxuriously. He seems to be over the whole Suki thing, but if he could talk he would probably say, "I miss her." But then if he could talk, he probably could have talked her out of leaving.

Akiko has added a lively element to our household. She owns more beauty supplies than Paris Hilton and she has her own extensive collection of CDs. She constantly dazzles us with her wardrobe choices, and her shoe and boot collection should be in a museum. She also doesn't seem to mind the mess but she does insist that we vacuum from time to time to keep Pierre's dander to a minimum. She's learned to say the word *allergic* really well. The vacuuming has reunited us with a lot of lost items.

Zach and I are moving tentatively toward something

that could be conceived of as a relationship if you don't look too closely. We see each other whenever we can and, while he may not be Joey Spinelli or M/Joel/William, Zach knows a thing or two about the female anatomy. Who knew that Zachary Joseph Zimmerman, a totally neurotic, skinny nerd with OCD, could have me sighing with pleasure? He also has a way of making me feel beautiful, and let's face it: He's seen me at my worst. We openly admit that our love for each other is primarily based on the fact that we're the only two people we know of who can talk about music for fourteen hours straight and wake up in the morning ready to start all over again.

My blog is going strong. I've had over forty thousand hits, and a steady stream of new readers arrive daily, and Elliot and I are designing a *Vinyl Princess* T-shirt. A few days ago, I got an email from this guy who runs a couple of big-time music blogs with tons of ads on them. He told me that he'd been reading my blog and watching it explode and he wanted to know if I was interested in selling it to him and I could still write it. He called it a "partnership." He said it could be a real moneymaker if we sold some ads on it. I deleted the email. There's only one Vinyl Princess.

The day that Bob finally closed Bob & Bob's for good, Zach and I took a blanket and we hiked up the long hill to the Lawrence Hall of Science and sat on a bluff watching dusk fall over all of Berkeley and the bay beyond that. It was a clear autumn night, the first of many to come. We didn't say much. Lights started to come on below us and stars flickered into the sky. The neon sign at Bob & Bob's stayed dark for the first time in twenty-three years. Zach took my hand in his.

"You got a blog figured out for tomorrow, Veep?" he asked. He calls me Veep now, short for Vinyl Princess.

"Bob Dylan, *Nashville Skyline*, and Bob Marley, *Uprising*."

Zach nodded. "Cool."

Eventually, a chill crept over us and we folded up the blanket and made our way down the hill together in the dark.

That night I finally finished Zach's mix CD, and I was right: It blew his mind.